Stunned by Roman's betrayal, Chase could hardly bear to look at him...

"You cold-hearted *bastard*. How could you do that and still take me to bed? If you didn't want me as a mate, you should have just left me alone. But no, you had to seduce me and then put me on display like a slab of meat in a butcher shop. And now you've had me, you don't want me anymore, so you're handing me off to someone else."

"No! Chase, that's not true."

Shock and pain filled his eyes, hunched his shoulders, but she ignored his reaction and plowed on.

"I trusted you. You made me believe I could."

She turned toward the patio door. "You could've been honest with me, Roman. You could've been fair. You didn't have to break my heart." The need to run, to get as far away from him and the pain as she could, overwhelmed her. Then the anger rose up again. It crowded out the hurt, so she grabbed onto it and let it grow. "I'll be damned if I'll submit to you or anyone else who tells me I have no choice. I'm an American. And in case you've forgotten about the Revolutionary War and the Boston Tea Party, we don't like being told we've got no options." Sliding open the glass door, she placed her foot on the threshold and braced herself. "So, you can go straight to hell!"

She shot out the door and gave into the sheer joy of running. The overlarge robe flew out behind her like a cape. She didn't know where she was heading, but God, getting there felt so good.

She didn't stop when Roman called her name or when she heard him chasing her. She didn't even slow down until she reached the edge of the forest—and came face to face with a huge, snarling tiger.

She didn't know what she was—or that what she was could get her killed...

A struggling private detective in Los Angeles, Chase Alcott has no idea about her unique genetic makeup. So when she takes on a new client—an old man with ulterior motives—she's unaware of the danger she'll soon face. Traveling to England to solve a mysterious murder at the request of her new client, Chase encounters terrifying creatures she thought only existed in her nightmares—only to find out she's one of them. Caught in a web of evil and deception after learning some terrifying truths about her long dead parents, Chase doesn't know who to believe. Does she dare trust the enigmatic Roman, a man with dark secrets of his own?

He knew what she was—he just had no idea what to do about her...

English nobleman, Roman Fernwood, half-werewolf/half-Vampire, doesn't want a mate, especially not a half human/half-weretiger with no knowledge of what she is. But there's something about Chase Roman can't resist, in spite of his determination not to fall in love. Is it her fascinating American spunk and courage or her stunning cinnamon eyes? Or could it be the passion he senses just beneath her calm, unruffled demeanor? Whatever it is, Roman must keep her safe from those who want to kill her—and find a way to show her what she is without driving her into the arms of the other Weres who also want her for a mate.

KUDOS for *Blood Fest: Chasing Destiny*

This story is different...which is why it's so appealing. I think one of the reasons why I don't care for paranormals is because in stories with Vampires and werewolves, things usually get bloody and violent or downright gross and disgusting. This story has a light-handed touch to it, even though it's presenting dangerous situations. – *Judith, member of crit group*

The story hooks me because I have the feeling that something's going to prevent the powders from working, and Chase is going to take that walk. And I want to go with her. – *Florence, member of crit group*

Blood Fest: Chasing Destiny is different from other paranormals. Instead of just the usual vampires and werewolves, O'Neal's added weretigers and half breeds. The hero, Roman, is a Vampire/werewolf cross, the heroine, Chase, a human/weretiger cross. He's British, she's American. So not only do they have to get past British/American cultural difference, they've also got to deal with the cat/dog problem. Chase's very much an alpha in her own right. She's not about to submit to anyone, male or female, and especially not because Mother Nature says so. – *Regan, reviewer*

As an admirer of smart heroines and alpha heroes, the attraction of *Blood Fest: Chasing Destiny* is the connection developed between our two leads. Chase and Roman's banter reminded me of a classic Hepburn and Tracey montage. Unwilling to surrender yet captured by each other's persona, they battle not only each other but some serious evil foes that are hell-bent on putting a serious kink in their romance. – *Taylor, reviewer*

Blood Fest
Chasing Destiny

by

PEPPER O'NEAL

A Black Opal Books Publication

GENRE: PARANORMAL/ROMANTIC SUSPENSE

BLOOD FEST: CHASING DESTINY
Copyright © 2011 by Pepper O'Neal
Cover Design by Dawné Dominique
Copyright © 2011 All Rights Reserved

Hard Cover ISBN: 9781644370995

First Publication: April 2011

Published by Black Opal Books **http://www.blackopalbooks.com**

DEDICATION

To Gary for always believing in me,
and for being my biggest fan.

And to my family for their unfailing love and support.

ACKNOWLEDGMENTS

I feel like this book was a group effort as I have so very many people to thank.

I want to give a big, heartfelt thank you to paranormal author, LJ DeLeon for her enormous help with my world-building. Without her, this story would never have been told.

Thanks also to my unofficial editors, Linda and Fiona. You guys were a tremendous help.

A big thanks to my online crit group, Internet Writing Workshop, especially to Amy, Beth, Carol, Daryl, David, Dawna, Deb, Deborah, Fe, Florence, Francene, Greg, Lauren, Jackie, Judith, Judy, Mark, Nik, Rhonda, Sandra, and Svetlana. Your help and suggestions made a big difference.

And finally, thanks to my editor Lauri and her staff at Black Opal Books, not only for believing in the story, but for giving me a chance to tell it. And thanks for your never-ending patience. I know there were times when you wanted to throttle me.

.

Chapter 1

Los Angeles, California, April 14th:

Damn it, he's getting away!" Scrambling into the passenger seat of David's Honda, Chase watched Steve Nolan's Porsche zigzag through the afternoon traffic and zip around a corner. "Do you have any idea how long it took me to track that bastard down and convince him to come talk to us?"

"Yeah, about as long as it took me to ferret out his name in the first place." David peeled out of their office parking lot, inundating the car with the smell of burning rubber. "Guess we should've tied him to the chair before we told him what we were really after."

"You think?" She braced her arms on the dashboard as he squealed through a left turn. "I'll keep that in mind. Not that it'll do us any good if you lose him."

She didn't have time for this shit. The client wanted results. Yesterday. Yet, even if they caught up with Nolan, then what? How the hell could she make him talk?

Like an idiot, she had *guaranteed* her client she'd clear his name. But without the information Nolan refused to give her, the investigation was dead.

And she'd been so close. Now she'd have to return the client's deposit—money she needed to keep her struggling PI business afloat.

Just once, couldn't things go right? No, that'd be too much to ask.

Brakes squealed. Horns blared.

"Jesus," she snapped. "That was a red light you just ran. Are you deliberately trying to kill us?"

"You told me not to lose him," he said, swerving out of the path of a car. "If I'd stopped for the light, we would have."

"My bad." She shot him a dirty look. "Just don't scrunch us. Okay?" Turning back to the window, she scanned the traffic. "There! Two blocks up. Looks like he's turning right at the light."

Nolan suddenly whipped across three lanes of traffic and headed for the freeway.

"He's seen us. Hit the gas. If we lose sight of him again, we're screwed." When he didn't respond, she groaned. "You can't turn into a wuss on me now. Come on, damn it, *punch* it."

He cursed but stomped on the gas. The car shot forward, zipped around a truck, and darted into the right lane—just as an elderly man stepped into the street from between two parked cars.

"Look out!" She held her breath, prayed.

David slammed on the brakes. The Honda screeched to a halt, but it was too late. The old man bounced off the right front fender, crumpling out of sight.

"Oh, my God!" She jumped from the car and rushed to the man's side. "I'm sorry. God, I'm so sorry."

His face was pale and pinched with pain, his eyes closed. His left leg stuck out at an odd angle, obviously broken. But at least he was alive.

Weak with relief, she sank to her knees beside him. "Everything's going to be okay," she promised, though she didn't like the look of his aura. It was faint, a pale gray tinged with a hint of muddy blue.

David hurried over, talking on his cell phone.

"If that's nine-one-one," she said. "Tell them to hurry."

"They said their ETA's five minutes." He snapped his phone shut. "Christ, Chase, I'm sorry."

She shook her head. "It was more my fault than yours."

The old man's eyes fluttered open then widened as he stared up at her. A look of triumph flashed over his worn, pain-contorted features. "Chase?" he asked in a clipped British accent. "Would you be Chase Alcott, the private detective? With an office three blocks down?" She nodded. "Splendid," he said. "I was on my way to see you."

She blinked. "You were? What did—" The question died on her lips as the man's eyes rolled back in his head. "Shit."

Sirens screamed in the distance. *Looks like we're going to be stuck here for a while.* Tears burned the back of her throat. Nolan was long gone. Why the hell couldn't she ever get a frigging break?

ფოჯ

Radlett, England, April 15th:

Rain dripped down the back of Roman's neck and trailed along his spine like cold, wet fingers. Forcing himself to ignore the disturbing sensations, he focused instead on the preacher's droning voice and the coffin being lowered into Melinda's grave.

"This wasn't an accident, Andy," he whispered to his solicitor. "I tried to tell Chief Inspector Clayton that, but he wouldn't listen."

Stepping closer to Roman, Andrew Wright shifted his umbrella to shelter the both of them. "Have you considered going to his superiors?"

"Yes. But I doubt it would do any good. They'd be as stumped by the lack of motive as Clayton."

The parish priest closed the graveside service with a prayer. Finally. Breathing a communal sigh of relief, the two dozen mourners headed out of the dismal little cemetery.

Roman slowed his pace until he and Andy fell behind the others. "I'm also afraid this may have been done by one of *my* kind."

Andy stopped walking and stared at him. "A Lycan or a Vampire?"

"Vampire."

"If that were true, wouldn't there be marks on her—" Breaking off when Roman made shushing gestures, Andy shot a quick, darting glance around the graveyard. "Sorry," he said in a lowered voice. "But wouldn't there be some evidence of that?"

"Only if the killer was feeding."

"Oh. Right." Andy gave a slight shudder. "Would you like me to hire a private investigator for you? There must be someone we can trust to look into this."

"Not until we have a better idea of what we're dealing with." Roman started walking again. "Besides, my father will be home soon. And I'd like to discuss the matter with him first."

"Er, ah—" Andy cleared his throat. "Lord Fernwood's stay across the pond has been extended. He was involved in a motor vehicle accident yesterday."

"Oh, Christ!" Roman cringed at the images flooding his mind. "Not him, too."

"Re—relax. He's not bad—not seriously injured, I mean." Andy's words rushed out, tumbling over one another. "I—I'm sorry. I should have told you that first. He has a broken leg, two broken ribs, and a fair-sized collection of bruises. But that's all."

"Thank God." Overwhelmed by relief, Roman stumbled on legs that didn't feel attached to his body. He grabbed Andy's shoulder to steady himself. "How did it happen?"

"From what he told me when he called from the hospital, he was crossing a street in Los Angeles—apparently against the light and in the middle of the road—when he was hit by a car."

Roman sighed. "That sounds like Father." Then the implication of Andy's words hit him. "Wait a minute. Father's supposed to be in New York. What the hell's he doing in Los Angeles?"

"I'm afraid I can't answer that." Andy paused as they neared Roman's Rolls Royce. He waited until they were seated inside the limo before continuing. "All I know is what he told me on the phone. He said he'd postponed his meeting in New York and had gone to California to check out something. Or someone. It wasn't the best connection, so I'm really not sure."

Roman rubbed a hand over his face. "Well, knowing him, whatever it is, it's bound to make my life more complicated."

A chill skittered through him—one that had nothing to do with the weather.

∽∾∽

Los Angeles, California, May 21st:

"Why us, Mr. Wright?" Chase didn't like the way the British attorney's aura flickered. "You must have plenty of private detectives in England."

"Yes, I dare say we do. But Lord Fernwood's afraid a member of his family might be involved. And he's anxious to avoid a scandal. That's why he wants you to pose as interior decorators. The English press won't recognize you, of course, so his family won't expect you to be anything but what you say you are."

She glanced at David. He wiggled his eyebrows, rolled his eyes. Stifling a grin, she turned back to Wright. "Why did Fernwood bring you all the way from London to approach us? Why didn't he just ask us himself? After all, we spent almost two hours a day with him for nearly three weeks while he was in the hospital."

She got to her feet and paced, wondering why she'd been so restless and uneasy lately—other than the pile of unpaid bills in her in-box. "When I asked him why he'd been coming to see us just before the accident, he told me the problem had been resolved."

"Yes, well." He shifted in his seat, his pale blue eyes looking everywhere but into hers. "Lord Fernwood felt you'd been extremely kind under the circumstances. He didn't want to impose any further. But there was another incident last Saturday, and he decided he had no choice. By then he was in New York attending to the urgent business delayed by you—I mean, by the unfortunate accident."

"We didn't hit him on purpose," she retorted. "The old fart was jaywalking." *And you were going way too fast*, quipped a little voice in her mind.

"Oh, there's no question Lord Fernwood was in the wrong," he said. "Or that you were a big help in his convalescence."

"We felt sorry for him. All alone over here in the hospital." Snatching a pencil off her desk, she twirled it in her fingers as she paced. "I like him. He's a great old guy. But we can't afford to go chasing off to England right now. We took a serious financial hit on the case we lost because of the accident."

"And Lord Fernwood's offering you considerable compensation. To make up for what you lost on that case, as well as for the work you'd do on this one." He pulled a check out of an inside jacket pocket and handed it to her. "Here's half the offered fee up front, plus a generous allowance for expenses."

She gaped at the amount then passed the check to David.

His eyes widened. "This is in pounds, not dollars?"

"Yes. As I said, it's generous. Especially with the strength of the pound against the dollar."

Chase chewed her bottom lip. Damn, this was enough money to clear all their current bills, plus hold them over awhile if they didn't immediately find more clients. And this was only *half* of the fee?

Still, she didn't want Wright to think they could be bought so easily. "How can we go to England under the guise of redecorating the family's ancient manor? We aren't qualified for that."

"How hard can it be? After all, Lord Fernwood doesn't expect you to do any actual decorating. Your visit will be covered as observing what needs to be done in order to submit a plan and an estimate." He gave a little cough. "Though, I think you've misunderstood me. Lord Fernwood actually wants Mr. Bronson to pose as the decorator," he said, nodding toward David, "and you to pose as his assistant."

"Now wait just a minute—"

David flashed her a grin. "I think it's a great idea."

"You would."

Wright spread his hands. "You must understand, Ms. Alcott. We English are still very traditional. Most of us, especially the aristocrats, rarely credit women with enough intelligence for undercover work. So you'll have an advantage. No one will suspect you're anything other than what you appear on the surface."

He ran his tongue over his lips and swallowed. "Another reason we felt it best you should pose as the assistant and Mr. Bronson as the decorator is..." Stretching his neck, he pulled on the knot of his tie. "I understand Mr. Bronson is, er, ah..."

"Gay?" David asked with a chuckle.

"Quite. Such people are more the type English aristocrats expect decorators to be, so no one will suspect he's posing as someone else." He glanced from one to the other. "If you get my meaning."

Chase shot a look at David. His grimace told her he was biting his cheeks, trying not to laugh. That had her biting her own, but it didn't help. She burst into gales of merriment. Once she started, he joined in.

Wright looked appalled. "I fail to see the humor."

"I'm sorry." Leaning against the wall, she tossed the pencil on the desk and used both hands to wipe the tears off her face. "It's just that David poses as someone else all the time. Most of the gay men we know love role-playing. I can't believe the English don't know this."

"Most Englishmen give little thought to American peculiarities."

"Apparently not." Chase looked over at David again and raised her eyebrows. He nodded. Oh, what the hell. It wasn't like they had a choice.

"So how would this work? Do we just show up and say, 'Joe sent me'?" At his blank expression, she waved a hand. "Never mind. What I'm asking is, do we have a cover story? I mean, we can't just show up out of the blue."

"The blue? Oh. Yes, of course. If you agree to take the job, I'll contact Roman Fernwood, Lord Fernwood's, er...grandson and tell him you're coming. Your cover story is that Lord Fernwood asked you to take a look at the manor house." He grimaced. "Roman won't be happy about it, but I'm sure he'll cooperate. He's very fond of his grandfather, and he'll do whatever it takes to make him happy. He'll have to know the real reason you're there, of course, but none of the other family members or staff will know."

"Terrific." She glanced back at David. When he nodded again, she sighed. "Suppose we agree to do this, what's our timeline?"

"Lord Fernwood would like the matter settled before his return to England. As he'll be in New York for about a month, that should give you plenty of time."

She studied the attorney's aura. Once again, it pulsed with dingy gray. "There's something you're not telling us. What is it?"

"Well, yes." He smoothed his thick, white hair then studied his fingernails. "I, er, you'll, ah, have to know, of course," he said as he brushed some non-existent lint off the lapel of his jacket. "One investigator, a reporter named Melinda Carter, has been killed."

"Killed? How?"

"She fell over the railing of a third floor balcony."

David leaned back in his chair and crossed his legs at the ankles. "If she fell, why—"

"The balcony railing is at chest height for an average height woman. Ms. Carter was short, barely five feet tall, so the railing would have hit her at the shoulder. Could she really have fallen over something that high?"

"What do the police think?" Chase asked.

"Scotland Yard ruled it an accident. The woman had a habit of walking in her sleep, and they decided she must have tried to climb the railing while sleep walking."

"But you don't agree?"

Wright shrugged. "Personally, I haven't a clue. But Roman says it was murder."

"Does he have any suspects?"

"None that he's mentioned."

She turned to David. The relaxed posture of his rangy body belied the keen interest in his piercing gray eyes. "Still think it's a good idea?"

"I'm game. If we go as decorators, we should be safe enough."

She combed her fingers through her hair, an unconscious stalling technique she'd used all her life when her instincts said something wasn't right. Attuned to it, the fact she used it now told her not to rush into this. Not that she could afford to pass up the money Fernwood was offering.

"Very well," she said, despite her misgivings. "We'll do it."

"Excellent." Beaming, Wright handed her a business card. "Call me when you've made your flight arrangements. And send me the contract as soon as possible. I'll take care of getting it signed."

ဆာဆာ

Chase stared out the front window as the attorney left their office.

"He's lying to us about something. I don't know what, exactly, but something." She paused a moment, distracted by a man leaning against a building across the street. He looked familiar, but she couldn't place him. Shrugging it off, she turned back to David. "I'm concerned about what we may be getting into."

"How do you know he's lying?"

"You mean, aside from the fact he was as nervous as a mouse at a cat show?"

He groaned. "Aside from the bad jokes, yes."

She stuck out her tongue at him. "His aura flickered with splotches of dirty gray."

"Ah, his *aura*."

"Fine," she snarled. This was a familiar argument. "You don't have to believe me about seeing auras, but have I ever been wrong when I told you someone was lying?"

"Not as far as I know." He jammed his hands into his pockets. "At what point did his—did you notice he was lying? If you can recall the subject, it might tell us what he was lying about."

"I noticed it several times, but more strongly when he talked about the grandson."

"So, you don't think it's about the murder then?"

"No. I'm sure he told us the truth about that, at least as much as he knows it. It has something to do with Roman Fernwood. Although it may only be about how much cooperation we'll get from him."

She pressed her fingers to her eyes, troubled, and exasperated because of it. "I can't believe I'm even considering taking on a case when I've got a bad feeling about it."

"We don't have a choice, and you know it. We need the money too badly."

"And if it gets us both killed?"

"I'm not sure I understand your concerns." He held up a hand when she tried to interrupt. "Let me finish. The only reason someone'll want to kill us is if they think we're a threat, which they won't if we're posing as decorators."

"What about when we blow our cover?"

"Why should we?" When she rolled her eyes, he sighed. "Look. You know as well as I do, we can pull off a cover as decorators. Especially, if all we have to do is make notes about a project that isn't even going to happen."

She stuck out her tongue again and made a face.

He laughed. "God, Chase, you're such a lady." Perching a hip on the edge of her desk, he studied her. "Now, what's *really* bothering you?"

"I don't know." She rubbed a hand over her stomach. It felt like something trapped inside was clawing its way out. Digging in her pocket, she pulled out a roll of Tums and popped one in her mouth. "And not knowing bugs me. Plus, there're all the unanswered questions."

"Such as?"

"Such as, why the hell Fernwood would hire American PIs in the first place. Or why he'd pick two unknowns like us. Or why he came all the way from New York to see us then just happened to be on that street so we could hit him with the car." She paused, shook her head. "No, I don't see how he could've planned something like that."

The Tums hadn't done her much good, so she popped another. "Then there's the size of the deposit. It just seems too much like a setup to me."

"Maybe Fernwood feels guilty for causing us so much trouble," he said. "After all, I made no secret about the fact his carelessness cost us a client. And a simple credit check would've revealed our financial problems." When she opened her mouth, he held up his hand again. "But even if—and I think it's a pretty big if—he does have ulterior motives, we can still protect ourselves."

"Oh, really? How?"

"You know how you've been nagging me to update our standard agreement form?"

"That's not true," she protested. "I mentioned it once. And only in passing."

He grinned. "Okay, maybe nagging's not the best choice of words. Anyway, I've done a little research, and there's a clause I was planning to add to our boilerplate contract. It basically ensures that if a client misrepresents the facts to gain our services, we're free to back out without refunding the deposit."

Opening a file cabinet, he pulled out a stapled document and handed it to her. "Page three, paragraph six. We'll include that in all future contracts, starting with Fernwood's. Once we get to England, if things aren't on the up and up, we can walk away—*and* keep the money we've been given so far. Besides, Wright needs to learn not to lie to American PIs. Or not to lie to you, anyway."

He patted her shoulder. "So, does that make you feel any better?"

"No, but it's a start." She saw the yearning on his face and knew it had nothing to do with the money. "You want to go because it'll make a good case to fictionalize for those crime magazines you write for."

"So? It's also like a paid vacation to England, and I've always wanted to go there. Plus, with Fernwood as our client, we'll be rubbing elbows with the upper class. There'll be fancy parties and dress-up balls. Hell, we might even get laid."

"Oh, God, I'm really not going now."

"Chicken." He ruffled her hair, kissed her temple. "Afraid to have a little fun?"

"I think your definition of fun and mine are so different they're not even in the same dictionary."

"Ah, come on, Chase. What have we got to lose?"

"It boggles the mind." Another sigh escaped. She'd been sighing a lot lately. She wondered if it meant anything. "I'll probably regret it, but if Fernwood signs the contract, you can make the travel arrangements."

"Cheer up, girlfriend. Everything's going to be fine. You'll see."

She didn't answer. He was usually right. But for reasons she couldn't understand, she feared this time might be the exception.

൦൭൦൭൦

Fernwood Manor, near Letchmore Heath, England,
May 26th:

"Damn it, Andy." Roman paced in front of the fireplace in his study. "I wish to hell you'd talked to me about this before you went to California."

He shoved another log on the fire—more out of frustration than a need for added warmth. "The last thing I want is another damned woman prying into things she shouldn't."

"Your father specifically asked me not to mention it until the contract was signed." Andy sighed. "I'm actually *his* attorney, you know."

"Why does he think I need another woman here? One who might die trying to uncover secrets best left alone. At least by a human."

"You'll have to ask him that. But if I had to guess, I'd say he's matchmaking again. This one's beautiful: twenty-nine, tall, and slender, with shoulder length hair that's a lovely cinnamon color. The same color as her eyes."

The wistful tone in Andy's voice alarmed Roman. Women usually didn't affect the stalwart solicitor this way.

"It's quite unique. I've never seen anyone before whose hair was the same color as her eyes." Andy gave a rare chuckle. "Her language is quite something, though. I couldn't understand half of what she said."

Rising from his chair, he headed for the door. "Oh by the way, she thinks your father is your grandfather, so be careful what you call him."

Roman rolled his eyes. "Christ. Why does Father insist on this tomfoolery?"

Andy stopped on the threshold and turned to face him. "You know how he is. He's worried about you being alone after he dies. After all, he'll be eighty-six next month and won't be around much longer. He claims you need a wife. However, I suspect what he really wants is a grandchild."

He cleared his throat. "Maybe you should just marry one of these women. It might stop his interfering. Although, what he expects you to do with her when you..."

"When I feed?" Roman finished for him.

Andy winced. "Couldn't you call it 'hunt' or something?" He hesitated, his lips pursed. "I suppose you can always drug her on those nights."

"Yes, and you saw how well that worked for Melinda." Roman's hands rose and fell as frustration fought with annoyance. "I'm still not sure who committed that murder. So I can't promise I can prevent another one."

"If you want, I can tell Ms. Alcott the job's been canceled. However, I'd like you to be the one to tell your father she's not coming."

"No, I'll go along with it." Roman pinched the bridge of his nose with a thumb and forefinger. "The old coot's using his age and declining health against me. He knows I can't refuse him anything."

"He loves you, and he's never forgiven himself for the accident that killed your parents."

Roman sank into his favorite chair. "I've told him countless times it wasn't his fault—for all the good it's done. He considers it irrelevant that he saved my life by taking me in when none of my relatives wanted me." Shaking his head, he chuckled. "Amazing. A human raising a Vampire-Lycan cross-breed. But he's been a wonderful father to me. I doubt my own parents could have loved me more."

He raked his fingers through his hair. "Who knows? After this latest scheme fails, and the woman goes home in defeat, perhaps he'll finally give it up. I'll just have to protect her while she's here. And hope like hell I can prevent another murder."

Chapter 2

Heathrow Airport, England, June 2nd:

I've got a really bad feeling about this," Chase told David as
they waited in the Passport Control line.

"You should have mentioned that before."

"I tried. All the way across the Atlantic. But you were en-
grossed in your book and pretended not to hear me."

"Sorry," he said, not sounding the least apologetic. "It's a very
good book."

He studied her, his pale blue eyes shrewd. "Is it posing as my
assistant you don't like, or is it this whole caper?"

"It hardly matters, since we're here."

The hairs on the back of her neck prickled. She scanned the
crowded terminal. "I've got the strangest feeling someone's watching us."

David laughed. "Now you're being paranoid." He hesitated,
shooting glances up and down the lines of people waiting to have
their passports stamped. "Aren't you?"

Was she? No. The feeling was too strong for simple paranoia.
"Just keep your eyes and ears open."

Once through Passport Control, they collected their bags. She
had three.

"Let me help," he muttered. He grabbed his suitcase and one of
hers. "Christ, this is heavy. Did you bring every piece of clothing
you own?"

"That's strange. It didn't seem that heavy to me." She frowned then shrugged. "I just figured we'd be here awhile. And I had no idea what I'd need."

"So, naturally, you brought everything." He shook his head. "God forbid you should actually have to launder something while we're here."

She gave him a dirty look. How could she explain she'd felt compelled to pack as if she were never going back to Los Angeles? Trying to ignore her uneasiness, she led the way to where Wright had said he'd meet them.

"Mr. Bronson. Ms. Alcott." The attorney shook their hands. "The car's this way. Let me get your bags, Ms. Alcott."

He struggled but managed to carry the suitcases to a silver Rolls Royce parked by the curb. "Roman is delighted you agreed to take this assignment."

Chase bit back a sarcastic remark. From the way Wright's aura flickered, she figured Roman was anything *but* delighted.

"We've decided it would be most convenient for you to stay at Fernwood Manor," he continued. "It's just outside Letchmore Heath. About forty-five minutes from London. Roman has agreed to give you his full cooperation. Though, he really doesn't think you'll find any new evidence."

His aura sputtered again, this time adding an element Chase recognized as fear. Why? Did he know who killed the woman? Was he somehow involved? Or was his anxiety related to something else?

The Rolls ambled through the busy London streets and onto what Wright called the "motorway." Though it was late spring, the rain came down in sheets. Everything looked so green. And drenched. She shivered, wondering if it was the weather or the mission.

By the time they reached Letchmore Heath, the rain had slowed to a steady, gray drizzle. One look at the village and Chase fell instantly in love, charmed by the quaint little cottages tucked behind neat brick walls, tidy hedges, and white-picket fences. A pond in the center of town sported a small flock of ducks.

When they drove past the local pub, she couldn't suppress a grin at the funny looking little cars parked in front. As the Rolls crept through the picturesque settlement, she promised herself she'd come back and explore at the first opportunity.

A few miles past the village, they turned onto a long, curved driveway. Her breath caught at her first glimpse of Fernwood Manor. Built of beige stone, it was palatial, three-storied, and—from what Wright said—at least three hundred years old.

With the well-tended lawns, woodlands, and pastures surrounding it, the manor house looked like an island of pale rock in the midst of a vibrant green sea.

When the car came to a stop at the end of the drive, she noticed a man standing at the front door. Somehow, she knew this was Roman Fernwood.

He looked to be in his mid-thirties. Very tall and rangy, he had a rugged face that was handsome without being pretty. His pale, English skin contrasted sharply with his blue-black hair and dark, haunted eyes.

But it was his aura that held her spellbound. She'd never seen one like it. Its base, a clear red, was laced with feathery strands of yellow, orange-red, bright pink, violet, indigo, and green, as well as a hint of dark, murky pink. It also sparked with tinges of deep, muddy red as he watched them get out of the car.

The colors told her Roman was powerful, confident, and passionate. He had a strong sense of justice, as well as some dark secrets. Right now, he was angry. And dangerous. She wasn't sure why, or to whom, she just knew he was.

He stared at her in silence. His intense gaze made the heat rise in her cheeks. Appalled, she tossed her hair back and glared at him. A small, mocking smile lifted the corners of his mouth while his aura shimmered with a surge of dismay.

She shot a glance at David. He looked dazed. *Uh oh!* Was this going to be a problem? God, she hoped not. She'd have to talk to him.

With an unusual gracefulness, Roman approached the car. "Mr. Bronson. Ms. Alcott. I'm Roman Fernwood."

His indigo-blue eyes were striking, his scent heavenly—reminiscent of chocolate-chip cookies and fresh-baked bread. Her mouth watered. She swallowed, fighting the urge to step closer and inhale. *What the hell's wrong with me?*

He shook hands with David before moving on to her. His grasp firm, he brought her fingers to his lips and lingered, making her blush again. Infuriated with herself, she tugged her hand out of his.

His arrogant smile grew wider as his gaze locked with hers. "I'm so pleased you could come," he said, but his aura contradicted him.

"Sure, you are." She shrugged to show she didn't care. "It's obvious you don't want us here. And personally, I'd rather be back in California. So let's cut the bullshit, shall we?"

Surprise flashed in both his aura and his eyes. "As you wish." He gestured toward the front door. "Please go in. The butler will show you to your rooms and bring up your bags. After you've had a chance to freshen up, we can discuss the reason you're here."

ဢ

Stunned, Roman cursed under his breath as he watched Chase walk into the house. Could his nose be wrong? He sniffed the air again. No. There was no mistake.

He turned on Andy. "Damn it, man, that woman's a cross breed."

Andy paled. "A Lycan-Vampire? She can't be."

"No, of course not. She's a Tigris hybrid. Half human, half weretiger. And she's coming into heat, for Christ's sake. What the hell is her pride thinking, letting her come here right now?" He rubbed at the tension in the back of his neck. "And didn't you say she was only twenty-nine?"

When Andy nodded, Roman groaned. "Then this is her *first* heat. Good lord, don't they realize how dangerous this situation is?" Jamming his hands into his pockets, he paced beside the car. "She needs to be home with her mate."

"I don't think she has either. No pride and no mate. I found no mention of any family or significant other in the research I did on her. Of course, I only did my routine investigation." Andy glanced toward the house. "What about her business partner?"

"Bronson doesn't count. He's one hundred percent human."

Roman couldn't understand what she was doing here. Even if she didn't have a pride or a mate, she should know better than to be among strangers so close to her first heat. Unless...Was it possible she didn't know what she was?

"Dig deeper," he told Andy. "Find out everything you can about her. Immediately."

"Do you think your father knows?"

"He has to. This can't be a coincidence." He paused to think. "Being human, Father couldn't have told by her scent. So someone in New York must have mentioned her."

"Who? None of the Weres in the U.S. know who your father is. To them, he'd be just another human."

"I know, but what other explanation—" The wind shifted, and Roman tensed, catching the scent of danger. "Another Tigris," he whispered. "He must have followed her here. Christ, I told you this was dangerous. If he catches her alone, he could force a claiming."

"What are you going to do?"

"Nothing. For the moment. His scent is faint, so he's not on our property. And if he's letting me smell him, he's too stupid to be a problem." He tasted the air again. "Or else he's acting as bait. Either way, going after him is a bad idea."

"What will you do about Ms. Alcott?"

"Protect her. What else can I do?" *And resist her.* If he could. Why the hell did she have to be so stunning? Or her scent so intoxicating? Not to mention those cinnamon eyes. He sighed. What the hell *was* he going to do? "Just get me as much information about her as you can. And fast."

Clamping down, hard, on the lust raging through his blood, he headed inside. The damn woman was trouble.

Her aura told him she was stubborn, courageous, independent, confident, and passionate—though if she hadn't had her first heat, she probably wouldn't know that. Yet. While he'd made her blush, twice, she'd been unaffected by the hypnotic power of his Vampire eyes. Oh, yes, she was most definitely trouble.

She'd need someone to guide her through her heat. Not him—not a wolf half-breed who'd be her natural enemy in the animal world. Dogs and cats were hardly a preferred match.

He should send her home. Immediately. But he couldn't. Not if she didn't know what she was and had no pride or mate to help her. He refused to let any Were flounder alone.

He sighed. The next month wasn't going to be pleasant. Not for anyone, but especially not for him. For him, it was going to be hell.

e⁄ɔe⁄ɔ

"Fernwood's attorney met her at the airport, so I followed them." Standing in the parlor of Ileana's elegant mansion, Dillon Butler struggled to control his anger. "He took her to Fernwood Manor. Apparently, they intend for her to stay there while she's in England."

"Perfect." The Vampire's smile made the hair on the back of Dillon's neck stand up.

"Perfect? Hell, Ileana, Chase is *my* mate, damn it. What if Roman decides to claim her before she comes into heat?"

"He won't. Your little Yankee pussycat doesn't know what she is." She waved a hand, as if dismissing his concerns. "Roman would consider it unethical to claim a mate who doesn't understand the rules."

Dillon turned to stare out the window at Ileana's luxurious gardens. He didn't believe her. She was a Vampire, for Christ's sake. What the hell did she know about Weres?

Roman was no different from any other man. If he got the chance, he'd force a claiming on Chase. It's exactly what Dillon would have done—what he still intended to do. Even if he had to kidnap her to do it. Hell, he should've snatched her in California when he had the chance, instead of just observing and keeping his distance like he'd been told.

He glanced over his shoulder at Ileana and saw her watching him with glowing red eyes. Swallowing hard, he turned around to face her. "You promised her to me."

She patted his cheek. "You'll have her, my pet, as soon as I get my revenge on Roman. And once you have the papers I'm arranging, you'll also have control of all her lovely money." With a shrug, she turned away and poured a glass of blood red wine from a crystal decanter. At least he hoped it was wine. "If she's as close to her heat as you claim," Ileana continued. "Roman won't be able to resist her. He'll fall like a stone. Once he does, the half-breed's all yours."

She gestured with her wine glass. "Besides, if you hadn't wasted so much time before going to New York to tell old man Fern-wood about her, you'd already have her."

"Now, look, damn it." He took a deep breath, reining in his temper. It didn't pay to get angry at a Vampire. "I flew to New York as soon as you called me, and I made contact with the old goat the day after I got there. And *he* flew to California that same day. It wasn't my fault the dumb bastard got hit by a car."

"No, I suppose not. Well then, I guess we're both lucky my plan allowed for the unexpected."

He didn't like her plan, especially since she held all the cards. While Dillon was a full-blood Tigris, he was a Bengal, second class Weres to the Siberians. If he wanted to raise his status in the local pride, he had to mate above his station. Although Chase was part human, the Tigris part was Royal Siberian.

Plus, a match with her meant he'd never have to work again—provided Ileana made good on her promise to arrange for the papers declaring Dillon executor of the trust that controlled Chase's money.

"So what's our next move?" he asked.

"Watch the house and keep me informed. But be careful. Roman's half Vampire. His senses are far superior to yours. So keep your distance, and don't let him know you're there."

"I don't care if he's half God." Dillon headed for the door. "If he tries to claim my woman, I'll kill him."

⁊᷈᷈

Roman gave Chase and David an hour then asked them to join him in his study. She looked even more dazzling than before. She'd changed into soft gray slacks and a pink Angora sweater that complimented her ivory skin and made the highlights in her dark red hair gleam like an autumn sunset. He poured her some wine, cursing the fact he'd ever laid eyes on her.

"So, tell me about the case," she said as he handed her the glass.

He frowned. "Didn't Andy explain it?"

"Only that someone was trying to complicate your life, and strange things were happening here."

"Yes. Very strange. Items belonging to guests are stolen.

Threatening notes left on their pillows. Dead animals appear in the garden whenever guests are staying here."

He handed a glass of wine to David then set the bottle back on the hutch. "None of it makes any sense."

"And the murder?"

"Melinda was a newspaper reporter who was a friend of my fa—" He covered his slip with a cough. "A friend of my grandfather's. She came to stay for a week at his request."

Wishing she'd focus those eyes on someone else, he turned his back and poured himself a glass of burgundy.

"Since Melinda was a sleepwalker, she had her apartment rigged to wake her before she could hurt herself. While staying here, she consumed some sleeping powders at night, which should have made it impossible for her to get out of bed."

Taking a sip of wine, he turned back around. "The night she died she was found on the ground beneath the balcony of the third floor guestroom where she was staying. The inspector who investigated assumed she'd been climbing the balcony railing in her sleep and fell off."

"But you don't agree?" David asked.

"No. The pathologist who did the autopsy told me the sleeping powders would have prevented her from getting out of bed. And she *did* consume the powders. He found the drug in her system." He hesitated, wondering how much to tell her then decided to stick with the facts. "Not only that, but except for some seepage from broken skin, she didn't bleed."

"Which means she was dead before she went over the balcony." Chase stared at him, her eyes unfocused.

He knew she was checking his aura. Cats' eyes could see auras even better than wolves' eyes could. *So you'd better be careful, or she'll know you're holding back.*

She sipped her drink, licked her lips. "Did you discover any motive for the murder?"

"None that made any sense." Again, he wondered if he should tell her what he suspected. No, now wasn't the time.

She studied him as if trying to read his thoughts. David, he noticed, watched him with undisguised lust. That didn't concern him.

He could handle David, but he wasn't so sure about Chase.

She rose from her chair, walked over, and looked him in the

eyes. "Then tell me this, why did your grandfather want us involved? You obviously have all the contacts you need. You know what the pathologist found, what the police think."

Turning away, she paced—no, he corrected, she prowled the room like a caged tiger, spreading her scent and taunting his inner beast with her pheromones.

"There isn't any need for us," she continued. "Your attorney said it was because your grandfather didn't want a scandal, but I don't buy it. He had to have some other reason for wanting us here."

Surprised by her question, he didn't attempt to conceal his disbelief. "You don't know?"

She shook her head. "Do you?"

Her aura didn't change. So she really didn't know. Interesting. Could Andy have misread the old man's intentions? Melinda had certainly been aware of his father's motives.

"I thought I did," he said. "Now, I'm not so sure."

"What did you think the reason was?"

"Knowing the old man," he confessed with some reluctance, "I assumed he was matchmaking."

David rolled his eyes, but Chase laughed. Enchanted with the sound, Roman found it hard to remember just how much he wished she were in California.

"Don't you have enough women in England to choose from?" she asked. "Why does he have to import them from America?"

Roman refilled David's wine glass then Chase's, trying to ignore her effect on his senses.

"Perhaps I misjudged him. If so, I have no idea why he picked you." He concentrated his gaze on hers, but she seemed immune to the power of his eyes. With a sigh, he looked away. "Have you solved many murders?"

"No. Fraud, embezzlement, missing persons, runaways, stuff like that. Things our clients want handled discreetly. We've helped locate evidence and witnesses in murder cases. And we've helped clients put pieces of the puzzle together to decide if a family member was involved. But most murders in the U.S. are solved by the police." A sardonic smile curved her mouth. "PIs there don't get the access to police records an English nobleman might get here. I understand class can open a lot of doors in England, making this much easier."

"I can see where you Yankees might find our aristocracy amusing. But you're right. It can open a great many doors." From his desk drawer, he pulled out a slim gray folder. "Since you're here, you may as well see what you can do."

He handed her the folder. "This case file contains everything I've been able to gather about the murder." Might as well let her try. Especially since he didn't want her to return to The States until he knew there was someone there who could help her deal with what she was. "Perhaps you'll see something I didn't."

"Perhaps."

Her smile, this one genuine, made Roman catch his breath. Christ, what was he going to do about her?

She scanned the file then passed it to David. "All those people mentioned as being in the house on the night the reporter died, are they available? Can we meet them without it looking suspicious?"

Roman stifled a groan. "If you think it's absolutely necessary." At their blank expressions, he clarified. "The only way to do it without causing unwanted questions is to have a party. We had two the week Melinda was here. That's the reason there are so many names on that list. She died three hours after the second one ended."

Chase cocked her head and studied him. "I get the impression you don't like parties any more than I do."

"No. I don't."

"I think it's a great idea," David quipped. "I love parties. It's the perfect way to meet these people." He looked from one to the other and laughed. "You should see your face," he said to Roman. "You and Chase have identical expressions of horror."

Roman studied David's aura. It was very different from Chase's and, in its own way, as surprising as hers. The colors told him David was loyal, honest, realistic, adventurous, and self-confident. Not what he'd expected. Especially since Andy said David wrote "true-crime" stories based on cases he and Chase had worked.

Roman had assumed there'd be insecurity and creativity coloring his aura, but instead it pulsed with the more grounded earth tones.

From the flickers of passion that occurred now and then when he looked at Chase, David was probably more bisexual than homosexual. Though he might be surprised to hear it. He was also what humans considered an Adonis—tall, golden blond, and handsome—but Chase showed no passion in her aura when she looked at him.

Disturbed by the relief that gave him, Roman suppressed a groan. The more time he spent with her, the less rational his thinking became. He'd have to feed tonight if he wanted to have any hope of resisting the raw lust she aroused in him.

He shook his head at the direction his thoughts were taking and focused on the subject at hand. "I suppose a party is the best way to handle it."

"I can do the mingling." David grinned. "If you two don't want to come."

Roman's lips twitched as he imagined how the British aristocracy would react when they met David, who was posing as a gay interior decorator. From California. It might be worth having a party just to watch.

"Unfortunately, since I'm the host, I'll have to be there." He shrugged. "We usually have them on the weekends we have guests. So I'll arrange one for Friday and Saturday next and invite all the people who came to the ones with Melinda."

"Let's do it backward," Chase suggested. "Switch the people who came to the one the night Melinda died to Friday, and the others to Saturday."

"I've no problem with that," Roman said. "However, do you mind if I ask why?"

"Two reasons. First, if the murderer was one of the people at the party the night she died, we might see something about them we'd like to investigate further. If so, we can ask them back on Saturday."

Impressed, Roman nodded. "And the second reason?"

She grinned. "If we get what we need on Friday, we can cancel the one on Saturday."

"Good thinking."

Going back to his desk, he jotted a note on his calendar. Not that he needed to, but it made him appear more human. Out of the corner of his eye he noticed both Chase and David watching him. She seemed suspicious, David looked dazed.

Roman sighed. "Why don't you both take it easy for the rest of the afternoon? Think about what we've discussed and go over the file. If you come up with anything, we can talk about it in the morning. Dinner's at seven in the small dining room. I'll have one of the servants come and get you."

"You won't be joining us for dinner." She made it a statement, not a question.

"Not tonight, I'm afraid. I'm sorry to be such a poor host, but I've a meeting I can't reschedule."

"Tomorrow then." She rose and collected the file from the table where David had placed it.

As she passed Roman on the way to the door, her scent shot straight to his loins. He shoved his hands into his pockets to keep from reaching for her. Yes, he would definitely have to feed tonight.

After she and David left the study, he headed for the kitchen to make sure the butler remembered to put sleeping powders in his guests' tea at dinner.

He wanted them both sound asleep. Not only so they couldn't follow him, but he dared not risk the chance she might decide to take an evening walk. In her condition, with the other tiger around, the consequences could be disastrous.

Chapter 3

So much for Roman's complete cooperation." Restless, Chase paced in front of the huge, stone fireplace in her bedroom, where she and David had convened after leaving the study. "There's an awful lot he's not telling us."

She pressed a hand to her throbbing stomach. "I didn't detect any outright lies, but I'm sure he's keeping secrets."

David hunched his shoulders. "So you see auras in England too?"

She glared at him. He sighed.

"Look, I'll admit you're uncannily right about your impressions of people. But I still think it's due to the fact that you're highly observant, rather than there's some mystical force field surrounding all of us."

She tried to overlook the pain his words caused her, but she couldn't. "So you think I'm lying about what I see?"

He blinked. "No, of course not. You're one of the most honest people I know."

Exasperated, she threw up her hands. "Then how the hell do you explain what I say I see?"

He cleared his throat. "Do you really want to get into this now?"

Running his index finger along the inside of his shirt collar, he swallowed. He looked so uncomfortable, she almost said no, but her pride wouldn't let her back down.

"Sure. Let's hear it."

"I've always assumed there's something wrong with your eyes." He rubbed his neck and cleared his throat again. "Sometimes they don't look quite, um—quite human."

Realizing he was serious, she stared at him in shock. "Not human?"

"Yeah, they, um, sometimes they seem to reflect light. You know, like cats' eyes do at night."

"That's ridiculous," she said, ignoring the ice that skittered down her spine. "Why haven't you ever said anything about it before?"

"I don't know. I guess because your eyes never seemed to bother you. And you don't have any trouble seeing. Besides, I wasn't sure what to say. Or even if what I saw was real. I'd have thought I imagined it if you hadn't said you saw auras."

"Other people see them, too."

She refused to believe there was anything wrong with her eyes. Her vision wasn't just good, it was excellent. Whatever he'd seen had to be an optical illusion.

Frustrated and uneasy, her stomach churning, she dug in her pocket for a Tums. "Try doing some research on the Internet. There are tons of websites on auras."

"True, but I doubt any of them are legit." Before she could respond, he shook his head and put his hands on her shoulders. "Look, let's not argue about it. Okay?" He kissed her forehead. "You're still my best friend, despite your strange eyes. I'll take your word for what you see. Now, when did you notice these flickers?"

"My eyes aren't strange," she muttered, but she figured that was all the apology she'd get from him and let it go. "For one thing, I'm not sure that Lord Fernwood's really his grandfather. Roman was also holding something back when he talked about motives and about Melinda 'consuming' those sleeping powders." She tapped her bottom lip with a finger. "'Consumed.' Interesting word to use, don't you think?"

"The toxicology report's in the file, and it says some drug I can't even pronounce was in her system."

"Oh, I'm not questioning whether she had it in her system." She poured herself a glass of water from the pitcher someone had left on the vanity. "I'm just wondering whether she took it herself or if it was given to her without her knowledge."

"You think the murderer gave it to her? But why?"

"It's a lot easier to kill someone who's sound asleep and can't fight you." She took a testing sip of the water. It tasted better than she'd expected, so she drank several swallows to ease her dry throat. "Even a small woman could do some damage when fighting like hell to save her life."

She wiped her mouth on the back of her hand. "Not to mention people don't make much noise if they're sound asleep. Awake, even if she couldn't fight off the murderer, Melinda could've screamed for help and woken the whole house. And did you catch what Roman said about her not bleeding?"

"She died of a broken neck, so that's not surprising."

"David, she was dead before she went off the balcony. Had to be. If the fall had killed her, she would've bled from broken skin, if not a crushed skull. But dead people don't bleed because their heart's not pumping blood. It might leak out of wounds, but they don't actively bleed."

"And you think Roman had something to do with that?"

"No, not with the murder. But he knows something. I'm just not sure what. The only times his aura flickered with dishonesty were when he mentioned his grandfather, the motives, and the sleeping powders." She chuckled darkly. "Except when he told us how pleased he was to have us here."

"What about when he said he couldn't join us for dinner?" he asked, a slight pout to his lips.

"No, that was the truth. He has something pressing to do tonight." She gave him her best "senior-partner" scowl. "And speaking of our host, I don't want you trying to jump his bones. That kind of problem, we *don't* need."

He gaped at her, and she narrowed her eyes. "I saw the way you looked at him. I also saw the lust in your aura, so don't try to tell me you weren't thinking of doing the nasty with him."

He conceded the point with a shrug and a grimace. "That doesn't mean I have plans to do anything about it. He's obviously straight, Chase, and not even the least bit interested in me. Now, *you* on the other hand."

Her hand jerked, slopping water on her sweater. "*Me?*" She brushed off the drops with her sleeve and shook her head. "No, you're mistaken. I didn't see any flares of lust in his aura at all. Not when he looked at you and not when he looked at me. He's definitely got a very passionate nature, but his aura says he's in total control of it." She paused. "Unless I missed it, but I don't think so."

"Well, it may not have shown up in his—whatchamacallit. But take it from me, he looks at you like you're some kind of yummy dessert he wants to devour whole." He shot her a sideways glance. "What about you? Does *he* turn *you* on?"

"Why would I bother with a man whose aura says he's not interested in me?" She kept her face blank, not wanting him to know how much Roman really affected her. "If he was, who knows? He's not bad looking. And his English accent's to die for."

David laughed. "'Not bad looking.' God, Chase, with such a talent for understatement, I'm surprised you're not British." He just laughed harder when she rolled her eyes. "Besides, I've never seen you interested in a man, even when one was *very* attracted to you. I bet you've never let anyone even get close enough to be a lover. Have you?"

"That's none of your damn business."

So what if she'd never met a man who aroused her until now? If it meant there was something wrong with her, so be it. Her life was rich and full just the way it was. She didn't need a lover, especially not a rich, arrogant playboy like Roman Fernwood.

"I didn't think so." He kissed her cheek and wrapped an arm around her shoulders. "Someday, girlfriend, you'll meet a man who'll breach those walls you've constructed." His face grew serious. "When he does, there'll be no going back, and I'm afraid you're really going to get hurt."

She laughed it off. "You make it sound so appealing, I can hardly wait. But don't hold your breath for it to be Roman Fernwood."

"That's okay," he assured her as he headed for the door. "I've got enough dirty thoughts about the man for both of us."

Alone in her room, she wondered if the reason she was so uneasy about this case was because she sensed Roman could get to her.

In a way, she wanted it to happen, wanted to know if she was capable of passion, and if so, how much. In another way, it terrified her, because she suspected David was right. She was in for a great deal of pain.

࿇࿇࿇

Aghast, Roman stood frozen in the ground floor corridor. He'd just left the kitchen after speaking with his butler when his ultra-sensitive hearing caught the conversation going on two floors above.

Chase was a virgin. Not only hadn't she mated one of her own kind, she hadn't even taken a human lover.

Christ! How much more bad news was there? Though, he supposed he shouldn't really be surprised. Most female Weres felt little or no passion until they experienced their first heat. Still, they knew if they'd never had sex, the heat would be a great deal harder on them. At least they *should* know.

He'd obviously been right. She didn't have a clue what she was. If she did, she'd have understood why David thought her eyes looked strange. She also never would've risked a trip away from home at this critical time. And she sure as hell wouldn't still be a virgin.

How could her parents, or whoever had raised her, allow her to grow to adulthood without understanding her unique genetics? And, more importantly, how was he going to help her? She had to be told, not only to prepare her for her heat, but to prevent her from exposing the existence of Weres. Chase was intelligent and perceptive and obviously shared most of her thoughts with David.

That had to stop. Immediately.

Roman could hardly sit her down and explain she was half Siberian Tigris/half human, and she needed to have sex as soon as possible because she was coming into heat. He snorted. *Oh yeah, that'll go over swell.*

The thought of her innocence fired his blood. Would it be so wrong to seduce her? Then, at least, he could assure she'd had sex before her heat. Or was that just an excuse to satisfy his own needs?

He could have almost any woman he wanted since very few could resist the hypnotic power of his eyes. Yet, while those seductions satisfied his physical needs, they did little for his emotional ones. For that, he needed a *willing* partner—one who could resist his eyes and was there because she wanted him as much as he did her.

Chase had not only resisted his eyes, she'd been unimpressed with his wealth or his manners and had seen right through his evasions.

Lust surged again, and he was glad she wasn't around to see his aura now. If he seduced her, he'd have to be careful. Unprotected sex between Weres meant claiming, and he had no intention of claiming anyone. Ever. He didn't want a mate. Especially a cat who didn't know what she was or what claiming meant.

He shook off his disturbing thoughts, like a dog shaking off water, and headed for his bedroom. Since Chase and David were occupied getting ready for dinner, this was the perfect time to check out the Tigris intruder he'd scented earlier. He grinned. It'd be easier—and a lot more fun—to do it on four feet instead of two.

Stripping down to his skin, he slipped outside. On his patio, veiled in the dusk of early evening, he morphed into a huge black wolf. He treated his muscles to a long, luxurious stretch and growled with pleasure.

God, he loved this part of himself. How boring it must be to be human. Life without the abilities and enhanced senses of his Lycan-Vampire heritage held little appeal for him. In fact, it seemed hardly worth living. He felt an upsurge of sympathy for David and wondered if Chase would be thrilled or horrified when she found out about her special genetics.

ഉഹരു

Dinner was scrumptious, the entrees rich with garlic and herbs. Martin, the elderly butler, told them the cook was French, so Chase assumed the food was as well. Afraid to ask what the strange-looking dishes were, she just enjoyed each tasty morsel. Martin served tea rather than coffee with dinner, but even that was delicious.

Roman didn't appear, either during dinner or afterward when she stopped by the library to borrow a book. Her disappointment surprised her. Of course, she wondered about him. He was a stranger. Or was it more than that? No, it couldn't be. She refused to let it be.

She was here to solve a murder, nothing more, and she never got personally involved with clients. Still, he filled her thoughts as she wandered around the huge library, looking at all the different books and stifling yawns.

Even considering jet lag, this fatigue and lack of energy was unusual for her. Hopefully, it would pass by morning. Selecting a science fiction novel, she plopped down in a chair.

ભ

Roman returned to the house shortly before midnight and found Chase in the library. Sound asleep. She made a lovely picture, curled up with her head on one arm of the chair and her hair splayed out around her. A book lay open on the floor.

"I found her like this right after dinner, sir," Martin told him. "But I didn't think I should try to move her until you got back, in case it woke her. Perhaps I put too much of the drug in her tea."

"Perhaps, but it's better to be safe than sorry. And you did the right thing by not moving her." He gathered Chase in his arms and carried her up to her room. "Christ," he muttered as he paused to adjust himself. Just holding her like this had him hard as iron.

Once in her bedroom, he laid her on the bed and covered her with a quilt. Then after a moment's thought, he lifted the blanket and removed her shoes so she'd sleep more comfortably. Bad move. The delicate shape of her feet entranced him. It was all he could do not to nibble on her toes. Biting back a curse, he turned away.

"Roman."

He'd almost reached the door when he heard her moan his name as she shifted in her sleep. The sound was so seductive it stopped him cold. A fierce longing seized him. Almost against his will, he went back and sat on the bed beside her.

She looked lovely in the moonlight coming through the open drapes. Her lips were slightly parted, as if waiting for his. He couldn't resist. Just once, he told himself and mated his mouth to hers.

Her response startled him. Slipping her arms around his neck, she met his lips with enthusiasm. So much enthusiasm, for a moment he thought she'd woken.

He let the kiss continue for several seconds, sinking deeper than he'd intended. Stifling a groan, he tore his lips away and gently removed her arms from around his neck. Unable to help himself, he lay next to her on the bed and held her, breathing in her scent. After a few moments spent fighting for control, he released her, rose, and rearranged the quilt over her.

Cursing himself for his foolishness, he hurried from the room. Where had these blasted feelings for her come from? He could understand the lust. After all, she was a beautiful woman and coming into heat. But the tenderness and the longing for much more than sex from her—these were not only unexpected, they were unwelcome.

It'll be even harder to stay away from her now, you idiot. Kissing her had been the height of folly and not at all like him. Maybe in the morning he should send her and David home. There was no *maybe* to it. He knew he should send them home. He also knew he couldn't.

And not just because she was a Were with no one to help her.

He wanted to claim her for his own.

He could no longer fool himself he'd be seducing her for her sake. Bloody hell! With one passionate kiss, she'd undermined decades of self-control. *What am I going to do now?*

♥♥♥

Chase jolted awake. Had she heard her door open? She glanced over. The door was closed. No one was in the room, but Roman's scent drifted on the air. She'd been having a very passionate dream about him, and her system was reeling from disappointment and thwarted lust.

Through the open drapes she saw the moon, high in a black velvet sky. *It must be close to midnight.* She adjusted her sweater then stared at herself in shock. How had she gotten into bed fully dressed? *Roman!* She'd fallen asleep in the library, and he'd obviously carried her up to bed.

No wonder she'd been dreaming about him. His scent was all over her. Damn, she'd been carried in his arms and hadn't even been awake to enjoy it.

No, don't go there. She meant what she'd told David about not sleeping with clients. No way would she let Roman destroy her professional reputation. Besides, all a man like him wanted was sex. As gorgeous as he was, he probably had women lined up for miles. He had money, looks, and breeding—stuff that was important to some women.

Chase got undressed and crawled back into bed, seized by an unreasonable yearning for him to walk through the door and join her.

"Oh, for crying out loud. Stop thinking about it and go back to sleep."

c⁄ɔc⁄ɔ

On his way downstairs, Roman heard Chase get up, move around, and go back to bed. She'd probably gotten undressed. He tried to force the picture from his mind—without success. Though he did manage to stop himself from going back to kiss her again now that she was awake.

He chuckled at her frustrated muttering, wondering what exactly she was thinking about that wouldn't let her go back to sleep.

Were her thoughts on him? He hoped so. It would make seducing her so much easier.

Entering his room, he stretched out on his bed and slipped into the trance that constituted sleep for his Lycan-Vampire body, wishing he could dream of Chase and hoping she was dreaming of him.

c⁄ɔc⁄ɔ

June 3rd:

When the first gray light of dawn stole through the windows of his room four hours later, Roman roused himself and headed for the shower. As the hot water beat down on his body, he analyzed the situation with Chase, trying to come up with solutions to the various challenges she presented.

First problem was the intruder. Roman had found the spot at the edge of his neighbor's estate where the Bengal had spied on Fernwood Manor. From there he'd tracked the weretiger to the road where his scent suddenly disappeared. He caught a whiff of transmission fluid and motor oil and figured the man had driven off.

How had the guy even known Chase was here? And why had he been following her? Well, that was obvious. She was an unmated female.

Did the Bengal and Chase know each other? Then why the hell hadn't he told her what she was? Or had he just noticed her at the airport and followed her? Either way, given that he'd been sneaking around, rather than making his presence known, his intentions probably weren't honorable.

Roman's temper spiked. He still didn't know what he was going to do about her, but he'd be damned if he'd let anything happen to her while she was under his protection.

Drake Gatos, the leader of the local Tigris pride, had to be told. Roman didn't relish the job, but wouldn't shirk it. Drake, a pure-blood Siberian, was a good man, a fair man, but he was also unmated, as were many of the males in his pride. Drake would see Chase first as a potential mate and second as an innocent Were in need of protection.

Still, the pride leader would have to be told. Withholding the information could start a war.

At the thought of her belonging to someone else, Roman growled in rage and snapped off the water so hard, he broke the knob. *Jesus, I've got it bad*, he decided, staring at the mangled piece of plastic in his hand.

He stepped out of the shower, tossed the broken knob on the counter, and grabbed a towel. He'd be safer away from the house today.

If he stayed away from her, maybe his head would clear so he could think. Less than twenty-four hours ago he'd resented her presence and worried about how to get rid of her. Now, he was trying to find a way to tell her what she was and seduce her. Christ. He rubbed his hand over his face. What a bloody mess.

He dressed and went to find Martin, instructing him to drug the tea again this evening.

"I won't be back until late, and I don't want Chase wandering around outside alone at night."

Martin nodded. "And if the young lady heads back to the library after dinner and falls asleep again?"

"We can only hope," Roman said with a smile. "Oh, and have Wilson replace the broken knob in my shower."

Chuckling at Martin's look of surprise, Roman slipped out the side door and drove off the estate.

ಌಌಌ

When Chase came down to breakfast with David, Martin informed them Roman had been called away early on some family business and would be unable to join them for dinner again this evening.

She swallowed her disappointment with her coffee and told herself it was all for the best. She needed to stop obsessing about him, do her job, and get the hell out of England while she still had her sanity.

After breakfast, she and David wandered the mansion pretending to take notes on decorating, while surreptitiously interviewing the staff and looking for anything that could explain the mysterious happenings here. She used a good deal of flattery and "sucking up," asking the staff's opinions on the décor of the ancient house.

Everyone was courteous and more than willing to gossip, but no one had any real information to give her. The only significant thing she learned the entire damn day was that each mysterious event happened during a weekend when parties were given at the estate.

Martin and Sandra, his wife, who worked as a maid, were the only staff living in the house with the family. Everyone else, including the cook, lived in the village and seemed to have little personal information about the Fernwoods.

The cook told her Roman rarely ate meals at the house. Even when he joined Lord Fernwood or guests for dinner, he seldom ate. He'd drink a glass of wine or two, but that was all. When the old man was away like this, the cook only came in to feed the staff and any guests of the estate. David asked if perhaps Roman was on some special diet for medical reasons, but the staff didn't think so.

Martin insisted Roman had very definite tastes and ate out often so as not to make it harder on the staff. "He was always a picky eater, even as a child," he said. "Drove his grandfather half mad."

Martin and Sandra had been with the Fernwoods for years. The rest of the staff had been hired three years earlier when the Fernwoods moved back to their ancestral home, which had been vacant for many years.

Chase studied the auras of the staff as they answered her questions, but only the butler's and his wife's showed any deceit—and only about Roman's grandfather. What it was they were hiding, she couldn't tell.

She asked David his opinion when they convened before dinner, but he was as confused as she was.

"It's probably something very simple," he said.

"Like what?"

"Maybe Roman and his grandfather aren't actually related. Maybe the old man was lonely, found an orphan, and took him in as his grandson without the proper court approval. After all, Roman and his grandfather don't look anything alike." He shrugged. "You can't tell me that if an English nobleman wants to take custody of a child no one else wants, anyone's going to hassle him over it. I doubt there's much an English aristocrat can do the authorities will complain about. The way the English still revere their upper class, I'll bet some of them even get away with murder."

"But Roman's an adult now. It shouldn't matter anymore."

"These upper-crust families keep secrets for years, even after they don't matter anymore," he said. "Or so I've always heard."

"You may be right. I just hate not knowing for sure. Also, I didn't think adopted children could inherit under English law, and Martin said Roman will inherit when the old man dies."

"Maybe they changed the law. But if it bothers you so much, why don't you ask him?"

"When? We've only seen him for a couple of hours when we first got here. The rest of the time he's been gone."

When David didn't react, she knew she'd managed to hide her disappointment. And her passionate dream last night was no one's business but hers.

"He'll be at the parties on Friday and Saturday," he pointed out. "As the host he has to make an appearance. Tackle him then."

"So how are you doing?" she asked him, impressed by his matter-of-fact tone. "Is it hard on you?"

"Oh, I'm fine when he's not around," he said with a dismissive wave of his hand. "Then it's easy to concentrate on the mission."

He looked so feminine when he used that gesture, it never failed to make her smile. It was the only thing she'd ever seen him do that shouted to the world he was gay.

Martin called them to dinner, which was just as tasty as the night before, though the menu was completely different. And she had just as much trouble stifling her yawns afterward.

Determined not to embarrass herself for the second night in a row, she took the book up to her room. She managed to get undressed, into her pajamas, and into bed. But although the novel she'd chosen was a page-turner, she couldn't keep her eyes open.

Something was definitely wrong.

കൈ

"Damn it, Drake." Roman's words hissed out between his clenched teeth as he fought to control his rising temper. "I've already told you. The woman's under *my* protection, and I'm not turning her over to anyone."

His lips curled back in a snarl, the pride leader glared at him. "You're telling me you have a half-Siberian, Tigris female staying at your estate, yet you refuse to surrender her to me?" He paced the parlor of his Victorian mansion, his fluid grace a striking contrast to his anger-contorted face. "And you expect me to just sit back and let you keep her?" His harsh laugh contained no humor. "I can only assume you're on drugs."

"Hear me out, will you?" Roman watched Drake pace. With his shoulder-length crop of dark blond hair, deep-set golden-brown eyes, weretiger physique, and rugged facial features, the man could give him some serious competition for Chase's attention. No, he decided as his gut clenched. Not going to happen. "Chase doesn't even know what she is. She thinks she's human."

When Drake opened his mouth in astonishment, Roman sighed. "Don't ask. I've no idea how it happened, but I've already begun an investigation into her background.

"However, regardless of how it came about, it's a fact we have to deal with. She has to be handled carefully. I just need a little time."

Anticipating another argument, he hurried on. "I know. I know. With her coming into heat, we don't *have* much." He jammed his hands into his pockets. "Christ. She's still a virgin. Can you even imagine how terrified she'd be if I abandoned her in the middle of your pack of horny bachelors?"

"What the hell do you take me for?" Drake growled. "Do you think I'd allow them to treat her like a normal Tigris female? Give me a *little* credit."

"I know you could and would protect her. But she doesn't know that. She barely trusts me. Give me a few days. That's all I ask."

"So you can claim her yourself?"

"You know me better than that." Roman grimaced. The comment hit a little too close to the bone. "I wouldn't claim someone who has no idea what she is. It would hardly be fair, since it can't be undone once it happens."

Knowing he had to convince the man, but not wanting to tell an outright lie, he chose his words with care. "I hadn't intended to claim her at all," he said, making it past tense.

"However, if it makes you feel any better, I give you my word, I'll make no attempt to claim her before you've had a chance to meet her and talk to her. Or," he added quickly, catching Drake's frown, "before she knows what she is, what I am, and what other options she has for her choice of a mate."

Drake pursed his lips, obviously looking for any loopholes in the promise. He was as thoughtful and visionary a pride leader as he was a clever and resourceful one. So Roman wasn't surprised his words weren't taken at face value.

"You said you *hadn't* intended to claim her. Does that promise still hold if you change your mind?"

"You don't miss much, do you? Yes, it holds."

"All right. How much time do you need?"

"You mean, I won?"

"No. I'm conceding she'll have to be handled with kid gloves." Drake grinned. "It's bound to be awkward and difficult trying to convince her of the truth, so I'm willing to let you bear the brunt of that."

"Thanks. I think."

Roman reached for the decanter of burgundy on the table and held it up in a silent question. When his host nodded, he poured two glasses and handed one off to him.

"As I said, I need a few days. Today's Monday. I'm giving parties for Chase and David on Friday night and Saturday night. Come to the one on Friday. I'll make sure you get some time with her."

"I'll be there."

"There's another issue." Roman sipped his wine, inhaled the rich bouquet. "The day she arrived, one of your pride, a pure-bred Bengal from the smell of him, watched her arrive at Fernwood Manor. I'm assuming he followed her there from the airport. But since you weren't aware she was even here, he obviously didn't share the information with you."

"No, he didn't. You're sure it was one of my pride?"

"I didn't recognize his scent, but having two new weretigers in the area is a little too much of a coincidence."

"Unless the Bengal followed her across the pond."

"I thought of that. But if he knew of her when she was in California, why didn't he tell her what she is? Why let her come over here just before her heat?"

"You're right. It doesn't make sense." Drake studied his wine a moment. "Where did the Bengal watch your place from?"

"Due north of my duck pond, in the woods on Ileana's estate. He never actually came onto my property. Why?" Roman asked then answered his own question. "You're going to go see if you can recognize his scent, aren't you?"

"If the man is a member of my pride, I need to know. Whether he's one of mine, or he followed Chase from California, there's a reason he was watching her."

Drake clamped his hand to the back of his neck and rubbed. "And since the bugger didn't make his presence known, that reason can't be good. She could bloody well be in danger."

He paused by the window and stared out. "I hope you've taken adequate precautions."

"I have." Roman finished his wine and set the goblet on the table. "But they're only temporary until I have a chance to explain things to her."

"Then do it fast. In the meantime, I think you're acquainted with Gray and Duncan, aren't you?"

"I'd recognize their scents, if that's what you mean. It wasn't either of them." He grinned as he realized what Drake was planning. "You're going to have them watch my place, aren't you? To protect Chase from danger? Or to make sure I keep my promise?"

"Both." Drake slapped him on the back. "It's not that I don't trust you, old chap, but unmated females are few and far between. And I'm not giving up a royal-Siberian without a fight."

Chapter 4

Drake waited until the tail lights on Roman's car had disappeared from view before pressing the intercom.

"He's gone, Gray. Come on in."

A hidden panel opened, and his second-in-command, Grayson Hunter, stepped through it. A tall, slender, half-Siberian, half-Bengal, Gray's lanky frame belied his remarkable strength and endurance—traits Drake had depended on more times than he could count, along with his friend's unfailing loyalty.

"You heard?" he asked as Gray helped himself to a glass of burgundy.

"Of course." Gray took a long swallow of the blood-red wine. "Do you trust him?"

"Who, Roman?" Drake shrugged. "For the most part. I've never known him to go back on his word. But even so, he's a Lycan-Vampire cross, and Vampires aren't noted for their integrity."

"If you ask me, it's the man, not his species, that's trustworthy or not."

"Then, yes, I trust the man." Drake sighed and rubbed a hand over his face. "Still, we're dealing with an unmated, royal-Siberian female who's coming into heat. And under those circumstances, I'm not sure I'd even trust myself."

Gray chuckled. "Point taken." He pulled a comb out of his pocket and ran it through his mop of wavy, dark-amber hair, though the comb did nothing to tame it. "So what's the plan?"

"Take Duncan and see if you can recognize the scent of the Bengal who was watching Roman's place. Then set a guard on Fernwood Manor. Not intrusive, mind you, just to keep an eye out for any trouble. Keep them on Roman's property, but near the border with the Vampire, Ileana's." He shrugged at Gray's raised eyebrows. "I've no reason not to trust her. I'm simply being cautious."

"Understood. Are you really letting him keep the female to himself until Friday?"

"How'd you like to tell a royal-Siberian female—an *American* female, no less—not only is she a creature straight out of a nightmare, but she has to take a life mate in less than three weeks? Yankee women don't like being told what to do." Drake chuckled, imagining Roman's predicament. "By Friday, her temper should've run its course. Hopefully." He grinned. "Then when I move in, all I'll have to do is comfort Chase—and clean up the mess."

❦❦❦

On his way home from Drake's, Roman stopped by to see Andy. "Any news?"

"I'm afraid so. And none of it's good." Andy led him into the study and motioned him to a chair. "You'd better sit down."

"Shit."

As Roman took a seat, Andy opened his briefcase and withdrew a sheet of paper. "When you told me to dig deeper, I pulled out the name of that contact you once gave me—the guy in New York, Aaron Matthews."

"The half-Lycan-half-human private detective?"

"Right. He found out what you wanted to know, but it's going to cost you." He handed him the invoice he'd taken from his briefcase.

Roman glanced at it, shrugged, and sighed at the anxiety etched on his old friend's face. "For Christ's sake, Andy, I'm not going to eat you just because you bring me some bad news."

"That's good to hear." Andy gave a weak smile and sank into the chair behind the desk. "Chase Alcott is the child of a human female and a Tigris male. She was orphaned at the age of four when her parents were killed in a house fire."

Running his fingers around his collar, he loosened his tie.

"Damn it, Andy! Just tell me."

"I *am* telling you." He shuffled the papers on his desk, cleared his throat. "Her parents were murdered by intruders. They—and Aaron's sure there was more than one—tied up the adults with silver wire and torched the house. But apparently they didn't know about Chase. She either escaped unseen, or her parents hid her before the intruders subdued them. At any rate, she was found the next day, wandering in the woods behind the house."

"Oh, Christ." Roman felt a rush of sympathy for Chase and her parents. He knew only too well what fire could do to flesh and blood. Bound with silver wire, the Tigris wouldn't have been able to do anything to save himself or his mate. "Why were they killed? Was it Were hunters or ordinary humans?"

"Aaron doesn't think it was either. He thinks it was members of her father's pride."

"His own *pride* killed him? Why?"

Andy got to his feet and crossed to the wet bar. Pouring himself a double shot of bourbon, he downed it in one long gulp.

Roman knew him well enough to know he'd cough up the information sooner if not distracted or allowed to change the subject. So he stifled his impatience and waited in silence while Andy poured himself another double shot then gestured with the bottle.

"Do you remember the story of Prince Leopold Skawronski?"

"Vaguely. As I recall he was the leader of a pride of Siberian Tigri in Eastern Europe." Roman searched his memory. "Didn't he disappear forty years or so ago in the midst of some scandal or something? There were rumors he'd been assassinated, but no one really knew for sure."

Andy nodded. "That's him. He hadn't been assassinated. Not then, anyway. Leopold fell in love with a human, Alexis Daniels, an American novelist who'd gone to Eastern Europe to research the 'man-tigers' the peasants told stories about."

Sipping his drink this time, he returned to his chair. "Apparently, someone told her that if she went into the woods at night, she might see one of these creatures. Well, she did. And she did."

"She saw one?"

"Yes. She came upon one of Prince Leopold's people changing from animal form back into human form. And of course, being an

American, she pulled out her camera and began taking pictures. With a flash, no less."

"Jesus." Roman shook his head. "Was she crazy or just stupid?"

"Neither, according to Aaron. He figures she'd simply romanticized the situation and didn't recognize the danger. Anyway, the Tigris grabbed her and dragged her to Leopold, who was required by pride law to kill her to protect the secret of their existence.

"But one look at Alexis and Leopold fell head over heels in love. He stalled the pride for as long as he could, hoping he could talk them into letting her live."

Confused, Roman frowned. "I don't understand. It's not uncommon for a Were to take a human mate. Besides, we've always allowed certain *trusted* humans to know our secret."

"Not at that time, in that part of the world. At least not in that pride. Leopold's father hated half-breeds, and most of the pride agreed with him. During his rule, pride laws were enacted that gave humans and half-breeds no quarter.

"By the time Leopold took control, these laws were accepted as an unbreakable code of behavior by the pride members. Any half-breed unfortunate enough to happen upon the pride was attacked and destroyed.

"Any human who learned their secret was immediately killed. No questions asked. That is, until Leopold met Alexis.

"The pride was enraged, to say the least. It was unthinkable for their leader to even consider mating with a human, especially when the pride had several available females vying for his attention. When Leopold couldn't persuade his subjects to see things his way, he took off with Alexis, killing several of her guards in the process."

"So they ended up in America." Roman rose and poured his own glass of bourbon. "Where the pride members found them."

"Well, they managed to keep ahead of the pride for over a decade. When Chase was born, they changed their identities one last time and put down roots, obviously thinking enough time had passed that the pride wouldn't bother them."

Andy studied the amber liquid in his glass. "Chase went to an orphanage after her parents' death because the pride members didn't know she existed, and no one else knew what her father was. They hadn't had any contact with other Weres for years."

Roman pinched the bridge of his nose with his thumb and fore-finger and clamped down on his frustration. "So what haven't you told me?"

Andy flinched and looked away. "I'm really sorry, Roman, but it never occurred to me to tell Aaron to be careful who he talked to or what he said while he was digging."

Shifting uneasily in his chair, he plucked miniscule pieces of lint off his pants. "Chase was an unknown entity before the investigation." He hesitated then glanced up, his expression wary. "Now, she's not."

Roman tensed. "Go on."

"The pride fell on hard times after they killed her parents. Leopold was smart enough to have an insurance policy—of sorts—in the form of one of those 'In the event of my death' things. When Leopold died, a Tigris attorney in Stockholm, Sweden confiscated the majority of the pride's assets.

"The money was Leopold's in the first place, but he'd left most of it for the use of the pride in the mistaken belief that if they had the money, they wouldn't come after him.

"But upon his death, everything went into a trust fund for Leopold's offspring should any be unearthed, or if not, then for his blood kin who weren't, and never had been, members of his old pride.

"If none of those could be found within fifty years after Leopold's death, the trust fund was to be used to start a foundation that would benefit all Weres."

"That was twenty-six years ago. What does it have to do with now?"

"Things got so bad that a few years after Leopold's death the majority of the pride members rebelled and killed those responsible for the murders, but they were unaware that Leopold had any blood kin outside the pride.

"They assumed the money was lost forever. Now they know about Chase—and that she's an unmated female.

"The current pride leader is also unmated and doesn't care if she's a half-breed. If he mates with her, the pride would have access to the trust fund through him, and for the approximately thirteen million dollars she'd bring them, they're willing to forego their former prejudices."

"Generous of them," Roman growled. He set his drink aside. "And now they're coming here."

"Yes. And they're not the only ones."

"*What?*"

"The Southern California Tigris Pride—the one Chase would have belonged to if she'd known what she was—also has a shortage of available females.

"They're extremely upset she was enticed away from her rightful pride by your father, and they're insisting she be sent back to them on the next flight out. If she doesn't show up, they're also coming here."

"But that means—"

"Exactly. If you're still determined to protect her, you'll be fighting the California pride, Leopold's pride, and the local pride. That's a three-front war you—"

"Can't win."

എഎഎ

June 4th:

Roman couldn't keep his mind off Chase—and the problems her presence in England caused—so it was almost dawn by the time he finished his hunt. Arriving home, he stopped by the library then, finding it empty, went upstairs to check on her.

She was sound asleep, propped up on her pillows with the light still on and a book in her lap. At least she'd made it into bed this time. He switched off the light, moved the book to the bedside table, and stood looking down at her, wondering if he could get away with kissing her again.

If he had any sense, he'd walk away from her—right now—and send her back to her rightful pride. Let them deal with it all. He forced himself to turn for the door. Then Chase whimpered softly in her sleep. Realizing it was already far too late, he walked back to the bed.

Though the moon was hidden by the clouds, he could see her quite well in the dark. She was sprawled on top of the pillows in a half-upright position.

What the hell. He leaned over and gently touched his mouth to hers. As before, her arms wound around his neck and her lips moved beneath his. Then she stiffened.

Christ, she's awake! Veiling himself, Roman pulled away and slipped out the door. With luck, she'd never realize he'd even been there. After all, he was supposed to be spending the night in London.

He heard her call his name but didn't go back. He wasn't willing to put her into a trance, even if he could, which he doubted.

As much as he wanted her, if—no, when—he took her, he wanted her aware and willing and knowing what he was. Telling her what she was could come a little later.

Halfway down the first flight of stairs, he surprised himself by turning around. When he got back to her room, he could see light through the crack under the door. He knocked.

"Come in."

"Is everything all right?" He kept a tight leash on any guilt or lust, in case they showed in his aura. "I saw the light under your door and thought you might need something."

She pulled herself into a sitting position, with her knees drawn up, and wrapped her arms around her legs, watching him warily.

He sat on the end of the bed as far away from her as possible. "Is there anything I can do for you?"

At his question, she looked away. He pretended not to notice her discomfort—or the passion flickering in her aura. At least this time he'd gotten a reaction he understood.

"Chase?"

She shook her head. "No, I'm fine. I just woke up with the feeling there was someone in the room, so I turned the light on to look. I didn't see anyone, but I know someone's been in here. I fell asleep reading. The light must have been on, and the book would've been on the bed. But when I woke up the light was off, and the book's on the nightstand."

He couldn't respond to her statement without lying, so he changed the subject and tried a line he'd been thinking about earlier.

"Are you sure you're okay? Your aura looks a little strange." He chuckled at her small gasp. "It's not as clear and bright as it was yesterday."

"*You* see auras?"

"Yes." He watched the amazed relief spread across her face. "You see them too, don't you?"

"I've seen them since I was a child, but I've never met anyone who believed me."

"I believe you. Your aura shows no deception at all."

Tears welled up in her eyes. She blinked them away. "I'm not a freak."

"No, you're not a freak. You're just different."

She picked at a thread in the duvet. "People have told me I'm crazy for years. Even when I could tell them things about people I had no way of knowing, they still didn't believe me."

"Let me guess. They told you that you were just highly observant."

"Or they just assumed I was a charlatan, and it was all an act. It's gotten to where I never mention it to anyone I don't trust completely."

"David must know."

"Yes, but only because I use it so much in my work. I had to tell him. He concedes that I'm always right about people, but he doesn't actually believe in auras." She paused, her lips thinning. "In fact, he told me he thought there was something wrong with my eyes."

"That's why you don't like social functions and parties, isn't it?" he asked, trying to ease her into a discussion of the paranormal.

"Yes. I feel like I'm being bombarded. It's just too much information for me."

"With me, it's not so much the auras as it is that my hearing's so much more acute than most people's. That many people in a room can be disorienting. It's also why I avoid crowds in general."

"Why is your hearing more acute?"

"My kind are different from most other people."

"What do you mean by your *kind*?"

"That's a question for another time."

Knowing he'd given her more than enough to ponder for one night, he stood up to leave.

"Can I ask you something else?" she said before he got more than a step away.

"Certainly."

"Is Lord Fernwood really your grandfather?"

He gave mental shout of triumph. This subject would do very well to get her thinking along the lines he needed her to. "No, he's not my grandfather. How did you know?"

"One of the only times your aura showed deception yesterday was when you mentioned him."

"*One* of the times? What were the others?"

"Well, there was when you told me how pleased you were that we came."

He laughed. "Yes, I remember you saw right through that. If I answer your question, will you keep this strictly to yourself?"

When she nodded, he continued. "Lord Fernwood is my father, not my grandfather." It wasn't strictly true, but close enough for his immediate purposes. "And the reason I wasn't pleased to see you was, as I told you, I thought he was trying to play matchmaker—again. I apologize if I was rude. It had nothing to do with you personally."

Chase ignored his apology. "He's your *father*?"

"Yes."

She stared at him, and he knew she was checking his aura. "But why does he pose as your grandfather?"

"Because he looks so much older than I do, he's afraid people will think I'm illegitimate. Not that it would bother me if they did, but Father's very concerned about appearances, and he wants to be sure I inherit his title. Besides, he doesn't want anyone to know I'm so much older than I look."

"How old are you? And why do you look so young?"

"It's complicated."

She rolled her eyes. "I'm sure I can keep up."

Sighing outwardly, he cheered mentally. "Those are also questions for another time. Before I answer them, there's something you need to think about. There are things about me you may not like. That you may wish you'd never found out."

He reached out a finger and gently stroked her cheek. "Things that could be dangerous for both of us."

Dropping his hand, he gazed into her eyes. "Some information comes with a price, Chase. Once you know something, it's not always possible to forget it, even if you want to. In this case, there's no going back." He sighed again, this time for real. "It's late, and you probably should try to get some more sleep."

He hoped her curiosity would keep her searching until she got the answers. "Let me know if you want to continue our discussion another time. But think about it carefully before you do."

Her eyes were wide as he turned and headed for the door.

"Wait," she called just as his hand reached for the doorknob. "Can I ask just one more question on a different subject?"

Certain he was getting in too deep, he returned to the bed. "Of course. What do you want to know?"

When she hesitated, he wondered what she could possibly want to ask. Her aura gave him no clue.

"When I woke up, I thought someone was in my room," she finally said. "Was that you? Did you kiss me?"

Roman decided on the truth. "Yes, that was me, and yes, I kissed you." He grinned. "I apologize if I offended you. But I won't apologize for kissing you. I enjoyed it too much. And to be fair, you did kiss me back."

"Why did you do it?"

He took a seat on the edge of the bed, but this time his hip brushed hers. "Does it matter?"

"Not really, but I'd like to know. Your aura isn't as easy for me to read as I thought it was."

Again he decided on the truth. "I found you in the library when I got home last night. You looked so adorable, asleep in the chair, and you smelled so...so delicious when I carried you upstairs, that I couldn't resist kissing you."

She kept her eyes on her knees as he talked, but there was no trace of anger in her aura, so he continued. "I came up here tonight to check on you. Watching you sleep, once again I couldn't resist kissing you to find out if it would be a repeat of last night. When you woke up, I slipped out of the room."

She raised her gaze and met his, but neither her eyes nor her aura gave any sign of what she was thinking.

"Do you think I'm a cad?" he asked. "I can't tell what you're thinking, but since you haven't jumped up and attacked me—" He flashed her a grin. "—it's obviously easier for you to resist me than it's been for me to resist you."

Her sudden laughter took him by surprise. "No. I don't think you're a cad, though I'm not even sure what that is." Shaking her head, she smiled. "As to what I was thinking. I was wondering—if you have as much trouble resisting me as you say, why it doesn't show up in your aura, and—"

She took a deep breath and studied the thread she pulled from the duvet.

"And?" he prompted.

He hooked his finger under her chin and raised it until she met his eyes.

"And," she repeated as her face filled with wicked amusement. "If you wanted to try it again, now that I'm awake."

∽◑∽

Chase held her breath, wondering what the hell had come over her. Laughing quietly, Roman rose, took her hand, and pulled her into his arms.

"Yes," he whispered as he crushed her against him. "I'd like that very much."

At first, his kiss was tender and sweet, but it quickly built into something stronger, more demanding. She slipped her arms around his neck, entwined her fingers in his hair, and returned the kiss with a passion she didn't know she had in her.

When they eventually broke apart, she clung to him, reluctant to let go. He lowered his head and kissed her again.

She wanted more, though she wasn't sure exactly what 'more' entailed. While she knew enough to comprehend what sex involved, she couldn't understand the strength of what she was feeling. Was passion supposed to make you feel like there was an animal inside, clawing to get out? She had a sudden urge to bite his neck, to leave her mark on him so the world would know he was hers.

Mine. All mine, rang in her head.

If this was a normal part of passion, she hadn't run across its description in any of the books she'd read on sex.

When he deepened the kiss, she felt a growl of lust rise up in her throat. It came out as a purr, making her sound just like a cat. *Where the hell did that come from?*

❧❧❧

He could take her now, and she'd be willing. Probably. She was so unpredictable, Roman couldn't be sure.

Even if she *was* agreeable, he didn't want her like this. He needed her to know and accept him for what he was—and still desire him.

At last, he raised his head and let her breathe. "Yes. I much prefer having you awake."

She chuckled. "I rather thought you might." Snuggling into him, she kissed his neck. "It works better for me this way, too."

"If I'd known you'd be this accommodating, I would've woken you last night."

"I might not have reacted this way last night. But I've been dreaming about this for both of the nights I've been here."

"Well, I only hope when you know me better, you'll still want me to kiss you." He leaned back to gaze into her liquid cinnamon eyes. "I'd never hurt you, Chase, but you may be frightened of me when you find out what I am."

"What you are?" She took a step back and crossed her arms over her chest. "Try me. I've known you could be dangerous since the minute I saw you. But you're not a threat to me. And you're not evil."

She locked her gaze on his. "Trust me, Roman. Tell me what you are."

He raked his fingers through his hair in frustration. He had to be careful how he handled her. Not only his life was at stake, but hers was as well. He needed a little more time.

"Not tonight," he said.

She looked like she wanted to argue, so he shushed her with a finger to her lips. "It's late, and I've been up for almost twenty-four hours. I need to rest so I'm coherent when we talk."

He pulled her back into his arms. "I *will* tell you, Chase," he whispered into her hair, filling his nostrils with her scent. "After we've both had time to think about this—and if you can't figure it out on your own."

She kissed him lightly then stepped away. "Fair enough. But don't expect me to give up. I'll have you know I'm fairly stubborn."

Relieved, he laughed. "I can tell. It shows in your aura. And I'm actually counting on it." He headed for the door once more. "Good night, Chase. I'll see you in the morning."

✧✦✧

Chase lay in bed, fighting the urge to go after him. She didn't know if she wanted to force him to tell her his secret or convince him to make love to her. Both sounded equally appealing and terrifying.

She'd never met a man like him before, passionate, yet totally controlled. She didn't know if he lost that restraint when he made love but suspected he did. He certainly wouldn't be much of a lover otherwise. Instinctively, she knew he was. She might not have had much, okay, make that any, experience with sex, but some things you could just tell.

What was the dark secret he seemed so afraid to reveal? He wasn't an evil man. His aura assured her of that. He'd implied he wasn't human, and there was certainly something not *normal* about his beauty, his grace, his scent, and his strength. Oh, and his speed. If he meant what he said about slipping from the room when she woke up, he must be inhumanly fast. She'd have noticed any ordinary man.

Was it really possible he wasn't human? If so, what was he? She could come up with all kinds of ridiculous theories—from Peter Parker to Clark Kent—but educated women didn't believe in comic book characters.

What about mythology? Could he be part Fairy or some other mythological being whose names she couldn't even remember?

Did those creatures really exist? There'd been legends about them in every culture on Earth since the beginning of recorded history.

"'There are more things in heaven and earth, Horatio,'" she muttered. "God, I can't believe I'm even thinking this stuff."

Getting out of bed, she pulled her laptop computer out of its case, booted it up, and plugged in her wireless card. In her browser's search window, she typed: "mythological creatures resembling humans" and waited to see what would come up. Several options appeared.

Clicking on a likely-looking site, she typed: "beauty+strength+grace+speed+(enticing scent)" into the site's search window. The response was, "no answer found to match your parameters." So she entered the characteristics one at a time and searched them individually.

The results came back: Elf, Fairy, Angel, Mermaid, Druid, Valkyrie, Lycan, Tigris, and Vampire.

She discounted the last one out of hand. Vampires were evil. Everyone knew that. Valkyrie and Mermaid didn't work as those were usually female. And Angel was just...silly, she decided, exhaling in a huff.

Elf, Fairy, Lycan, Tigris, or Druid—one of those might be a possibility.

Could Roman really be a mythological creature? While her rational mind said no, her gut told her there was no other logical explanation. Unless he was from another planet.

She sighed and shook her head. Still, that made just as much sense as anything else she'd been thinking tonight. Exasperated, she shut down her computer and paced the room.

Did it matter what he was? No, it really didn't. She wanted him regardless.

Why him and why now? She rubbed a hand over her churning stomach. *And what the hell is happening to me?*

Unaccustomed to the lust searing her blood, she did the only thing she could think of. She grabbed fresh clothes and headed into the bathroom to take a long, *cold* shower.

Chapter 5

Roman paced his room. *What the hell's happened to me?* He'd never felt like this about anyone. So why her and why now? Was it fate? Or was it the challenge because she could resist the power of his eyes?

What if she wanted a tiger mate, instead of a wolf? Knowing he might lose her when she found out what they both were kept him on edge, unable to settle.

He heard her start up her computer. Okay, so she was researching it on the Internet. *I wonder if she'll understand what she finds.* Hopefully, she'd figure it out—at least part of it—and he wouldn't have such a hard time getting her to accept the truth.

Of course, convincing her they were both Weres was only half the battle. He still had to tell her she needed to take a mate before she turned thirty. If she didn't, once she came fully into heat, she'd accept the first male who offered—and probably regret it as soon as her hormones ebbed. But by then, the damage would be done. The image of her trapped and unhappy sent waves of nausea spiraling through his gut.

At last, he threw himself on the bed and forced his trance. If he didn't get some rest, he'd be in no condition to handle the situation no matter how it turned out.

❧❧❧

Dillon yawned, rose from where he'd been sitting with his back against a tree, and paced at the edge of the forest. He'd been watching Fernwood Manner for hours and hadn't seen a sign of Chase. Except for Roman's arrival a few minutes ago, there'd been no action all night. *Big effing deal*. His temper spiked. "Shit. What the hell am I even doing here?"

Damn Ileana and her stupid plan! The bitch could stuff it. All she'd done was ensure he'd lose Chase to another Were. Probably Roman.

Dillon sneered. No way would he let that happen. If Chase stepped one foot outside the mansion, he'd grab her, screw her, and make her his.

In fact, he could wait until Roman left again then drive over to Fernwood Manor and demand to see her. He only needed a few minutes alone with her in private to—

A faint sound reached his ears. He tensed, listened. Footsteps. His nostrils twitched as the scent of danger assaulted them. *Oh, shit.* Grayson Hunter and Duncan McCoy.

What were *they* doing here? Did they know he'd been watching Fernwood's place? They must. Drake's two enforcers turning up here was no fluke. Should he stay and face them or take off and wait till they approached him for an explanation? "Shit, shit, shit!"

He wasn't at his best when suffering from lack of sleep. Better to slip away and save the explanations for when he wasn't at such a disadvantage. He grabbed the pack he'd brought with him and high-tailed it out of there.

☙❧☙

"Do you recognize his scent?" Gray asked Duncan as they tracked the rogue Bengal through the forest.

"Yeah. And I imagine you do, too."

"Dillon," they said in unison.

"What do you suppose he was doing here?" Duncan said.

"Oh, I think it's obvious what the scumbag was up to. I just want to know what cock and bull story he's going to give Drake in an attempt to save his worthless ass." Gray smashed his fist into a tree, welcomed the pain. "Whatever he comes up with will have to be confirmed by that bitch, Ileana. Which means *someone* has to go talk to her."

He shuddered—and not entirely for dramatic effect. "I hope to hell it isn't me."

ɔɔ

When Chase left her bedroom to head downstairs for breakfast, David was standing in the hallway, his arms folded across his chest, his expression a cross between a glare and a pout.

"Who spit in your cereal?" she asked him, pretending not to notice the jealousy and suspicion in his aura. "What's the matter? Didn't you sleep well?"

"I heard voices and laughter coming from your room early this morning," he accused. "Are *you* jumping our host's bones, Chase?"

"No. I'm not jumping his bones."

Not yet anyway. At least not in reality. David didn't need to know about her dreams. Or her intentions. She cast about in her mind for an answer that would sidetrack his interrogation.

"Roman came upstairs to check on something last night and saw a light under my door. So he came in to see if I needed anything."

"I see." He didn't sound convinced. "And did you? *Need* anything?"

She laughed at his tone. "No, silly." For the first time since she'd known him, she was grateful he couldn't see auras and wouldn't detect her lies. "I just couldn't sleep. So when he came in, we talked for a while."

"About?"

"Well, for one thing, I found out that Lord Fernwood isn't really his grandfather."

"Then what is he?"

"It's like you said. An informal adoption. Without the proper paperwork. Something the butler and his wife have promised not to reveal."

"Oh. And you think that's why you saw the flickers in their...thingies?"

"Of course. After all, you're the one who said it was probably something simple."

She found it much harder to act nonchalant when she entered the dining room and saw Roman waiting for them—especially since he'd see the same flare of passion in her aura she saw in his. Turning away to hide her face, she headed for the coffee pot. Not that she could fool Roman, but then, she really didn't want to.

ぐうそ

Roman had listened to Chase's conversation with David, his emotions running the gamut of amusement, dread and, finally, relief that she hadn't revealed his true secret to David.

He wondered what she'd found in her Internet research and tried to think of some way to get her alone so he could kiss her again. Perhaps, if there was time, they'd even talk.

Should he seduce her before he told her what they were, so if she did choose another mate, at least he'd have the memories? No, that was only asking for heartache. Then he saw the lust in her aura as she looked at him, and his resolve faltered.

"Good morning," he said, as she turned away, blushing.

If her thoughts were anything like his, he knew why she'd blushed.

As she and David finished breakfast, Roman leaned forward, his elbows on the table. "How would you two feel about splitting up today?"

She stared at her plate.

David looked over at him and smiled hopefully. "What'd you have in mind?"

"Well." He used the full force of his eyes and voice. "Since you don't seem to mind meeting strangers as much as Chase does, I thought I'd send you to talk to some of my relatives on the pretext of getting their views on the decorating. And while you're at it, you can discuss the mysterious things that have happened here."

David beamed.

Roman felt a surge of guilt, though not enough to deter him. "You'll need a reason for asking the questions, of course. Let's see. Oh yes, you could say you're gathering information for a story for one of those magazines you write for. I've read your work, by the way," he lied. "I'm very impressed."

Out of the corner of his eye, he saw Chase press her lips together in an effort not to laugh.

David's gaze stayed glued to Roman's face. "That's an excellent idea," he murmured, totally entranced.

"Great. Why don't you grab a coat, some paper and a pen. Wilson, our chauffeur, will drive you around and introduce you."

David left the room in a daze. As his footsteps faded, Chase burst out laughing. "You shouldn't do that," she scolded. "It's not really fair. I'm surprised he didn't have an erection from the power of your eyes."

He chuckled. "They don't seem to have the same effect on you."

"You might be surprised."

"Really?" He stood and came around beside her. "I don't recall putting you in a trance when I gazed into your eyes last night."

"No. It was your kiss that did that." She turned her face away from him. "So why did you get rid of David?"

Placing a hand on her cheek, he tugged her head back around. "Why do you think?" Bending down, he kissed her. "I think we need to continue our conversation from last night." He kissed her again. "Don't you?"

Chase raised one lovely eyebrow. "You want to *talk* to me?"

He laughed and scooped her out of the chair, into his arms. "Eventually," he said with a grin as he carried her to his room and dropped her in the middle of his king size bed.

Sliding his body over hers, he ravaged her mouth, savoring her taste and her scent. She moaned softly.

He could feel her awakening hunger in the way she moved beneath him and the rapid firing of her heartbeat. His need for a willing partner overrode his common sense.

They'd talk later. Right now, he could only surrender to what she unleashed in him.

At first he feared she might stop him, afraid of being unprofessional. Then he realized her needs were overriding her common sense as well. She wanted him as much as he did her. His fingers moved to the buttons on her blouse while his lips nuzzled her neck. She trembled. It thrilled him.

"Did I mention how lovely you look this morning?" he murmured against her throat. "If this blouse weren't so nice, I'd rip it right off."

"I did bring other blouses, and you probably have other shirts."

Grasping the front of his shirt with both hands, she ripped it open. His buttons went flying. She laughed and ran her hands over his chest. "God, I can't believe I really did that."

Raging desire slammed into him. He wanted her *now*! He tore off her blouse and feasted on her creamy skin then flipped open the front catch on her bra to free her breasts.

"Women wear such convenient underclothes these days."

Had he ever seen anyone so lovely? He stared down at her until she flushed. Then he lowered his head and took a nipple in his mouth. She moaned again, punctuating this one with soft whimpers.

His hands and mouth roamed over her, tasting, touching, savoring, as he tore off the rest of her clothes then his own.

When they were both naked, he pulled her to him, marveling at the feel of her skin against his and her hands roaming over his back.

"I want you, Roman," she whispered. "I know this is totally unprofessional, but *God*, I want you so much."

Pleasure surged through him at the lust and the guilt flickering in her aura.

"Since I can tell you don't do this for your other clients, I think we can grant you a waiver on the professionalism, just this once. Besides, this client's really *okay* with it. So why don't you stop feeling guilty and let me show you how much I want you, too."

"Oh, yes. *Please*!"

His plan for a tender seduction flew right out of his head. No one had ever begged for him before—and meant it.

He crushed his lips to hers while his tongue pillaged her mouth. Slipping a hand between her thighs, he brought her to orgasm with his fingers. Her screams of ecstasy and the earthy smell of her juices drove him mad with lust.

Clamping down hard on his own needs, he watched her face as her trembling subsided. "You're beautiful, Chase. I've never known anyone like you."

Her smile took his breath away. "I could say the same about you."

She put her hands on his chest, pushed him down on his back, and started exploring his body with her tongue. "My turn to drive you nuts."

When she reached his genitals, hesitated, then awkwardly took his shaft in her mouth, he felt like a virgin. Only women in a trance had done this for him. No lover in his entire life, human or other, had ever done it willingly. Or wanted to. A low feral growl ripped from his throat, and he heard his own voice begging.

"Please, Chase, I need you. Now."

"Then take me."

Her throaty whisper sent him spiraling right to the edge. Grabbing a condom from the nightstand, he shoved it on, rolled over on top of her, and thrust into her, driving her deep into the mattress. At her startled gasp of pain, he froze. "Christ, Chase, I wasn't thinking. I'm sorry."

"Be sorry later." Her body arched to meet his. "Don't you dare stop now."

"I'm not sure I could, even if I wanted to."

She was everything he wanted in a mate, and by God, he'd win her, whatever it took.

With hard, deep strokes and tender nibbling kisses on her mouth and neck, he brought her to another climax. When she cried out his name and tightened around him in a death grip, he buried his face in her hair and surrendered to his body's own demand for release.

As their shudders eased, he lingered above her, his breath ragged. She opened her eyes and smiled at him. He kissed her with total possessiveness, the need to stake his claim driving him on.

If not for his honor, and a condom, she'd already be his. Hell, she *was* his, she just didn't know it.

☙❧

Chase woke in Roman's arms, his lips nuzzling her hair. She sat up partway and smiled down at him as the blanket he'd covered her with slid to her waist.

"Sorry I fell asleep."

"Don't be." He ran his fingers along her jawline and down to her breasts. "I'm flattered I exhausted you. And I enjoyed holding you while you slept."

She sighed and laid her head back on his shoulder. "How long was I out?"

It felt like she'd slept for ages, but daylight still filtered through the silken drapes on the windows.

"Just a couple of hours. We've got plenty of time. There's really not much investigating you can do until Friday when people start arriving for the first party."

"And David?"

"He won't be back for hours yet. Not the way my relatives like to talk."

She laughed. "He's going to be *sooo* pissed."

Roman chuckled and tightened his arms around her. "Ask me if I care."

She lay for a while, savoring his embrace, his warmth, and his scent. She knew they needed to talk and realized they were both putting it off. Time to bite the bullet.

"I guess this is 'eventually.' You wanted to talk?" He tensed, so she added, "We don't have to if you don't want to, but last night you said you did."

"Yes." He exhaled in a long sigh. "We need to. We probably should have talked first, but I'm afraid my brain wasn't functioning."

"I can relate."

Thrilled to learn she affected his ability for rational thinking as much as he did hers, she ran her fingers over his chest and heard him sigh with pleasure.

"So tell me," he said. "What theories did you come up with in your Internet research?"

She blinked. "How did you know about that?"

"I told you. My hearing's acute. I heard your computer start up from down here in my bedroom."

"Your hearing *must* be good."

"Stop stalling. What'd you come up with?"

"You'll just laugh at me."

He removed one arm from around her and stuck a finger under her chin, lifting her eyes to his. "I won't laugh," he promised. "Tell me."

"Well, the only thing I figured out for sure is you aren't human. At least not completely."

"Not completely?"

"You could be a hybrid. With one parent who was human and the other who was...something else."

"I'm not human at all. Neither were my parents."

"*Neither* of your parents—"

She broke off at the pain in his expression. Pain mixed with fear. Fear she'd reject him? The thought tore at her heart.

"Roman, I don't care what you are. I decided last night. It doesn't matter. I won't run. And I won't betray you. You can trust me."

"Christ, I really hope that's true. Because what I have to tell you is going to be hard for you to accept."

He tugged her close and kissed her until she pulled away, laughing.

"Stop trying to change the subject." She dropped her head on his shoulder so the desire in his eyes couldn't impede her ability to think. "If you're not human, what are you?"

"Oh, no. I haven't heard all your theories yet."

"The Internet only gave me a few possibilities."

"Such as?"

"The ones that seemed to fit your characteristics best were Elf, Fairy, Lycan, Tigris, and Druid. Though I did consider you might have come from another planet."

Though he made almost no sound, his suppressed laughter tickled her hair and bounced her off his chest.

"Hey." She whacked his stomach with the flat of her hand. "You promised not to laugh."

"I'm *trying*." His chuckles increased in volume, and she found herself laughing with him. "You really considered I might be an alien?"

When she nodded, he chortled. "Sorry, you're not even close."

"So, tell me."

The humor disappeared instantly. "You tell me. What nightmarish creature haven't you mentioned?"

She didn't answer. He sighed. "Didn't your research mention Vampires?"

"Vampires?"

"I'm only half Vampire. My mother was a Vampire. My father was Lycan."

"Half-Vampire, half-werewolf?"

Her mind rejected the image, even as her instincts confirmed its truth. His beauty, his grace, his scent, his strength and speed. It all made sense now. He was the perfect predator. So, why wasn't she afraid? She felt him waiting for her response, watching her aura, and looking for the terror he feared.

"I told you, Roman. I don't care. If you'd wanted to hurt me, you could have done it at any time since I got here." He didn't respond, not even to breathe. "I trust you. There's no evil in your aura."

She raised her head and met his eyes. "I'm sorry if that's not the response you were expecting, but it's the only one you're going to get. So deal with it."

He laughed and hugged her. "I can deal with it. I'm just not sure you can." Then he sobered again. "I'm afraid there's more."

"From your tone, I take it you think the more's even worse." A sudden chill ran up her spine, and she pulled away from him. "What could possibly be worse than what you've already told me?"

"This isn't about me. It's about you."

"Me?" Dread grabbed her by the throat, making it difficult to breathe. "It can't be. You don't know anything about me." She scooted off the bed and looked around for her clothes. They were in tatters on the floor. "Can I borrow a robe so I can get back to my room?"

He came up behind her and took her by the shoulders, turning her around. "I can't believe you have the courage to face what I am but not what you are."

"What do you mean? I'm human."

"Well, you're half right, anyway."

No. He was wrong. She refused to listen to this bullshit. There wasn't anything special about her. Being special meant bad things happened to you. Strangers came in the dead of night and—

"Oh, my God!"

Her legs turned to Jell-O, her head spinning, as images she'd long repressed flooded her mind. "Oh, God, my parents."

"Breathe, Chase." He caught her as she slid toward the floor and sat her on the bed. "Take it easy and just breathe," he ordered, pushing her head down between her knees. "You'd blocked it all out, hadn't you?"

She didn't answer, just concentrated on taking slow, deep

breaths. Yes, she'd blocked it out. Locked away the horror and the pain, the terrible longing for her parents to come back from where the bad men had taken them.

Her own survival had depended on keeping all that agony at bay. Now it was back. Suddenly, she felt four years old again. She curled up in the fetal position and wept.

⌘⌘⌘

Roman stroked her hair and let her cry, feeling completely useless. Not an emotion he was used to. He didn't know what to say, how to comfort her.

He hadn't realized she'd repressed the memories of her parents' death and had assumed they'd sent her away before she'd witnessed anything.

When her wracking sobs quieted, he pulled her onto his lap and rocked her.

"I'm sorry, Chase. Christ, I'm so sorry. I lost my parents by fire, too. And though their death was an accident, it still hurts."

"Mine were murdered," she sniffed. "By people they both knew."

"Yes, by his own pride."

"His what?"

"Did you know what your father was?"

She shook her head. "No, not exactly. But I knew he was different. And my mother—"

"Your mother was human."

"How the hell do you know that?"

"Chase, I smelled what you were on Monday when I met you at the door." She crawled off his lap. He tried not to let it hurt. "I could also tell you didn't know."

"So you did some digging to find out about me," she growled.

She jumped off the bed and rushed to his closet. Pulling out a terrycloth robe, she slipped it on. "Didn't my privacy mean anything to you?"

"Yes, it did." He grabbed a pair of jeans and pulled them on, just in case she decided to go storming through the house, and he had to go after her. "But your survival means more."

Her eyes widened. "My survival? No one else even knows I exist."

They do now. He decided to save that revelation for later and changed tactics. "I figured since you didn't know what you are, you wouldn't know where you came from. I thought you might like to, and I wanted to help."

He could see the struggle going on inside her, so he waited, hoping her natural curiosity would win out.

"I'm not sure I want to know." She met his gaze as if daring him to call her a coward. "It brought my parents only heartache and isolation from their own kind. And in the end it brought them a cruel death."

She headed for the door. "Maybe, I'm better off not knowing."

He beat her to the door and slapped a hand on it. "It's too late for that, I'm afraid. You're almost thirty years old. So you have no choice."

She tossed her hair back. The anger sparking her eyes and coloring her cheeks only made her more beautiful. He jammed his free hand in his pocket so he wouldn't reach for her.

"I'm sorry, Chase. I really am. There are things you have to know. Whether you want to hear them or not, you're going to have to listen. If you don't, in three weeks' time, you could end up trapped in a very bad situation."

She turned on her heel and paced the room, throwing him an occasional glare. He knew he was just as trapped as she was. He had to make her listen.

But the way he did it, the way she might force him to do it, could turn her against him forever. He could almost feel his heart breaking as he cursed fate, and his father, for putting him in this untenable position.

Chase said she trusted him, but would that hold when she heard everything he had to say? If it didn't—No. Screw that! He refused to let her walk away from him now.

Chapter 6

Don't go there, screamed a little voice in Chase's mind. *Don't listen to him.* That worked for her. Yet, what if he was right and her survival depended on what he had to say? Recently, she'd sensed her body changing, and it had to be because of what her father was. If the change was dangerous—to her or to others—she needed to know.

Released memories flooded her mind. Her father, a big, strapping man with a booming laugh and fierce amber eyes. Her mother, blonde, beautiful, and sweet. Much too gentle for the brutal way she'd died.

She could also remember her mother's screams and her father's roars as they burned alive. For twenty-six years she'd locked away the love she'd shared with them, along with the pain of their loss and the horror of their murders.

She'd never be able to repress it all again, even if she wanted to, and she wasn't sure she did. She didn't even know if her parents had been avenged.

Apparently, Roman knew something about who they were and why they died. She glanced over at him. He leaned against the door, his face calm. But his eyes burned with something she couldn't identify—something that said she wouldn't like what he had to tell her.

"What happened to your parents?" she asked to give herself time. "You said they died by fire."

His aura flared with anger and grief. "A car accident in the Alps. I was ten years old."

He pushed away from the door, walked to the window, and stood with his back to her. "It was winter. A cold, clear night. The roads were icy. Father—my adopted father, Lord Fernwood—lost control of his car, coming down a narrow mountain road. He slammed into the back of my parents' car."

He took a hard breath. "My birth father was driving. My mother was sitting up front with him. I was in the backseat. Restless and bored as I usually was, I was jumping around, playing with the door handle. It was all a game to me then. After all, we were special. Invincible."

His long, drawn-out sigh made her want to weep, and she regretted bringing it up.

"My door came open on impact, and I was thrown out of the car. But my parents..." His shoulders hunched. "Our car went off the road and over a cliff."

He swallowed audibly. "I waited for them to climb back up and see if I was okay. But they didn't. So I climbed down. Lord Fernwood came with me. This was fifty years ago, and he was much more agile."

"Fifty? You're sixty years old?"

"Yes, I'm sixty. Weres age very slowly after we turn thirty." He turned around, his eyes bleak. "Anyway, the car landed upside down at the bottom of a twenty foot ravine. A fire was raging in the engine compartment. I shouted at my parents to get out of the car. They were pinned inside. There was blood everywhere. Still, I felt certain they'd survive—if they just got out of the car. But they'd lost too much blood and didn't have the strength to free themselves."

His hands rose and fell in a gesture of helplessness. "I started over to them, but Father pulled me back."

"Of course he did." She hated the pain and guilt she heard in his voice and saw on his face. "To him, you were just a ten-year-old boy."

"Not for long." Pressing his fingers to his eyes, he turned back to the window. "I was angry at him and terrified for my parents. I lost it and shifted in front of him."

He cleared his throat. "To his credit, he didn't freak—much—when confronted with a wolf where a boy had been. He just went to the car and tried to help my parents. We could see them through the windshield. But the fire was too fierce. We couldn't reach them."

"Oh, Roman." She slipped her arms around his waist and pressed her cheek to his back. "I'm sorry. I'm so very, very sorry."

He covered her hands with his. "My mother was a Vampire and looked fairly human. Until you saw her canines. Which we did when the skin burned off her face."

A tremor ran through him. "My father was Lycan. Before he died, he shifted to his wolf form."

"Lord Fernwood knew you were...different, and yet he adopted you?"

"He blamed himself for the accident. Still does. Even though it wasn't his fault."

Unlocking her hands from his waist, he turned back around. "He was alone in the world, with no other close family. And he loves me." He took another deep breath, sighed. "That's my story. Now it's time for you to hear yours."

"One more question."

"I think you're stalling, but go ahead."

"I thought—I mean the literature. Well, I always had the impression that Vampires are sterile. How did—"

"You mean fiction says Vampires are sterile," he said dryly. "It also says you become a Vampire by being bitten and getting some kind of virus."

He waved a hand as if dismissing all the common theories. "Vampires are a species like any other. It's true, Vampire women rarely have children, but it's usually a matter of choice."

Wrapping his arm firmly around her shoulders, he guided her back to the bed. "Because a Vampire's life span's so long, we have to be careful not to out-populate our food supply."

"Oh."

Eeuuww. Not sure I wanted to know that. She shook her head and sat on the edge of the bed. He was right. She was stalling.

Wrapping her arms around her body in a vain effort to protect herself, she nodded. "Go ahead. Tell me."

As he described how her parents met, fell in love, and were betrayed by her father's pride, she was assaulted with a barrage of conflicting emotions—anger, grief, horror, and shock. Shock had outstripped the others by the time he'd finished the tale.

"Did you say million? You're telling me my parents left me a trust fund of more than thirteen *million* dollars?"

"Yes."

Before she could even begin to fantasize what she might do with all that money, she saw the look in his eyes and slumped down on the bed.

"There's still more, isn't there?"

"I'm afraid so."

"You may as well tell me and get it over with," she said heavily. "Since I have the feeling it's not something the thirteen-plus mil is going to help me solve."

"The money only adds to the problem." He sat beside her and took her hand, not looking at her, just studying her fingers. "I'm relieved you're able to accept what you are so easily, but since you finally remember your parents, it's not surprising."

Whatever was coming, it was clear he didn't expect her to like it. That fact alone was enough to have her jerking her hand out of his and hopping up to pace the room again. He sat watching her without speaking until she longed to punch him and relieve some of her frustration.

"For Christ's sake, Roman, spit it out. The suspense is killing me."

"Weres are different from humans in a lot of ways," he said. "But one very important way is in their sexual, or reproduction, cycle."

"What do you mean?"

"We live much longer than humans, and we aren't sexually mature until we reach our thirtieth birthday."

At his words a chill ran up her spine, but she bit back her questions and waited for him to continue.

"That's when our females are able to bear children, but they can only get pregnant during certain times of the year when they—"

Oh, God. "When we come into *heat*? Is that what I'm doing here with you? I'm coming into heat?"

The implications floored her, and she could almost hear her heart shatter. He'd only been attracted to her because she was giving off some maximum-strength pheromones or something, not because he cared anything about her personally.

"I thought—I mean, we—" She bit her lip and shook her head. "Never mind. It doesn't matter."

He was off the bed so fast, she didn't even see him move until he had her wrapped in his arms.

"Yes, it does matter," he whispered. "And no, I'm not attracted to you because you're coming into heat."

"What, you read minds, too?"

"No, not under most circumstances. But your thoughts were written all over your face."

"What do you mean not 'under most circumstances'?"

"Later." With a sigh, he led her back to the bed. "I wanted you from the moment I saw you."

He kissed her, easing some of the pain in her heart. "I still do," he said. "And it has nothing to do with anything but who you are. Understand?"

Because she wanted desperately to believe him, she swallowed and nodded.

"Good. Now, it's important for you to understand what's happening to you is a natural condition. But it still puts you in danger."

"But if it's natural, why should it put me in danger?"

Embarrassed at the thought of her "condition," she looked away and played with the belt of the borrowed robe, untying and retying it. *Coming* into heat had made her horny enough to sleep with a client. So when she was *in* heat, did that mean she'd act like an out-of-control slut?

"Am I going to chase men through the streets like a dog chases cars? I don't think I like the sound of this."

"Have you ever seen a cat or dog in heat?"

Closing her eyes, she shuddered. "So I *will* be a slut." Christ, how much worse could this get? "What can I do? Can you lock me in a cage until it passes?"

"Um, no. That won't work."

Uh-oh. The distress in his voice had her gaze shooting back to his. "What do you mean it won't work?"

"I'm sorry, Chase," he said. If the pain on his face was anything to go by, he meant it. "A female who's raised in a pride is taught what turning thirty means and how to control the heat as much as possible. If she doesn't have a mate lined up, the pride takes care of her until it passes. But you weren't raised in a pride, so—"

"So what? It doesn't pass?"

"No, it'll pass, but by the time it does, you'll have mated. And Weres mate for life."

"Mated?" She struggled to get her mind around the concept. "Look, just tell me like you were explaining this to a human."

"Okay." He tensed, and she braced herself. "You were still a virgin until a little while ago because female Weres don't usually experience passion until the onset of their first heat, or rather until a few weeks before the onset.

"When they come fully into heat, that's *all* they feel. Since you weren't trained to control the lust, and you don't have any pride members to…help you until it passes, you'll accept the first male that comes sniffing around."

He ran his hand up her arm and over her shoulder. "If he's less than honorable, or any less able to control himself than you are, you'll end up mated. Very probably to someone you won't want after the heat passes."

Another spasm of pain crossed his face. "And as I said, we mate for life. There is no divorce."

She jerked away from him. "You mean to tell me I'll end up stuck with someone I can't leave?"

No way was she getting trapped in some loveless marriage because her hormones were out of control.

"Bullshit. I don't know what kind of laws you Were people have, but that's just bullshit!"

"It's not the laws of Weres, Chase. It's the laws of Mother Nature. Once you mate, you'll become physically ill and could even die if you're away from your mate for too long."

"So if one mate dies, the other one's screwed?"

"No. Death cuts the mate bond. The surviving mate may still succumb to grief and depression, but there's also a chance they could snap out of it and live. With an enforced separation, there's no chance of survival for either one."

"Well, that's just great. So why can't you just lock me away until the heat passes? Surely you must have an old tower around here. Somewhere no one would hear my screams."

He snorted, but it didn't sound like humor. "I'm fresh out of old towers, I'm afraid. Besides, the lust would drive you crazy. Your psyche could be screwed up for life."

"Jesus. There has to be something I can do."

"You can choose a mate and let him claim you."

"And that's it? That's my only option? How the hell am I supposed to choose a mate?"

He didn't respond. She shook her head and prayed for patience. "You're the only other Were I know, so what am I supposed to do? Put an ad in the weretiger personals?"

"That won't be necessary." His voice was so low she could barely hear him. "It's being taken care of."

Stunned, she stared at him. "Taken care of? How? You told someone about me?"

Rage coated her vision in a red haze. "You put out the word that I needed a mate before you even told me what I was?"

Hurt mixed with the anger churning her stomach. She fisted her hands and shoved them in the pockets of the robe to keep herself from slapping his face.

"You cold-hearted *bastard*. How could you do that and still take me to bed? If you didn't want me as a mate, you should have just left me alone. Or sent me back to America and let me deal with this myself. But no, you had to seduce me and then put me on display like a slab of meat in a butcher shop. And now that you've had me, you don't want me anymore, so you're handing me off to someone else."

"No! Chase, that's not true."

Shock and pain filled his eyes, hunched his shoulders, but she ignored his reaction and plowed on.

"I trusted you. You made me believe I could."

Though she tried, she couldn't hold back the tears that spilled onto her cheeks and betrayed her. She swiped her hands over her face, hating herself for being weak enough to cry over a man like him. God, how could she have been such a fool? Emotionally drained, and disgusted with herself, she turned toward the patio door.

"You could've been honest with me, Roman. You could've been fair. You didn't have to break my heart."

She pushed opened the glass door. The need to run, to get as far away from him and the pain as she could, overwhelmed her. Then the anger rose up again. It crowded out the hurt, so she grabbed onto it and let it grow. Taking a deep breath of the damp English air, she straightened her spine.

"I'll be damned if I'll submit to you or anyone else who tells me I have no choice. I'm an American. And in case you've forgotten about the Revolutionary War and the Boston Tea Party, we don't like being told we've got no options."

She glanced back at him, still sitting on the bed and staring at her as if too stunned to register what she was doing. Ignoring the stab of guilt that pricked her conscience, she placed her foot on the threshold and braced herself. "So you and all the little Were buddies you've lined up to pawn me off on can just go straight to hell!"

With that, she shot out the door and gave into the sheer joy of running. The overlarge robe flew out behind her like a cape. She didn't know where she was headed, but God, getting there felt so good.

She didn't stop when Roman called her name or when she heard him chasing her. She didn't even slow down until she reached the edge of the forest—and came face to face with a huge, snarling tiger.

ᚱᚢᚱ

"No!" Roman shot to his feet and charged out the door after her. "Damn it, Chase, no."

He'd never meant to hurt her or make her think he'd wanted her for anything less than a mate. Christ, how had he screwed this up so badly?

He had to catch her and convince her to return to the house before she got into trouble. If he couldn't persuade her to come peacefully, he'd toss her over his shoulder and haul her back like a sack of flour. She was going to listen to him, damn it, if he had to tie her to the bed and sit on her.

Why did Yankees have to be so damned independent? Didn't she realize it was dangerous for her out here? If she'd wanted to go storming out of his bedroom, why couldn't she just have gone back to her room?

And where the hell did she think she was going dressed only in his terrycloth robe?

"*Chase!*"

If she heard him, she didn't let on. She was headed for the forest. He put on a burst of speed. Then the wind shifted, bringing him the scent of another weretiger—the one who'd been watching Fernwood Manor.

If he got Chase alone, he could force a claiming, and Roman had no intention of letting that happen. He'd protect what was his—to the death, if necessary. Shucking his jeans, he shifted and streaked toward the forest on four legs.

✑✑✑

Dillon had returned to his spot in Ileana's woods that morning as soon as Drake got through grilling him on what he was doing out here—and chewing his ass for not clearing it with him beforehand.

Like the scumbag needed to know what his pride members did twenty-four/seven. He sure hoped Ileana confirmed she'd hired him to investigate some suspected poaching on her property. Otherwise, there'd be hell to pay, and he didn't intend to be the one footing the bill.

Cursing himself for getting caught up in the Vampire's grand scheme, he sipped coffee from an insulated mug and paced back and forth at the edge of the forest.

He'd been watching Fernwood Manor all day but hadn't seen any sign of Chase. If Roman would just leave the damn house, Dillon could drive up and demand to see her. She didn't know who he was so she shouldn't object to giving him a few minutes in private. And a few minutes was all he'd need to—

He heard a shout and spun around. Chase came flying out of the house, wearing a terrycloth robe several sizes too big. She was running straight for him. Perfect. This way he'd get more than a few minutes with her.

Roman was chasing her, but she had a good lead on him. No problem. By the time the bastard reached the trees, Dillon would have Chase spirited away to someplace quiet. Then Roman shifted to his wolf form. Even better.

Dillon stripped and shifted, too. Now he could exact Ileana's revenge on Roman and claim Chase all in one throw. After all, a wolf was hardly a match for a tiger.

ᥱᠥᥱᠥ

Drake glanced up from his paperwork as Gray slammed into the study, temper sparking off the fireworks in his eyes. Ducking his head to hide his smile, Drake continued entering figures in his ledgers. "How'd it go with Ileana?"

"How the hell do you think it went?" Gray shuddered—one quick jerk. "Fucking Vampire gives me the creeps. Don't know why you wanted *me* to go talk to her in the first place."

"Because of all my enforcers you have the most charm and the best social skills." At Gray's snort of disbelief, Drake swallowed a laugh and kept his head bent over his accounts. "So, what'd she say?"

"Oh, she confirmed what Dillon told us. But that just means they're both lying."

Drake raised his head and watched his EX-O pace. "I can see why you'd question Dillon's veracity, but what reason could Ileana have to lie for him?"

"I don't know." Gray pulled out his comb and raked it through his hair in a gesture that shouted of frustration. "But her eyes were awfully shifty when she was explaining how she'd hired Dillon to investigate some poachers because 'tigers are such good trackers.'"

"A Vampire's eyes are always shifty," Drake said with a chuckle. "And tigers *are* very good trackers. So the explanation makes sense."

"Yeah? Then how come we only found Dillon's scent in that one spot on the edge of Roman's land, except for a narrow path from there to the road?"

Gray slapped his hands flat on the desk and glared at him. "Unless these alleged poachers limited their hunting to just one small strip of land and then spread their wings and flew away when they'd finished, Dillon should have tracked them all over the bloody property. Instead, he's confined his search to the few square yards where he has an unobstructed view of Fernwood Manor."

"That's an excellent point." Drake scratched his chin with the eraser on his pencil. "Did you put a guard on Fernwood Manor?"

"Sort of." Gray sighed, shook his head. "It's supposed to start tonight." He held up a hand before Drake could interrupt. "I assigned a couple of guys, but they asked if they could finish up the job they were on first. And since it was only another twenty-four hours, I didn't think it would matter. Guess I was wrong."

"No harm done. Where's Dillon now?"

"A good question. Apparently, he disappeared right after you spoke with him this morning. I stopped by his work on my way here, and not only isn't he there, he hasn't been for over a month. Claimed he had a freelance job and took a leave of absence."

He perched a hip on the edge of the desk. "There's no sign of him at his house. Now, it seems to me if he were really hunting poachers, he'd want to sleep during the day and traipse around the Vampire's woods at night. That's when most poaching gets done. Unless we're talking about some very eccentric poachers. Interesting, don't you think?"

"Yes, I do." Drake stood and fished the car keys out of his pocket. "What do you say we cruise on out to those woods? See what's what?"

Gray's grin was quick and wicked. "Sounds like a plan. I could use a good fight."

∾∾∾

Chase gaped at the tiger confronting her. He—it was way too big to be female—was larger than any she'd ever seen in a zoo or on The Discovery Channel.

She rubbed a hand over her throat at the sight of his four-inch-long canines. One bite to her neck and she'd be a goner.

Instead of attacking, the monster growled softly and motioned with his head toward the trees. He wanted her to *follow* him? Fat chance!

She thought about running then dismissed it as foolish. He'd catch her before she'd gone a yard. Easing backward, she glanced around for anything she could use as a weapon—a tree limb, a rock. Nothing caught her eye. *Great. Now what do I do?*

She'd almost decided running might be her only option when a gigantic black wolf charged from behind and skidded to a stop in front of her. Head down and hackles raised, he stalked toward the tiger.

Roman. Somehow, she recognized him. Though grateful for his intervention, her first response was a feline aversion to his wolf side, and she hissed at him before she could stop herself.

Oh God, had she actually *hissed?* This must be why she'd never been comfortable around dogs. *I'm a frigging cat!*

The tiger fixed his evil amber eyes on Roman and began to circle. Roman woofed and jerked his head at Chase in a gesture that told her to get her ass away from there.

"Like hell." She refused to abandon him but did scramble backward, giving him more room to maneuver.

The snarls and growls the two creatures emitted as they circled made her cringe with fear, but not for herself. As huge as the wolf was, the tiger was bigger, more powerful, and likely had longer, sharper teeth and claws. He sprang, landed on Roman's back, and dug those claws into his hide.

Roman yelped in pain, dropped, and rolled, clamping his jaws on one of the tiger's legs. The tiger screamed then sank his teeth into the wolf's rump. Roman whimpered, losing his grip on the cat's leg.

His body contorted into impossible positions as his teeth fought for purchase on any part of the tiger he could reach. Blood streamed over his fur, like red paint on black velvet.

She had to help him or that monster was going to kill him. Before she realized she intended to move, she'd jumped on the tiger's back.

Wrapping her arms and legs around him like a vice, she grabbed one of his ears with her teeth, clamped down as hard as she could, and held on.

Chapter 7

S hit!" Chase cursed her own stupidity as the tiger suddenly abandoned his attack on Roman and took off for the woods— with her on his back. "No way, buster."

She didn't know what he had in mind, but she didn't want any part of it. Unwrapping her arms and legs, she pushed herself off him and landed on her ass on the hard ground.

"I don't care where you're going," she said, rubbing her bruised rump. "I'm staying here."

The tiger skidded to a halt. He whirled and grabbed the neck of her robe in his teeth. Then he pulled her toward the trees.

"Stop it!" She pounded on his head and chest and dug her heels into the ground, but it did little to halt his progress. "Get your grubby teeth off me."

His saliva dripped down the back of her neck. She heard the terrycloth robe rip then a fierce growl as Roman, still in his wolf form, launched himself at the tiger.

"No!"

The stiffness of his movements, and the blood on his fur, told her Roman was badly injured. Still, he was risking his life to protect her.

The two animals rolled over the ground in a melee of snarling, growling, raking claws, and snapping teeth. Tossing safety aside, Chase plowed into the fray. She tore at the tiger, pinching and twisting handfuls of his hide as hard as she could.

"Get away from him and leave us alone, you sick bastard."

He swiped a paw at her. His claws slashed through the robe and scored her chest and abdomen. She hissed in pain and stumbled backward, Roman's furious snarl echoing in her ears. Before she could rejoin the fight, two more tigers leaped onto the field.

The newcomers headed straight for Roman and his opponent. *Oh, God. He can't fight them all.* He wouldn't stand a chance.

Panicked, she scanned the ground for a weapon. This time she spotted a baseball-sized stone. She grabbed it, raised it over her head, and pitched it at the tiger fighting Roman. The rock missed his head but landed a glancing blow off his hip. He yelped, whirled, and hissed at her. Then, to her shock, he turned and fled toward the woods.

"One down, two left," she muttered and looked around for another rock.

The other two cats didn't attack. Instead, they chased the first monster into the trees. Chase dismissed them, for the moment, and focused on Roman—human again, naked, and struggling to his feet.

"Lie down, you idiot," she ordered, running to his side. "You're hurt."

"Really?" He sank back to the ground. "What gave it away?"

His sarcasm did nothing to mask his pain and exhaustion.

"Don't be a smartass." She ripped a piece off the bottom of the robe and wiped the blood from his wounds. "He sure did a number on you."

"Are you all right?" He cupped her face in his hands, stilling her movements and causing her breath to hitch. "Did he hurt you?"

"I'm fine, but you're not."

The sight of his battered face brought tears to her eyes. She forced them back and concentrated on wiping off the blood.

"What the hell were you thinking, attacking that monster?"

"It's not as bad as it looks. Once we turn thirty, Weres heal fast. So I'll be good as new in a few minutes."

He parted her robe and exposed the claw marks. "I thought you said he didn't hurt you."

"It's just a scratch. Now stay still, damn it."

"Shut up and let me hold you," he ordered, pulling her into his arms. "Christ, I thought I'd lost you."

"But I—you—" She felt the relief pouring off him in waves and didn't understand. "You didn't want me."

"Damn it, Chase," he said, his voice ripe with exasperation. "I do *so* want you." He gave her a small shake. "You're the first woman I've ever wanted as a mate."

His lips crushed hers, the kiss more frustration than passion. "I said I'd taken care of notifying the local Tigris pride. I didn't say I intended to let you choose anyone else but me."

"Then why the hell did you tell them about me at all?"

"I had to. My honor demanded it."

"Honor?" She shook her head and pulled away from him, crossing her arms over her chest. "What is it with you English and your frigging honor? Christ, an American who wanted me would've been thumping his chest and shouting, 'Mine.'"

His lips twitched. "I'm up for a little chest thumping." He reached for her again. "In fact, why don't—"

"This looks like fun. Mind if we play, too?"

Chase twisted out of Roman's arms and looked behind her. Two naked men stalked toward them, their blond hair disheveled. The other tigers, she realized.

She absolutely refused to blush at their lack of clothing. If they didn't care, why should she? Besides, they were both prime specimens.

She glanced back at Roman. He looked furious, but not worried. So apparently, these cats weren't a threat. At least not a physical one.

"Goddammit, Drake," he growled. "Put some fricking clothes on, why don't you? What the hell's the matter with you two?"

"Considering you're buck naked, too," one blond hunk responded. "I'd say that's the pot talking to the kettles."

"I didn't have any choice. You and Gray are just doing it to impress Chase."

"Is it working?" the darker blond asked.

He flashed her a grin, adding charm to his rugged good looks. Although, tall and slender, he was well-built—and hung like a horse. Chase tore her eyes away from his...attributes and got to her feet.

"If you guys are going to get into a pissing contest, I'm going back to the house."

She studied the one called Drake, deliberately running her eyes up and down his body—she had to admit it was a damn fine one. He grinned. Roman growled.

Tossing tossed her hair back, she pivoted on her heel and marched toward the house. If she had to choose a mate, at least her options were all hunks. Still, how could she be sure they wanted her and not just her money?

She shook her head in wonder. That was a problem she'd never expected to have. Now that she did, she wasn't giving up control of her trust fund to anyone. If these English studs thought she'd capitulate just because they told her she had no choice, they all had another think coming.

When—if—she chose a mate, it would be someone she couldn't live without and someone who couldn't live without her. If Roman wasn't man enough to step up to the plate and go after what he said he wanted, so be it. She'd be damned if she'd let her hormones force her into anything.

Mother Nature might have other ideas, but if so, She could go to hell, along with all the men in England.

✌✌✌

Watching her go, Drake could only shake his head in admiration. "Lord, she really is a stunner and, obviously, a handful."

"She's mine," Roman announced. "Get that through your thick skull right now. Both of you," he added, shooting Gray a dirty look.

Drake stroked his chin and studied him. "You gave your word not to claim her."

"I haven't. Yet." He headed back toward the house. "You'll get your promised time with her," he called over his shoulder. "But I suggest you put some clothes on first."

Picking up a pair of jeans from the ground, he pulled them on. "We've all agreed this will be Chase's decision. So you might want to find out what your pride member was doing here, trying to drag her off. Because whoever he is, I don't think he's gotten the message."

As Roman continued toward the house, Drake sighed. "I was afraid of this."

"I thought you said you trusted him."

"He didn't break his word. Chase is still unmated. But it looks like she's fallen for him."

"So you're just giving up?"

"Hell, no. I'll talk to her and try to convince her to choose a tiger." Drake shrugged. "But if she still wants Roman, it's pointless to fight the inevitable."

He clapped Gray on the shoulder. "You have to learn to pick your battles, my friend, because you sure as hell can't win them all. Especially when a woman's involved."

∽∾∾

Dillon picked the lock on Ileana's back door and slipped inside. She'd bloody well better hide him from Gatos and Hunter, or there'd be hell to pay. As he started across the kitchen, the Vampire suddenly appeared, blocking the doorway that led into the rest of the house.

"What are you doing here?" She waved a hand at his nakedness. "Especially like that."

"I got into a fight with Fernwood, but before I could finish—" The look in her eyes had him reconsidering what he'd started to say. "—the discussion, we were interrupted by Drake Gatos and Grayson Hunter."

"You *showed* yourself to them?"

"Well." He swallowed hard. "Not intentionally, but Chase came running out of the house. Fernwood was chasing her, and I thought—"

"Oh, I'm well aware of what you thought." She stepped toward him. He moved away. "You figured you could ignore my orders and abduct her, didn't you?"

"No. No, that's not true. I was...bringing her to you," he said, backpedaling furiously. "Just like you wanted me to."

"What I wanted was for you to simply keep an eye on her until Roman was head over heels."

She moved farther into the room, the whites of her eyes turning blood red.

"He was—is head over heels. He was chasing her, for Christ's sake." He glanced around quickly, looking for an escape that wasn't there. "Everything worked out just like you planned it."

"Not quite yet." Ileana's voice was soft, hypnotic. She came at him so fast he didn't even realize she'd moved—until she had him by the neck. "But it will."

℘℘℘

Roman couldn't help but whistle when Chase walked into his study twenty minutes later, wearing a rust-colored silk jumpsuit with a cowled neckline that dipped to the top of her breasts and almost to her waist in the back.

"Wow."

"Thanks." In her hand was the gray case file. She waved it at him. "We need to discuss Melinda Carter's murder."

He blinked. With everything that had gone on since she arrived, he'd completely forgotten her purpose in coming here. "Fine. I'll tell you anything you want to know. But first—"

He reached for her just as the butler appeared in the study doorway.

"A Mr. Gatos and a Mr. Hunter to see you, sir."

"Are they clothed?"

Martin raised an eyebrow. "They appear to be, sir."

Chase laughed. Roman sighed.

"Send them in." He turned back to her. "Drake wants to talk to you."

"Uh-huh. And, of course, he's going to try to convince me to choose a tiger for a mate." She stepped closer to him. Her gaze scoured his face, searched his eyes. "Do you want me, Roman?"

"More than I can say."

"Then why—"

"I hope I'm interrupting."

Drake's deep voice from the doorway made Chase jump and Roman curse.

"Oh, you are. Believe me." He slipped his arm around her shoulders. "Drake Gatos and Grayson Hunter," he told her, motioning at one then the other. "Chase Alcott. Drake's the local Tigris pride leader, and Gray's his second-in-command."

"I'm very pleased to meet you, Chase." Drake gave her a wide smile then took her hand and brought it to his lips. "I thought Roman was exaggerating your beauty, but he was clearly understating it."

He had to give Drake credit. The bastard was charming. Roman hoped Chase wouldn't be swayed by the fact he was a feline and not a canine. When she murmured a thank you, tugged her hand free, and wrapped her arm around his waist, a surge of relief swept over him.

Now if she could just resist the logic Drake was bound to throw at her. He knew from experience how convincing the man could be.

"I assume Roman's told you I need to talk to you, Chase." Drake flashed that smile again. "In private."

To Roman's surprise and delight, she tightened her hold on him and shook her head. "I don't think so. Roman may trust you, but I don't. I don't know you. So, you can talk to me if you want to, but he stays."

"I could insist."

"You could try," she corrected. "But since I don't recognize your authority, you wouldn't get far. I also don't think you want to piss me off. Especially if you're hoping to convince me of anything."

Roman covered his snort of laughter with a cough. Well, he'd warned the pride leader Chase was stubborn. "Why don't you all sit down while I pour us some wine?"

Looking disgruntled, Drake and Gray sat on the sofa. Chase pointedly remained standing. Roman poured the burgundy and handed it out. When he gave her a glass, she winked at him and eased the tension balling in his gut.

Christ, she was a jewel. Mother Nature couldn't have picked a more perfect mate for him if She'd tried, except for the cat and dog thing, of course. But they could live with that. Somehow. He took up a position behind her right shoulder and waited for Drake to speak.

"Roman says he's told you about your situation."

"We've discussed it, and I've—" She hesitated. Roman ran a hand down her arm, offering what comfort he could. "—remembered my parents," she continued in a small voice.

"Remembered?" Gray asked.

"She'd blocked it all out," Roman said. "Which is understandable, considering she was only four when they were murdered."

Drake looked from Chase to Roman and back again. "And you've told her everything?"

"Yes," they said in unison.

"Then you understand why you have to choose a mate immediately?"

"No."

"No, you don't understand?"

She shook her head. "No, I don't have to take a mate."

Roman tensed. If she'd decided she didn't want him after all, he'd...just have to convince her.

She reached back and took his hand, gave it a gentle squeeze.

"Roman and I are discussing it. But since we've only known each other for three days, I doubt either one of us is ready to make a lifetime commitment at the moment." She lifted her chin. "Besides, I refuse to let my hormones be a factor in such an important decision."

Though he held himself in check, Roman wanted to grab her and shake some sense into her. She might not be ready to commit, but he sure as hell was. Even though, now they were lovers, he could help her through the heat without claiming her, that was no reason not—

"Christ, man, I thought you said you told her everything." Drake's snarl cut through Roman's thoughts like a scalpel.

"I—bloody hell." A small groan escaped as he realized what Drake meant. "I was going to tell her. I—we just got distracted."

"Distracted, huh?" Gray scoffed. "Is that what they're calling it these days?"

"Tell me what?" Chase spun around to face him, and his heart broke at the fear in her eyes. "Roman?"

"Don't worry," he said, pulling her into his arms. "We won't let anything hurt you."

He wanted to shelter her, to protect her from what she needed to know. But he couldn't. He opened his mouth to tell her, but Drake beat him to it.

"If you're not mated before the other two pride leaders get here," he said, his calm voice belying the storm in his eyes, "Roman will end up fighting a two-front war. One he can't possibly win."

℃℃℃

"A war you can't win?" Chase jerked out of Roman's arms and stared at him. "What's he talking about?"

Roman sighed. "There are two other pride leaders, both of whom think they should be the one to claim you."

"And the only way to keep you from getting killed is for us to mate before they get here?"

"Yes," said Drake.

"No," countered Roman.

She shook her head and glared at them. "That's not exactly helpful, guys."

Terrified for Roman, she paced the room, trying to relieve the churning in her gut. "Apparently, you disagree with Drake's answer," she said to Roman and reached in her pocket for a Tums. "So would you mind explaining?"

"Drake's right. In a sense. If we're not mated, they'll fight me for you. However, I doubt they're going to just give up and go home if you're claimed before they get here. So either way, they're going to fight me."

"Terrific."

She rubbed her forehead, where a headache had formed to rival her indigestion.

"How did these other two pride leaders even find out I exist?" she asked. "They can't have known about me prior to my coming to England, or they would have approached me in America." She paused when Roman grimaced. "Christ, just how many people did you tell?"

"I only told Drake. The others found out by accident."

"As I'm the local pride leader, he had to tell me. I had a right to know there was an unmated female in my territory." He rose and stepped toward her as if trying to establish his authority. "In fact, you should have informed me you were coming before you left California." When she opened her mouth to tell him off, he added, "I'm not taking you to task for it because you didn't know what you are, and you don't understand the rules."

"The *rules*?" Who the hell did this guy think he was? She jabbed a finger into his chest. "Let me tell you something, buster. I don't give a rat's ass who you are or what position you have with the locals. The only rules *I* have to follow are the laws of whatever country I happen to be in at the moment. Furthermore, I refuse to be ordered around by a bunch of oversexed he-men just because my father wasn't a human."

Instead of matching her temper as she expected, Drake grabbed her hand and gave her a condescending smile, the kind he might give a child who asked why it was dangerous to play in the street.

"Without a pride leader's protection you won't stand a chance against the Siberian males who are coming."

"Oh, really?" With a snort, she jerked her hand out of his. "You wanna bet? I may have trouble getting a handgun in England, but shotguns and hunting rifles are easy enough to come by. And I'm more than willing to shoot the assholes, if necessary, to defend myself." Unless...

She turned to Roman. "You said Weres heal fast. Does that mean you can't be killed?"

"No. We can be killed. It's just a bit more difficult. Normal bullets won't do it. You'd need silver."

So that myth was true at least. Something to remember. "And you have some?"

"I do."

"If you go that route," Gray warned. "You'll be shunned by every pride in existence."

"He's right," Drake said. "There are certain...traditions, let's say, since the word 'rules' offends you, that must be followed if you and Roman intend to interact with your own kind ever again." As she started to protest, he raised a hand. "At least let me finish before you bite my head off again. Traditions, I might add, that have been followed by our kind for centuries."

She closed her eyes briefly, struggling for patience. "What kind of traditions?"

"The right to challenge another male to a fight over a mate, for one," Gray said. "You should be grateful Drake hasn't challenged Roman for you already."

"Damn it, Gray," Drake growled. "Keep your mouth shut."

Chase glanced from one to the other. "And your females have no choice in the matter?" she asked Drake.

"It depends on the pride leader. Despite what Gray says, I personally believe both mates should choose freely, and I wouldn't pick a fight over someone who didn't want me. But with the shortage of female Tigris in most parts of the world, not all leaders agree."

He sighed, and some of his arrogance dissipated. "The rules are there for a reason, Chase. Humans vastly outnumber us, and with the advent of modern weapons, it's easier than ever to kill us. Our survival depends on humans not learning our secret.

"Even though tigers are solitary creatures in the animal world, Weres gather in clans, or tribes if you will, for protection—and so we can be ourselves around others without worrying about revealing our existence to humans.

"Although most of us today live in cities and among humans, we still belong to the local tribe of weretigers, which is our pride."

He crossed his arms over his chest. "When there's trouble, as there is now, my pride members know they can come to me for help and protection. But without a pride, weretigers are on their own, and few of them survive for long."

"Which means unless I join your pride, Roman and I are screwed, is that it? What about Roman's pride?"

"Pack," Roman corrected. "Wolves gather in packs, but my father's pack abandoned our family when he mated with a Vampire."

Chase heard the pain in his voice, though she doubted anyone else did. At least they gave no sign of it. Though her heart ached for him, she kept her face blank, her voice matter of fact, and her sympathy well hidden.

"And your mother's family?"

"The same, for the most part, though my cousin Tatyana's a possibility."

"There's still the matter of you coming into heat," Drake said. "By June twenty-first, your hormones are going to be raging out of control. If you're not mated by then—"

"Back off, Drake," Roman ordered, nearly at a shout, obviously thinking this was between the two of them, not Drake. "You know damn well, I can help her through that. You have no right to put pressure on her to—"

"You won't be much bloody help to her if you're fighting every unattached male Tigris on three continents," Drake argued, his voice rising in volume to match Roman's. "Besides—"

"Why June twenty-first?" she demanded, drawing the men's attention back to her. "Because it's the summer solstice? Does every female Were turning thirty this year go crazy on that day?"

They fell silent and stared at her like they'd never seen her before. Finally, Roman cleared his throat.

"June twenty-first's your birthday. While it's not always exact, the heat usually hits within the one or two days either side of the day you turn thirty, so you'll—"

"Wrong." She ran her fingers through her hair, imagining how they'd react when she told them. "My first caseworker must have transposed the date when I entered the foster care system at age four, and the mistake followed me all the way to adulthood. But a few years ago when I ordered a copy of my birth certificate so I could get a passport, I discovered I was actually born on June twelfth."

A stunned silence followed her announcement. Then they all started talking at once.

Chapter 8

Roman watched as Chase paced the study, her hand pressed to her stomach. Nothing had been settled before Drake and Gray left, except they now knew they had even less time than they'd thought.

"Why didn't you tell me about your birthday?" he asked.

"Probably for the same reason you didn't tell me the other pride leaders were coming. Like an idiot, I went ballistic and took off running before we got that far."

She hesitated, shooting him a sheepish smile. "Sorry about that, by the way. And then there's the fact I'm not real comfortable with the idea of turning into a raging slut."

"That really bothers you, doesn't it?"

She stopped pacing long enough to glare at him. "How do you expect me to feel?"

"The heat is a natural part of being a Were, Chase, and it's certainly nothing for you to be ashamed of."

"Easy for you to say. You're a man. But for someone like me, who didn't even know what I was, it's...mortifying."

She sighed, her shoulders slumping. "Oh God, Roman, what are we going to do?"

Opening his arms, he enfolded her and crushed her against him. "We'll figure it out, together. Now, that we're lovers, I can get you through the heat without claiming you."

"And you're okay with that?"

Hell no! He wanted the world to know she was his, but she didn't need that kind of pressure. Not now. He could wait—for a day or two—to let her get used to the idea.

"Let's just say, I'd rather not force you into something you're not ready to accept."

"But what if the other pride leaders come?"

"Drake will tell them to turn around and go home." He nuzzled her hair, breathing in the scent of honeysuckle and jasmine in a sun-splashed meadow.

"And if that doesn't work?"

"We'll cross that bridge when we get there."

She pulled away from him, dug in her pocket, and brought out a small roll, her other hand once more pressed to her stomach. Taking two tablets from the end of the roll, she popped them into her mouth.

"What are those?" he asked.

"Tums. Antacids for my indigestion."

"Do they work?"

"Not all that well." She went back to pacing. "But I keep hoping."

"Does it feel like something's trying to crawl out through your navel?"

Her footsteps faltered as her gaze shot to his face. "It's not indigestion, is it?"

"No." He bit back his chuckle, sure she wouldn't quite see the humor. "It's your body trying to change into your animal form. After you shift the first time, the pain will lessen to just a twinge."

"Will it get worse until then?"

"Most likely."

"Terrific." She rolled her eyes then nibbled on her lip. "So how do I shift the first time?"

"It's instinctive. If you'd been raised in a pride, it would've happened naturally when you were a youngster and saw others shift. As you weren't, it'll probably come when your animal side feels threatened enough to go into survival mode."

Closing her eyes, she sighed. "This just gets better and better, doesn't it?"

He wanted to take her mind off the pain—and everything else assaulting her—and cast about for a change of subject. The gray case file caught his eye. Perfect.

"What was it you wanted to discuss about Melinda's murder?"

"You're trying to change the subject, aren't you?"

"I think you've absorbed enough surprises for one day, and David will be back soon."

"Oh, God. David. What am I going to tell him?"

"Chase—"

"I know. I know. He can't learn about the woo-woo stuff."

"Woo-woo stuff?"

"Yeah, you know." She fluttered her hands and hummed a familiar tune. "The *Twilight Zone* stuff." Walking over to the desk, she picked up the file and opened it. "You said you'd tell me everything you knew about the murder, right?"

"Yes."

"Okay." She took a deep breath and stretched her neck, as if shifting gears. "You mentioned the other day Melinda took sleeping powders. In fact, I think the word you used was 'consumed.' I noticed flickers of dishonesty in your aura when you said it."

Oh, Christ. If he'd known what she was going to ask, he'd have changed the subject again. But he had to tell her. As clever as she was, she could probably find out another way. He wanted her to accept him as a mate, and having her see flickers of guilt in his aura wasn't the way to build trust. Besides, she'd keep asking questions until she was satisfied with the answers.

"I was hoping I wouldn't have to tell you this." No kidding, but he figured it'd take her about ten seconds to guess the rest of it, so he'd better confess up front. "I had Martin put the sleeping powders in Melinda's tea. Without her knowledge. Just as I have him doctor the tea of every overnight, human guest we have. So they won't wake up and find me gone when I feed, or worse, try to follow me."

Her laughter came as a shock. "No wonder I've been so tired every night since I got here."

Stunned by her response, he stared at her. "You're not angry?"

She chuckled. "I probably should be, but I understand why you did it. Besides, it's the best sleep I've had in months."

Cocking her head, she studied him. "It also explains the flickers I saw in your aura when we discussed the murder the first time. You blame yourself."

"No, but I do wonder if Melinda would have survived if she hadn't been drugged."

"Well, you can stop wondering. One thing I've learned as a private detective is that if someone wants to commit a crime, they'll find a way to do it. Drugging Melinda might've made it a little easier to break her neck and throw her over the balcony, but—" She sliced her hands in front of her for emphasis. "—a determined murderer would have found some way to kill her, regardless."

Her words eased a weight from his heart he hadn't realized was there.

"Come here."

She arched an eyebrow, pursed those tempting lips.

"Please."

Grinning, she placed the file back on his desk, sauntered over, pulled his head down, and nibbled his bottom lip. He yanked her closer then changed the angle of the kiss, deepening the hunger and plundering her mouth with his tongue.

When he finally let her breathe, she sighed and rested her head on his shoulder. He saw confusion in her aura that instinct told him had nothing to do with the murder.

"Your aura's cloudy. You still have questions about me?"

"It boggles my mind to hear someone talk about *my* aura."

"Boggles your mind? What—No, don't explain. I don't think I even *want* to know what it means."

He kissed her again, couldn't stop himself. "Reading your aura is what got us into trouble this morning. If I hadn't seen the lust in it when you looked at me over breakfast, I might have been able to resist you."

Crossing to the hutch, he poured himself more wine. "Go ahead, ask your question."

She hesitated.

"What is it?" he prompted. When she didn't respond, he ran a hand through his hair, nerves fraying. What could she possibly want to know she'd be reluctant to ask? "Talk to me, Chase. I'll tell you anything."

"Something you said earlier made me wonder—" She cleared her throat. "When you say 'feed,' do you mean on humans? Is that myth true?"

Ah, so that was it. "Yes. Vampires live on human blood. But as I'm half Lycan, I can also eat solid foods."

"So then you don't need to...to drink blood?"

"I do. My Vampire half requires it. But I don't need as much as I would if my father hadn't been a Lycan."

"I see." She frowned, her eyes searching his. "Does the person you drink from die?"

"Yes."

"Oh." She paced to the fireplace and back, chewing her bottom lip. "And that doesn't *bother* you?"

"Considering the type of humans we feed on, it doesn't bother me at all."

"I don't understand."

"Other than the basic rule of keeping our existence a secret, Vampires have only one law we must obey without exception. We can't kill innocent humans—well, ones that aren't evil."

"But it's impossible to tell if someone's evil just by looking at them. Unless you only feed on people you know."

"Hardly. But Vampires can see auras, just as Weres can."

He sipped his wine and watched her pace, while his mind wove fantasies about how he'd soon channel some of that restless energy.

"Have you ever seen anyone with a black aura?"

She frowned, shook her head. He wasn't surprised. If she had, she'd understand.

"The more evil the person, the darker his or her aura becomes. Vampires only take people with very dark auras. And humans should be grateful we do. Without Vampires, there'd be a lot more serial killers, pedophiles, and rapists than there are."

"So the Hollywood version of Vampires drinking the blood of virgins is all wrong?"

"Unless the virgin is also a serial killer, yes."

"Most of them are probably safe then. We virgins like to start our criminal careers by breaking the small laws first and working our way up. So by the time we get to be serial killers, we're no longer virgins." She chuckled. "And since I only lost that title a few hours ago, I guess I'm getting started a little late."

That she accepted it enough to joke about it, both amazed and thrilled him. He couldn't begin to explain what a gift she was. Snagging her by the arm as she passed, he maneuvered her up against him and kissed her, long and deep.

"Any more questions?"

"Hmmm," she murmured distractedly. "I might've had some if you hadn't just destroyed my ability to think."

"Perhaps I should kiss you again and make it better."

"Oh, yeah, like that'll really work." She put her arms around his neck and pulled his lips back to hers. "But thinking's way over-rated, anyway."

"Absolutely."

"So tell me," she said, several minutes later. "Are Vampires immortal?"

"Under normal circumstances, we are." He nibbled along her jaw and sucked her earlobe. "We can't get sick. Poisons won't hurt us, nor will a gun, a knife, a cross, holy water, sunlight, garlic, or a stake through the heart. Or any of the other stuff legends talk about.

"So daylight and sunshine don't hurt you?"

"No. But we *can* be killed by decapitation or by completely destroying our bodies with fire. Anything else will heal. Hollywood missed the mark on that one, too."

His sensitive hearing caught the scrape of tires on gravel. "Time to face David. I can hear the car coming up the drive."

"It really shouldn't be a problem. He'll be pissed at me, seeing as how I told him not to try to take you to bed, and I ended up doing it myself. But he'll get over it."

"If I recall what happened this morning, it was *I* who took *you* to bed, not the other way around."

She laughed. "Either way, it's me he'll be pissed at. There's no way I can hide what's happened between us, so he's just going to have to deal with it."

"Hmmm. Well, why don't I let you handle that while I go see Martin about dinner?"

"Coward."

He headed for the door. "Guilty."

"Wait. I have a question."

"You always do," he said, retracing his steps back to her.

"Is it safe for me to drink my tea at dinner tonight?"

"Are you saying there's something you'd rather do than sleep?"

She wrapped her arms around his waist. "Something like that."

"Actually, I intend to tell Martin not to drug your tea at all," he murmured, nibbling on her neck. "I have other plans for your nights."

∾∾∾

Chase braced herself when David came into the study a few minutes later. He stopped dead, dropped his notepad on the floor, and stared at her.

"What?" she demanded.

"You *didn't!*"

She rolled her eyes. "Didn't what?"

He flopped down next to her on the couch. "You slept with Roman, didn't you?"

She almost said she hadn't *slept* with him then realized she couldn't, since she'd taken a two hour nap. Still, for some reason, she wasn't quite ready to confirm David's suspicions.

"What makes you think that?"

He gave her a shrewd look. "You're glowing. I've never seen you look more killer—or more guilty."

With a laugh, she gave up. "It just happened. I didn't do it on purpose." Grinning at his raised eyebrows, she corrected herself. "Okay, I guess I did do it on purpose, but I didn't *set out* to do it, if you know what I mean."

"Well, I can't say I'm surprised. I told you he looked like he wanted to eat you."

She suppressed the giggles that threatened to explode at his words and studied his aura. He was jealous, but not angry.

"Thanks." She threw her arms around his neck for a hug.

He hugged her back. "For?"

"For not being pissed. And for not giving me the same lecture I gave you when we first got here."

"Look, sweetie." He leaned back and gazed into her eyes. "The very fact you actually slept with a client tells me this is a special circumstance."

He shrugged. "And there's no point in being pissed. Roman's

not gay, so even if he wasn't interested in you, he still wouldn't want me." Pouting a bit, he pulled her back into the hug. "However, I *am* jealous as hell."

He held her a few seconds before getting up and pouring himself a glass of wine. Walking back to the couch, he frowned at her. She could see flickers in his aura that meant he was trying to say something not easy for him.

"Spit it out," she ordered. "Before your aura explodes."

"Very funny," he grumbled, but he did it with a grin. "I'm just worried about you, girlfriend. Roman's a man of the world, and you're pretty naïve when it comes to romance. I just don't want you to get hurt."

"You don't have to worry about me."

"Oh, really." With a snort, he sat back down on the couch. "Did he fill your head with pretty nonsense while you were having sex? Or maybe you think *because* you had sex, it means he loves you? Or are you just assuming it was love and not lust you saw in his...*aura?*" He spit out the word as if it burned his lips then leaned toward her, a five-alarm scowl on his face. "Is that why I shouldn't worry?"

"No, he didn't fill my head with 'pretty nonsense,'" she snapped. "And I'm not *assuming* anything. I know because I asked him."

"Really?" His head jerked in surprise. "What did he say?"

"What do you think he said?"

She got up and wandered over to the fireplace, stared at the flames. There was no way she could tell David the things she and Roman had discussed. She could never tell anyone.

"I just know I don't have to worry about him hurting me. At least not intentionally."

"Well, that eases my mind," he muttered. "Those *un*intentional hurts are always so much less painful than the intentional ones."

"Don't be an ass, David."

He chuckled. "You say that like it's possible for me to stop."

With a sigh that told her he was conceding, but only because he could see it was no use to argue, he rose and kissed her on the cheek. "Just be careful, okay. I have a bad feeling about this."

She flinched and looked away. David was right so much of the time. No. Everything she saw in Roman's aura, and in his eyes, told her he wouldn't hurt her.

She hoped.

Uneasy with David's dire prediction, she changed the subject. "What did you find out today? Anything interesting?"

"Interesting, yes," he said, collecting his note pad from the floor. "Useful as far as solving the murder? I'm not sure." He flipped through the pages. "I learned that Roman has some cousins almost as beautiful as he is. Too bad none of the guys are gay. I've seriously fallen in lust."

"Yeah, right."

But she was very glad the cousins were straight. The last thing she needed was for David to get involved with a Vampire. Or a Lycan.

"They had lots to say about the redecorating project. Mostly, that old man Fernwood was throwing money away. Money that should go to the family when he dies. Nobody seems to think the house needs any redecorating at all."

He grunted and looked around. "I must say I agree with them. For being nearly three hundred years old, this place doesn't have much wrong with it. At least nobody seemed to think I was anything other than a decorator."

She grinned. "Of course not. I told you we wouldn't have any trouble maintaining that cover."

He rolled his eyes. "Sure, you did. Anyway, I got some good information on the 'ghostly' events that've happened in the house."

"What'd you learn?"

"They think the servants are doing it. Guess the upper class doesn't trust their servants much."

"But these people didn't do it. I'm sure of it."

She decided not to mention she'd checked the servants' auras for that very thing when she'd interviewed them. David was being understanding about Roman, and she didn't want to push her luck.

"But what about the threatening notes? Do they think the servants were responsible for those, too?" She cocked her head as she considered it then nodded. "Of course they do."

"Of course," he confirmed.

"So did anyone you saw today act suspicious? Did you detect anyone lying?"

Chagrin flashed across his face. "No, not really."

"Not really?"

"Well, most of the relatives are so incredibly beautiful, I'm afraid I spent most of my time staring, rather than looking for lies."

"Well, don't feel bad. My day wasn't even as productive as yours." She laughed when David wagged his eyebrows. "You know what I mean."

"Well, you'll meet them all this weekend, I suppose," he said. "And then you can check their—auras."

Chase almost snapped at him for the disdain in his tone and was tempted to tell him Roman saw them, too, but stopped short as she realized his lack of belief didn't bother her anymore. She now understood why she saw them and knew she wasn't a freak. Well, okay, maybe she was, at least far as humans were concerned, but she wasn't a freak to Roman, and that was enough.

He picked that moment to come tell them dinner was ready. With the passion she saw in his aura, and the look in his eyes when he took her hand and smiled, she decided it really didn't matter what anyone but him thought about anything.

eɔeɔ

Roman had listened to the conversation between David and Chase with none of the concern he'd felt at breakfast. He knew he could trust her. He stayed in the dining room with them while they ate dinner, making small talk and drinking wine.

Martin had grumbled a bit about having to separate David's tea from Chase's but gave in good-naturedly when he realized the reason. Martin and Sandra worried about him finding a wife almost as much as his father did. The elderly couple had always been there for him, just like his father. He shuddered to think what would've happened to him without these three humans in his life.

After dinner, he took Chase aside while David yawned his way up to bed. "I need to leave for a few hours." He hesitated, reluctant to admit where he was going. "Will you wait up for me?"

"No problem. I'll wait in the library. If I fall asleep in the chair—well, you know what to do."

He laughed. "I'm sure I can figure something out."

"You're going to feed, aren't you?"

He stared at her in wonder. There was no contempt or disdain in her voice, aura, or expression. Just curiosity. "You're okay with that?"

"Of course." She looked surprised he would think otherwise. "You're not a monster, Roman. You're one of the good guys, helping the people who would become the victim of the bad guys. So stop feeling as if you have to justify yourself. You've nothing to be ashamed of."

He pulled her into his arms and crushed his lips to hers. "Thank you," he whispered. "You can't imagine how grateful I am you feel that way." He kissed her once more and left her to make her way to the library. Outside, on his way through the rose garden, he heard her voice from inside the house.

"I miss you already, Roman. Hurry back."

Laughing with delight at the wondrous creature fate had dropped into his life, he took off toward the slums of London— where someone with a black aura would soon learn human predators weren't the most dangerous beings on the streets tonight.

഻ഹ഻

The hunt took him three hours. When he returned to the house it was dark and quiet. Chase was asleep in the same chair in the library. Martin must have snuck in and turned off the light for her.

Roman picked her up, carried her down to his room, placed her in the middle of his bed, and kissed her awake.

"Hmmm," she purred. "You're back. You feel warmer than this afternoon. Is that from the feeding?"

"Yes. Now, hush and let me kiss you."

After several minutes, during which his tongue scorched a new path through the warm confines of her mouth, he raised his head and smiled at her. "I missed you. I don't like leaving you. I'm afraid you'll disappear while I'm gone."

"Not a chance." She pulled his head back down for another kiss. "Did you hear my goodbye tonight?"

"I did. I almost came back to tell you I missed you, too. Then I decided to just hurry back and show you."

With a chuckle, she began undoing the buttons on his shirt. "So, who was on the menu tonight?"

He almost choked on his laughter. "Do you really want to know?"

"Sure." She pushed the shirt off his shoulders and onto his arms, pinning them to his sides. Then she started kissing his neck and chest. "Tell me."

"A pervert following a young girl down a back street in the slums." He held his breath, wondering how she'd react.

Her kisses stopped for a fraction of a second then resumed as she worked her way down to a nipple. "Good. I hope you made him suffer."

His laugh was rough, half relief, half exasperation. With a growl, he ripped his shirt off, freeing his arms, then grabbed her and threw her down on the pillows. "Not nearly as much as you're going to suffer if you don't stop worrying about my eating habits and concentrate on what we're doing."

"Promises, promises."

❧❧❧

They rolled over the bed, pulling at clothes. Chase loved the feel of his body and tried to taste him everywhere, wanting to show him how much he pleased her. Using her tongue and mouth on his erection, she made him moan and growl with pleasure. When he twisted his hands in her hair and gently pulled her away, she yelped.

He froze. "Did I hurt you?"

"No, I just wasn't finished."

"Oh, well, that's too bad." He chuckled and pushed her down on her back. "Because David said something in the study this afternoon that intrigued me."

"David did?"

"Yes. He said I wanted to eat you." His mouth began tracing patterns of fire down her body. "I thought it was an excellent idea."

She couldn't think of a thing to say. In fact she couldn't think at all as his mouth moved between her legs and his tongue slipped inside her. A long low moan came out of him as he greedily lapped at her juices.

Clenching her fists in the bedding, she arched her body toward his tongue, squirming with pleasure, until a sudden hard climax gripped her, refusing to let go. She cried out. Roman eased up on top of her as she peaked, entering her with one sure thrust, sending her over the edge again.

As her shudders eased and she became aware of her surroundings again, he began to move inside her, slowly at first then faster, deepening each stroke. She wrapped her arms around him and met his thrusts with a passion she hadn't known she possessed. As his body tensed, heralding his own release, she plunged off the edge with him. Screaming out his name, she clutched him in a death grip, helpless under the onslaught.

Chapter 9

June 5th:

Drake glanced up from his computer as Gray entered the study, quietly closing the door behind him. At the look on his friend's face, the hair on the back of Drake's neck prickled.

"Trouble?"

"Not really sure," Gray whispered. "You've got a visitor. Danyer Spects, the Southern California pride leader."

"Oh shit. He's *here*?"

"Standing in your foyer."

"How pissed does he look?"

"He doesn't. That's what bothers me." Gray walked to the window and stared out. "I expected pissed. That, I can handle. But this guy..."

"This guy what?"

Gray turned away from the window and jammed his hands in his pockets. "He looks like a beach bum. A laid back, happy-go-lucky, surfer-type. Complete with ear-to-ear smile and enthusiastic handshake."

"I hear a 'but.'"

"Yeah. But there's something about his eyes. I look into them, and I get the feeling he could rip my head off my neck and shit in the stump before I even knew what hit me." He took a breath and let it out in a long exhale. "He scares me."

"Jesus." Drake stared at him in disbelief. He'd seen Gray take on three tigers at once without even flinching. "I didn't think anything scared you."

Gray shrugged. "This guy does. The whole time he was smiling at me and shaking my hand like a long-lost relative, I kept waiting for the knife to slip between my ribs."

"Great. Just what I need. Damn Roman, anyway."

"You want me to send this guy over there? Let him deal with him?"

"You know I can't do that. Regardless of the fact that they haven't mated yet, Chase has chosen Roman. That means she'll live here in England, which makes her part of our pride, along with him. I don't abandon my people when there's trouble. And I sure as hell don't send trouble their way just so I can avoid it."

"Yeah, I know, but it was worth a shot." Gray sighed. "Well, I guess we can't put it off any longer."

"No, we can't. Show him in, and let's get it over with."

Even with Gray's description, the man who was shown into the study a few minutes later came as a shock. Silver blond curls fell to his collar and framed a face tanned to gold dust by the sun. Straight white teeth gleamed behind generous lips that curved in a wide, apparently friendly, smile.

Skimming just under six-feet tall, Spects' rangy body rippled with muscle. He was dressed in stone-washed jeans, a bright yellow T-shirt—with the slogan, "Why work when you can surf?"—and well-worn sneakers. A pair of dark, wrap-around sunglasses were perched on top of his head.

But it was his eyes that drew Drake's attention. Though the man didn't look a day over thirty, his eyes were ancient. A deep, piercing blue, they didn't have the don't-fuck-with-me look, common to many skilled predators. Instead, they radiated a supreme, bone-chilling confidence that proclaimed this man was invincible, knew it, and had accepted it to the point he no longer considered it worth worrying about. The colors of his aura reflected this same unshakable self-assurance.

His gaze swept the room as he entered, leaving no doubt in Drake's mind he'd catalogued everything in it, noted the exits, and had already come up with any number of plans to use if he needed to in order to get his way.

It was obvious Danyer Spects had been alive, surviving by his skill and wits, for a long time. This was a man to be reckoned with—or better yet avoided all together. He certainly wasn't someone to underestimate.

With another mental "fuck" directed at Roman and Chase, Drake stuck out his hand, hoping the other pride leader would shake it and not bite it off.

"Drake Gatos, Mr. Spects. Pleased to meet you."

"The pleasure's all mine. And please, call me Danyer." His voice washed over Drake's senses like the finest, aged brandy—smooth, mellow, and warm. "I save the formalities for my enemies."

"Danyer, it is." As Drake motioned the American to a chair, Gray moved into a guard position beside the desk. "At ease, Gray. I doubt Danyer's going to eat me before we've at least had a chance to talk."

Danyer chuckled. Like his voice, the laugh was intoxicating. Drake wondered if he did it on purpose to put his victims at ease. Probably. There was no doubt both his voice and his laugh were effective weapons.

Figuring Danyer had most likely heard every excuse and evasion ever invented, Drake decided on the direct approach. "I could ask you why you've come, but we both know the reason. So why don't I start by asking you what you intend to do about it?"

With another soft chuckle, Danyer leaned back in his chair, crossed his arms and his ankles, and grinned. "You're smart, son. I'll give you that. You cut right to the chase with no bullshit. I appreciate it. So let me say upfront, you and your bodyguard there can relax. I'm not here to start a war."

Drake grinned but shook his head. "No offense, Danyer, but I seriously doubt either one of us will relax until you're on a plane headed back to California."

The Yank burst into genuine laughter, his eyes gleaming with mischief. "You're a straight shooter, kid. I like you."

He uncrossed his ankles and propped his right one on his left knee. "So here's the deal. You've got one of my pride members here, unauthorized, unmated, and about to come into her first heat." He held up a hand as Drake started to speak. "Not your fault. I'm aware of that. I'm also aware the girl didn't know who or what she was until she got here.

"It's unfortunate. And not the way I like to handle my pride. But her parents hid their existence well. We had no idea Chase Alcott even existed until someone started asking questions about her. Nevertheless, she *is* a member of my pride, she needs help, and I'm where the buck stops."

"Actually, since she's relocated to England, she's now a member of *my* pride."

"Relocated? I thought she was just here investigating a case for some client."

"She was. However, she's chosen one of the locals as a mate. That puts her in my pride and makes her my responsibility."

Danyer's eyes widened. "Check me on this. She got here on Monday, today's Thursday, and she's already chosen one of your local tigers as a mate? That's some pretty fast work."

Drake braced himself. "I didn't say she chose a local tiger. I said she chose one of the locals."

"Good God, man, tell me you didn't let her choose a human."

Gray snorted. "No. Roman's definitely not a human."

"Roman?" Danyer glanced at Gray then back at Drake. "From the way you two are bracing for a fight, I'd say whoever this Roman is, you don't think I'm going to be happy about it."

When neither one responded, Danyer sighed. "Something I learned a long time ago—bad news just smells worse the longer you keep it back."

Drake nodded. "Yes, I've learned the same thing, and lately, I've discovered that when an American female makes up her mind, not even God can change it."

Danyer chortled. "Ain't it the truth? Turned you down flat, did she? Well, let me have it. Who is this Roman, and why won't I like him?"

Drake had to laugh. Danyer sounded just like a father concerned about who his teenage daughter was dating. "Roman is Roman Fernwood, and I don't recall saying you wouldn't like him. He's actually a likeable guy. He's an English aristocrat and a man of honor. He's got money, land, looks, and before too much longer, he'll inherit a title."

"Un-huh. Now give me the rest of it.

"He's half Vampire, half Lycan."

Danyer digested this news in silence with no visible reaction at all, increasing Drake's respect for him.

After a few seconds, the American asked, "And you've given this match your approval?"

"My approval was neither requested nor welcome. Chase is more than capable of making up her own mind. In fact, when I did try to assert my authority, she told me exactly what I could do with it." Drake grinned at Danyer's grunt. "If you're worried that Roman influenced her with his vampiric powers, forget it. She appears to be as immune to them as she is to the advice of what she terms 'oversexed he-men.'"

Danyer shot him a sideways look. How the hell the man packed that much punch into a look, Drake had no idea. Despite his misgivings, he found himself liking the other pride leader and hoped fervently he wouldn't have to fight him—for a number of reasons, not the least of which was Danyer would chew him up and spit him out in pieces before Drake got in his first swipe.

"You seem like a smart young man, Drake. I think you mean what you say about this Roman character. But given Chase *was* a member of my pride, I'm going to have to check this out for myself. I want to talk to the girl, just to be sure."

Drake felt a smile spread across his face. "I've certainly got no problem with that. I'll take you over and introduce you."

"Now, hold on a moment. What is it you're not telling me? You think Roman can get the better of me?"

"Danyer," Drake said in all honesty, "I doubt there's a male alive anywhere who can get the better of you. But I can't wait to see how you fare with Chase."

e/3e/3

Chase glanced up and smiled as Roman entered the library. Then she noticed the anxiety flickering in his aura and set aside the case file.

"What is it? Is something wrong?"

"I'm not sure."

He slipped his arms around her and kissed her hair as she nuzzled his chest. God, he smelled good.

"Drake called to tell me he was on his way over here," he said. "With a man called Danyer Spects, the leader of the Southern California Tigris pride."

"Did Drake say what the guy wanted?"

"He wants to talk with you. I assume he wants to be sure I'm not hypnotizing you or something."

"Oh, for crying out loud. Why can't these people just leave us alone?"

"Just talk to him, Chase. Perhaps if he's satisfied you're here of your own free will, he'll go home and forget about you."

"And the thirteen mil?"

"Drake doesn't think he's motivated by the money."

"Yeah, right." She sighed and turned to the more immediate problem. "Where's David?"

"I sent him into London to talk to Melinda's friends, though that was before Drake called."

"Oh? Why?"

"Because," he murmured, pulling her closer. "I had plans for you today."

"Plans are good." She slipped her arms around his neck, nibbled his bottom lip. "I'm very fond of your plans."

"Me, too. As soon as you meet with Danyer Spects, we'll give those plans our full attention."

"Fine. I'll talk to him, but I don't want to meet with him alone."

"Not a chance." He nibbled on her neck and sent shivers down her spine. "I'm told the guy's a hunk, as well as formidable enough he could take both Drake and Gray before they lifted a hand. So I'm staying right beside you."

She ran her tongue along his jaw. "Good. How soon before they get here?"

"Too soon." He groaned when Martin knocked on the doorjamb. "They can't be here already."

"Afraid so, sir." Martin hesitated. "I could serve them tea in the parlor if you like, so you and the young lady can finish your...discussion."

Chuckling, Chase reached for the buttons on Roman's shirt. "That works."

He grabbed her hands and swatted her on the ass.

"Behave. We appreciate the offer, Martin, but we may as well get it over with. Go ahead and send them back."

"Spoilsport." She stepped away from him and straightened her shoulders at the footsteps thudding in the corridor. "Show time."

The man who followed Drake and Gray into the library was a good-looking son of a bitch. She'd say that for him. His aura warned her he wasn't someone to be trifled with. Not that it mattered. She'd no intention of letting him or any other man tell her what to do. She held her tongue as introductions were made and remained standing when Roman suggested they all take a seat. After all, a cat knows the value of looking *down* on her enemy.

"I sure do appreciate your hospitality," Danyer began as Roman handed him a glass of wine. "But I'm afraid I'm going to have to ask you fine gentlemen to leave for a bit so I can have a word with Chase in private."

"No," she said. "I'd like them to stay."

"Well now, little lady, I'd love to accommodate your request, but I really need to speak with you alone."

"That wasn't a request. Either they stay, or I don't."

"I'm afraid I'll have to insist."

"You go right ahead." Insist, her ass. Just who did this guy think he was talking to? "Let's be clear, here. I have no intention of following your orders. I've agreed to talk with you, but only on my terms. There's no way in hell I'm going to stay in a room alone with a male Tigris I don't know."

"What exactly are you implying?"

"Nothing. I'm just telling you what I'm willing to do."

"Now look. As your pride leader—"

"Don't even go there," she snapped, fighting a losing battle with her temper. "You are *not* my pride leader. Where was your pride when my parents were murdered? Where were they when I spent my childhood in foster homes, convinced I was a freak because I saw auras?"

She paced to the fireplace then whirled and shook her fist at him. "You sure as hell weren't looking out for my family. So don't you come in here and squawk about being my pride leader."

Roman stepped beside her and murmured in her ear, "You lose your temper, you lose the battle. So take a breath."

Although she knew he was right, she glared at him then reconsidered and nodded. Taking a couple of deep breaths, she let her eyes sweep over the three tigers. Drake shook his head. Gray winked. Danyer appeared calm and unruffled, though she could see a hint of anger in his aura.

"You wanted to talk," she told him. "So talk."

"The problem is," he said. "Roman here is half-Vampire. They have ways of influencing people. So with him in the room, how am I to know for sure this is what you really want?"

"If he's influencing me, that's my problem, isn't it? But in case you didn't notice, I'm not easily influenced."

"Oh yeah, I noticed that right off." Danyer glanced at Roman. "Is she always this stubborn?"

He gave a half chuckle. "So it seems, but she's made a good point, and I'm not talking about the fact your pride wasn't there to protect her and her family."

"Then what are you talking about, son?"

"We don't know you. You claim to be from California, and you look it. However, you don't talk like any Californian I've ever heard. Does he to you, Chase?"

"No, he doesn't." She shook her head, wondering how she'd missed that. "He sounds more like he's from Texas to me."

Danyer laughed. "Smart girl. Born and raised there. Spent my formative years there. Transplanted to California during the gold rush of eighteen forty-nine. You know what they say, 'You can take the man out of Texas, but not Texas out of the man.'"

Eighteen forty-nine? The guy looked like a young man in his prime. She made a mental note to ask Roman how long Weres lived.

"Well, young lady. I'd say what we have here is a Mexican standoff."

"Maybe in your opinion." She heard Gray snort and grinned at him. "If you're hoping to convince me to come back to California and mate with one of your pride, you're wasting your breath. I don't need to come back with you. I have plenty of options right here."

"Drake says you've chosen Roman, but it's obvious you haven't mated. Mind if I ask why?"

She shrugged. "You can ask. Doesn't mean I have to answer."

Roman slipped his arm around her shoulders. "If you must know, she wanted to be sure. Once it's done, she's stuck. And we've only known each other four days."

"Well now, son, maybe I've misjudged you." Danyer rubbed his chin. "Apparently, you're trying to do the right thing by this young lady. I have to say I approve of your actions, but I'm not sure I approve the match—yet."

Approve? What right did he have to approve anything? So furious, she could hardly control herself, she jerked away from Roman.

"What makes you think I want your frigging approval? You have no authority over me, so I don't give a rat's ass whether you like what I'm doing or not."

"Now, Chase—" Roman began.

She whirled and hissed at him. "Don't you 'Now, Chase' me. This asshole wasn't anywhere around when I needed a pride. If I hadn't come to England, I would've had to face what's happening to me without any help at all." Her hands clenched into fists. "If you think for one moment I give a tinker's damn about anything he says, you're crazy."

"I can understand how you'd feel that way," Drake told her. "But if you want Roman to live, it's not that simple."

"What the hell are you talking about?"

"When Zakhar Fedorov gets here, we'll need all the help we can get."

"Bloody hell, Drake," Roman growled. "I told you I didn't want you to pressure her."

"She has a right to know," Gray pointed out. "If Fedorov takes you out, and Chase doesn't have a pride leader, she'll be totally defenseless."

"What the hell are you talking about?" she repeated.

"That's a good question," Danyer said. "Who's Zakhar Fedorov, and what's he got to do with this?"

"He's the current leader of her father's old pride." Drake scrubbed a hand over his face. "He's on his way here, intending to claim Chase as his mate so he can take over her trust fund."

His lips pursed, Danyer looked from man to man as if sizing up their strength and skill. "So what's the problem? You telling me the three of you can't take out one lone tiger?"

"That's not the issue." Roman hesitated and glanced at Chase, frustration washing across his features. "He isn't coming alone."

Chapter 10

June 6th:

Friday morning after breakfast, Roman met with Chase and David in his study to go over the murder case. With everything else that was going on, he wanted to forget about the murder, but that wasn't fair to Melinda. Besides, as far as David knew, the murder was the only reason Chase had for remaining in England.

"Martin's invited everyone who was here the weekend Melinda died to parties both tonight and tomorrow night," Roman said, handing them the guest lists. "People from out of town will be staying here at the house. That way, Chase, you'll have plenty of time to study their auras and see if you notice anything I didn't."

David's head jerked up. "You believe she sees auras?"

"Of course, I do. I see them, too." Using the hypnotic power of his eyes, he caught David's gaze and held it. "You *know* Chase and *know* she's honest. Stop fighting your instincts and *believe* her. Besides, your attitude hurts her, and that I won't allow."

When he'd finished, he released his hold by blinking. David shook his head, coming slowly out of the trance.

"Thanks," Chase whispered softly.

"My pleasure," Roman whispered back. "Now," he continued, raising his voice. "Where were we, before we got distracted by the question of auras?"

"Chase can see auras," David announced proudly.

She snorted. "What was Melinda like? Perhaps, there's something about her that would indicate a motive we might have missed."

"Such as?" Roman asked.

"Hell, I don't know. Did she have a lot of money someone inherited when she died? Or was she messing around with someone's husband? You said she was a reporter. Did she write a story and piss someone off? Was she working on a story someone wanted killed—literally?"

Chase was obviously a good investigator. Roman hadn't considered any of that until she asked the questions. Running his fingers through his hair, he sighed. His suspicions sounded so vain. Startled by her chuckle, he looked up to find her grinning at him.

"What?"

"Your aura's about to pop. Just spit out what you're trying to say and stop worrying about how to say it."

"You'll probably think me incredibly vain, but do you remember when you first showed up? And asked me why my—" He shot a glance at David. "—Grandfather recruited you?"

"Oh yes. You thought he was matchmaking." She eyed him curiously, but with none of the disdain he'd expected. "So in her case, it was true?"

He nodded. "He'd been trying to get Melinda out to the house on some pretext or other for months. Kept telling me how lovely she was."

He grinned over at Chase and was relieved when she grinned back. "She was short, only about four foot ten, but exquisite, with dark hair and unusual violet eyes. She looked like a beautiful little Elf." His spirits rose when he noticed the flares of jealousy in her aura. "Right away she started talking about how I needed a woman in my life. How it was past time I settled down." He winked at her. "Maybe she was just trying to get in my knickers."

She laughed. He could hardly believe it. Here he was, making jokes about another woman, and Chase was amused. When she tapped her eye, he understood she was asking if Melinda had responded to his hypnotic powers. He nodded.

"I don't know if I would've been more receptive to her if she hadn't been so blatant about why she was here, but that's the way she was. She didn't mince words. So you could be right about her work. I'm sure her stories were just as blunt as her personality. I never considered any of the other reasons you gave as motives, but I'm sure Scotland Yard must have. And there's no mention of anything like that in any of the reports."

David flicked a concerned glance at Chase. "So she was killed because someone else was jealous and afraid you might be interested in her?"

Roman nodded as he fought down a surge of panic for Chase's safety, still afraid his suspicions were correct. "Until Chase brought up those other points, I could see no other motive for her murder. But now I don't know."

"It says in the file the woman had no enemies," she reminded them. "At least as far as C. I. Clayton could determine. Who's C. I. Clayton?"

"Chief Inspector Clayton of Scotland Yard," Roman replied. "And yes, when I insisted her fall wasn't an accident, Clayton told me he could find no reason anyone would want to hurt her."

She flipped to a clean page on her legal pad. "Okay, let's look at your idea for a motive. Who wants you so badly she'll kill to get you?"

Feeling like he was cataloguing notches on his bedpost, he ran through his female acquaintances in his mind but could think of no one who qualified. "That's just the trouble. I can't imagine anyone does. Melinda did get a threatening note, telling her to 'stay away from the Fernwoods or else' on Friday. Early the next Sunday morning she was dead. What else am I supposed to think?"

"You mentioned these notes—notes, plural—before, so I'm assuming that other guests got them as well." She tapped her pen on her pad. "Was the threatening note Melinda got any different from the notes anyone else received? And have notes been given to men as well as women?"

"I don't know why I didn't think of this before." He shook his head in disgust. "The answer to both questions is no."

"I think there's something to this." David leaned forward in his chair, elbows on his knees, and rested his chin in his hands. "If I understand it, the notes are only given to women guests, and only during the weekends you have parties, but no one else has been killed." When Roman nodded, he continued. "So, what happened with the other guests who got notes?"

"There were three, two before the murder and one after. The notes were identical to Melinda's, and they were sufficient for those guests to leave the next morning and not come back. Whereas Melinda laughed it off."

He looked over at Chase, just as David did.

"Oh, stop it you two," she snarled. "I can see fear in both your auras, but don't even think about sending me home."

"If this really *is* my fault, Chase—" Roman began.

"The only one at fault is the murderer. Besides," she said, shooting him a sideways look, "if someone's after me here, they're likely to follow me home, where I won't have *your* protection from a number of people."

"Fine," he snapped.

Lord, he hated it, but she did have a valid point. Not only might the murderer go after her at home, Zakhar Fedorov would find it much easier to force a claiming on her there.

"Starting right now, I'm not leaving you alone for a minute. If I can't be with you, David will be. Agreed?"

She nodded.

David shifted in his seat. "Maybe we should hire some body-guards. If I'm going to mingle and interview suspects and you're the host, Chase will be on her own at the parties. I mean, this Melinda was killed, and you weren't even interested in her. Chase won't stand a chance."

"I won't leave her side during the party tonight or tomorrow night," Roman said. "She and I will watch the auras while you mingle."

"Chase?" David turned to her. "How do you feel about this? Do you think you'll need bodyguards?"

"No. I trust Roman. If he says I'll be safe, I will be."

Humbled by her display of trust, Roman was overwhelmed with a sinking depression. She looked at him curiously, and he knew his distress showed in his aura. He shook his head and cast around in his mind for a change of subject.

"We should probably go over the names of all the female guests so you both know something about them before they start arriving this evening," he said. "David, you met some of these women yesterday, but Chase still has no idea who they are."

They went over the guest lists for the next few hours, Chase and David taking notes as Roman tried to think if any one of these women might harbor strong enough feelings for him to kill their competition. Trouble was, he couldn't remember anyone who'd shown more than a friendly interest in him, with the exception of the women who'd been threatened or killed.

"Who is Tatyana again?" Chase asked.

"That's one of Roman's beautiful cousins," David answered, before he could. "So are Ileana and Katia, the next names on the list. I met them yesterday."

"Hmmm." She rubbed her cheek with the end of her pen. "Well, since they're related to you, I suppose we can eliminate them."

"Not necessarily," he countered. "Not that I really think it's any one of them. But they're distant cousins. I think in America you call them kissing cousins."

"Meaning it's legal to marry one?"

"Yes. They're good at hiding their feelings, so I can't rule them out. Still, none of them has ever given me any sign she's interested."

Chase nodded, letting him know she understood. His depression spiraled as he looked into her lovely cinnamon eyes. She was in danger every minute she remained in England. Yet, as she'd pointed out, she wouldn't be any safer at home. Once there, Fedorov would have a clear shot at her.

⌒☽⌒

"Roman, what's wrong?" Chase asked softly, mindful of David next door. She and Roman were in her bedroom while she dressed for the party and he stood guard over her. "All day I've seen distress in your aura, but I couldn't ask you earlier because David was there."

She slipped into a long pink gown. Picking up a string of pearls, she held them up to her neck, decided against them, and dropped them back on the vanity. Then she turned to the mirror and ran a comb through her hair. "Talk to me, please."

He walked over to her and put his hands on her shoulders, turning her around to face him. "There are a couple of things going on," he said. "One is that I am truly worried about your safety. If a Vampire really was responsible for Melinda's death then I'm the only one here strong enough to protect you, and even I can't be in two places at once."

"Why do you think a Vampire's responsible?"

"The total lack of clues. Vampires can veil themselves so they don't leave a scent, and no one can hear or see them. If the murderer were anyone other a Vampire, I would've smelled traces of her at the scene of the crime. There wasn't the scent of anyone who shouldn't have been there."

"So maybe whoever's doing this is someone you think should have been there. Therefore you aren't suspicious of them."

"I'd trust Martin and Sandra with my life. They have absolutely no motive. They want me to find a mate, almost as much as my father does. They're also well compensated for their service, so it's doubtful someone could bribe them to do this."

"I see." She hesitated then asked the question she wasn't sure she wanted an answer to. "What else is wrong?"

He winced. "As much as I want you as a mate, I'm worried about how you'll adapt to being the mate of a wolf." Raking his fingers through his hair, he paced to the window and back, cleared his throat. "For lack of a better way to describe it, at age thirty, your inner beast will...awaken. Your senses will sharpen, and you'll be more in tune with your cat's needs and wants."

"So, you think I'll turn on you or something?"

"No, of course not, but while the human side of you has accepted me for what I am, your cat may have other ideas."

She sighed, tired of repeating herself to men who didn't seem to understand. "I know what I want, Roman, and neither my hormones, or some hidden part of me is going to control what my own heart tells me."

Placing her hands on her hips, she cocked her head to one side and studied him. "Now, if you don't want me, that's different, and you need to be man enough to tell me. But don't try to tell me what I want, or will want on June twelfth, and don't make decisions that involve both of us based on what you *think* might happen in the future. Decide if you really want me as a mate. We'll deal with the rest of it when it happens."

"Yes, we will."

He lowered his head and kissed her, his lips branding his possession and distracting her, if only momentarily, from realizing he hadn't answered her challenge. Breaking off, he cursed under his breath at the pounding on the bedroom door.

"If you two are ready. Martin says the first guests are arriving. We should probably all be downstairs," David said, pounding again.

"We'll be right there," Chase called, running her tongue over her still tingling lips. She gave Roman a rueful grin and turned back to the mirror to touch up her makeup. Finished, she asked. "Do I look okay?"

"Stunning." The hunger in his eyes made her blush. He grinned and reached for her hand, pulling her toward the door.

A thought occurred to her and she stopped him. "There'll be other Vampires here tonight, won't there?" she asked as low as she could and still make him hear. "Is their hearing as acute as yours?"

"Yes, to both questions," he whispered just as quietly. "We'll have to be very careful what we say."

"I wish there was some way we could communicate without words." She didn't understand the pained look on Roman's face, but there wasn't time to pursue it. At another bang on the door, she sighed. "Coming."

As they headed for the stairs, she trembled.

Roman wrapped an arm around her waist. "Don't worry, I'm right here."

"I know. I'm just nervous because it's a party."

Chuckling, Roman leaned in and whispered so softly she could barely make out the words. "You're not afraid of taking a Vampire/Lycan for a lover, but you're so scared of a party you're trembling?"

"Of course." She arched an eyebrow. "At least *I* have my priorities right."

They walked down the stairs hand in hand. She could hear the voices coming up from the first floor and took a deep breath, commanding herself to relax. It was only a party, after all.

❧❧❧

The evening wasn't as bad as she feared—it was worse. It was held in the grand ballroom, and at least sixty females attended. As Roman held her against his side, she examined the aura of every woman there.

While a good number showed jealousy in their auras whenever they looked at the possessive arm Roman kept around her, she couldn't tell if it was severe enough for one of them to try to kill her.

Drake, Grayson, and Danyer were there, but they kept their distance. Which was fine by her. Although all three were prime alpha males, each one radiating a raw power leashed tight by the constraints of a civilized world, it was the man beside her who had ensnared her in a trap she had no desire to break free from.

Midway through the party, four young women arrived, too beautiful to be anything but Vampires or Lycans. Every human eye, male or female, followed their every move as they flowed around the room. Chase checked their auras and gasped. Roman looked at her questioningly.

"Who are the four women who just walked in?" She pointed to her eyes, silently asking if they were Vampires.

He nodded. "Those are my cousins, Tatyana, Ileana and Katia, and Katia's friend, Katrina."

"Can you see their auras?"

"Yes. What about them?"

"Great," she muttered. How to do this so the Vampires' phenomenal hearing didn't pick it up? Tatyana, Ileana, Katia, and Katrina. *Lovely names*, she thought absently. *They sound Russian.*

She remembered how, in the movie, *Russia House*, Sean Connery had been trained to communicate silently in Communist Russia. Without saying a word, she took Roman's hand and led him out of the ballroom to his study.

Once there, she put a finger to her lips and drew him over to the desk where she took a piece of paper and wrote in block letters as fast as she could:

Three of the women's auras are okay, but one aura is just WRONG. I've never seen anything like it.

Roman took the pen and wrote much faster in an elegant script. *Do you know which one is which?* Chase shook her head. He nodded. *The one who's aura is wrong, what was she wearing?*

Silver gown with cutouts.

Ileana, he wrote. *What is it you think is so wrong?*

When she looks at you, it flashes with dark murky forest green, laced with muddy red and gloomy pink. I don't know what it means, but it doesn't look right to me.

No, it doesn't sound right either, he agreed.

What do we do?

Nothing we can do now. Let's go back to the party. We'll talk about this later. But first— He pulled her into his arms and kissed her.

As they slipped back into the ballroom, Roman held her even closer, almost as if he was afraid one of the Vampires would attack her in the middle of the crowd. When they came over to Roman, he introduced Chase simply as a friend. They smiled and shook her hand politely before moving on. She managed to suppress her shudders. At least until the end of the party.

At the close of the evening, the Vampires left with those guests who weren't spending the night. Martin came in and said tea was ready in the drawing room for everyone remaining, so if everyone would just follow him.

Roman snagged David by the arm as he trailed after Martin. Still holding onto Chase, he led them into his study.

"Well?" David demanded.

Roman ignored his question and turned to Chase. "What exactly did you see in Ileana's aura?"

"Well, as I said, it was a dark murky forest green laced with muddy red and dim, cloudy pink, but only when she looked at you." She shuddered. "I know what muddy red and murky pink mean, but I have no idea what that color of green stands for. I've never seen it in an aura before. There were also some soft blue flashes when you introduced me, which I've always related to wish fulfillment." She hesitated. "But I don't understand why you couldn't see what I did."

"That's a good question. I'll have to give it some thought." He glanced at David, and she knew there were things he wanted to say but couldn't. He got up from the couch and poured each of them a glass of wine. Chase could see guilt and despair in his aura.

"What is it, Roman?" she asked, alarmed.

"Dark murky forest green mixed with muddy red stands for resentment and anger. That accurately describes Ileana, and I'm afraid that a lot of it is my fault."

"Why?"

"I was driving Ileana and her husband home from a party at Tatyana's house one night and a horse jumped out in front of my car. I swerved, but it was raining. The car slid on the wet road and rolled over. Ileana and I were both badly injured, but we survived. Her husband didn't."

"But that wasn't your fault! It was the fault of whoever let the horse get out on the road."

"I know, Chase. However, Ileana still blames me. If I hadn't swerved, if I'd just hit the horse, I probably wouldn't have rolled the car. I thought she'd gotten over it. Apparently, she's just gotten better at hiding it."

His hand gripped the fine crystal goblet, his knuckles turning white. Chase marveled that the glass didn't shatter under such pressure.

"Swerving is the natural thing to do," David offered. "It's instinctive. Surely your cousin knows that."

"She may know it intellectually, but emotionally? Grief does strange things to people."

Chase pondered Roman's story. "You know, the motive we're looking for may be revenge. If Ileana thought you cared for Melinda, she may have killed her to hurt you. To keep you lonely like her. Revenge is more likely to cause murder than jealousy."

She hesitated, afraid to say this, but knowing she had to. "That would also explain the blue flashes when she saw you with me. She was happy to know she finally had a target you really cared about."

"Bloody hell." Alarm flared in Roman's aura as he ran his hand over his face. "David, I need to go out for a couple of hours tonight. Could you stay up with Chase till I get back?"

"It's almost midnight," David complained. "I mean, of course, I'll be glad to babysit her for you, but what can you do so late?"

"I need to see someone. I'm not worried he'll be asleep." He looked at Chase. "Chase, I..."

She assumed he was apologizing for leaving her alone while he went to feed. "I understand. I'll be fine. Go."

He kissed her on the forehead and hurried out the door. Chase and David left more sedately. By the time they got to her room, she was nervous and grumpy.

Since they had probably figured out who murdered Melinda, Roman might try to send her away so she'd be safe. Well, tough titties. She just wouldn't go.

"Stop fidgeting," David snapped. "Take a seat on the bed and relax."

Ignoring his complaint, she stomped over to the vanity to put her pearls away. They weren't there. "Have you seen my pearls? I left them here on the vanity when I went down to the party." She knelt and searched the floor.

"Maybe the ghost got them."

"Very funny." She glared at him a moment and returned to checking under the furniture.

"Chase, you're making *me* nervous. Get up and sit on the bed."

"I just hate being babysat," she growled. But she did as he asked. "I feel like I'm five years old."

David laughed. "Well, you don't look five years old. You look killer tonight." When she didn't respond, he added, "Don't think of it as being babysat. Think of it as me watching your 'six,' like they say in the cop movies."

"Right. Protective custody." Her hand brushed something that felt like paper. "What's this?" She picked it up and looked at it. Her insides froze. "Roman!"

"What is it?" David yelped, jumping up from his chair. She handed him the note. His face turned pale as he read it. "You want me to see if Martin knows where Roman went? I'm sure he won't have heard you. We could call him at his friend's when he gets there."

Chase shook her head. Martin wouldn't know where Roman feeds. "If he's anywhere near the house, he'll have heard me. If not, I'll have to wait until he gets back."

Provided whoever wrote the note let her live that long.

Chapter 11

R oman!"

Stopped and held captive briefly by a houseguest gushing about the party, Roman was less than a quarter of a mile from the house when Chase's scream turned his blood to ice. He spun and raced back.

Lord, if anything happened to her!

He didn't waste time going through the house but jumped to her third floor balcony from outside and exhaled a gust of relief at the sight of her, pale and strained, but alive.

Veiling himself, he slipped through the window and crossed the room, dropping the veil as he opened the door.

"What happened?" he demanded, bolting to her side.

The scent of almonds tickled his nose, trying to claim his attention, but he shrugged it off. David thrust a note at him. He read it with dread.

Leave this house immediately. Stay away from the Fernwoods or die.

"This is worse than the others," he said. "More threatening, I mean."

"More lust in my aura? Hold on, what do you mean, it's more threatening?"

"The others just said 'stay away from the Fernwoods or else.'"

Chase went over and poured herself a glass of water from the pitcher Martin left on her vanity. "What's different about me and

Melinda? I mean, a difference that would make me more of a threat or a target than her?"

"Well, I held on to you all night, and I never did that with Mel—"

The bitter almond smell coming from the glass of water Chase was lifting to her mouth finally registered in Roman's mind.

"Don't drink that!" He dashed across the room and knocked it from her hand. "Cyanide."

"Cyanide?" she and David gasped simultaneously.

"Yes. When was the last time you had water from this particular pitcher?"

"Just before the party," she said. "Martin brought me a fresh one when he put them in the rooms for all the others who are staying here. You were there, don't you remember?"

"Then someone has been in here between then and when you and David came up here a little while ago." His arms slid around her. "David, why don't you go to bed? I'll stay with Chase."

"That's fine with me, but what about the person you wanted to see?"

"I'll do it another time. Chase is more important."

David kissed her cheek. "Will you be okay?"

She nodded, and he left the room. Leaning against Roman's chest, she sighed. "I hate to have you go hungry for my sake. I could wait in your room while you hunt."

He shushed her with a kiss. "It's all right. I don't need to feed every night. It's just easier to be around innocent humans if I do. But one or two nights without won't matter. I have plenty of control. Don't worry." He kissed her again and led her out the door. "Besides, I'm *taking* you to my room."

"Oh, I forgot to tell you. Someone stole my pearls."

"It's the same pattern that happened with the other three. They'd notice items missing and find a note. I'll bet if we look in the garden, we'll find a dead animal."

"Yuk. Let's not look."

His hand tightened on hers. "Hadn't planned on it."

"Thanks for coming back. I didn't know if you could hear me. How far from the house were you?"

"I didn't leave immediately, so I was only about a quarter of a mile away, more or less. My hearing's good up to a half a mile.

That's why most of us live in the middle of large open spaces like this. So we don't have to listen to all the neighbors."

"And Ileana?"

"Her property's next door to mine." He scooped her up and carried her downstairs to his room. "Her husband was human. That's why he didn't survive the accident."

"She married a human? Why?"

"She claims they were soul mates."

"How awful for her to lose him like that."

"Yes, he was her life. She told me she wished she'd died with him." As they entered his room, he turned on the light and carried Chase to the bed. "Sit for a minute."

"Uh oh," she said. "I don't like the colors in your aura. This is bad news, isn't it?"

"Chase, I—"

She cut him off. "No! You aren't sending me home. I absolutely refuse. Besides, I'll be a sitting duck for that Zakhar guy."

"Danyer would protect you from him."

"Just like he protected my parents?"

"Given he didn't know about your parents, it was impossible to help them. But he can help you."

"No." She shook her head emphatically. "He'd expect me to mate one of his pride, and I refuse. If you don't want me to stay, I'll leave, but I won't go home."

"Damn it, Chase. I want you to stay, I just couldn't live with myself if anything happened to you. I'm already responsible for one death."

"That's not true! The accident wasn't your fault. Ileana may never have gotten over her grief, but that doesn't give her license to kill people." She crossed her arms and glared at him through the tears filling her eyes. "I'm certainly not going to be scared away by her. Assuming it *is* Ileana. We don't know for sure that it is."

"We don't," he agreed. "However, she seems the most likely suspect at this point. At least she has the most to gain by hurting me." He tried again. "Chase, please do this for me."

"No! Don't you understand? I'll die without you anyway. The only difference between my heart and my body is, if my body dies, I won't have to suffer too long."

She buried her face in her hands and wept.

His heart broke at her sobs. He shoved aside his plans to send her away—for now—and took her in his arms. Unsure what to say, he kept silent and held her while she cried, trying to think of some way to protect her—from Fedorov, from herself, and from whoever was trying to kill her.

◦◦◦

June 7th:

When Chase woke in the morning, the sun was high in the sky. Alone in Roman's bed and unwillingly to move, she mulled over last night. He'd held her until her tears dried then made love to her for the rest of the night. He hadn't discussed sending her home any further. Still, she was pretty sure he'd bring it up again. Maybe he'd even get David involved in trying to convince her.

She wouldn't go. She was determined on that.

"Your breathing tells me you're awake, so stop pretending."

She jumped at Roman's voice, opened her eyes, and looked at him. He had a tray of food and a smile.

"I come bearing gifts."

Coffee, eggs, bacon, and toast. It smelled delicious. Her stomach rumbled. She pushed herself up against the headboard. "I always heard you should beware of Greeks bearing gifts."

"True, but I'm not Greek, and my gifts don't have any nasty surprises in them." He set the tray across her knees and kissed her lightly. "How are you this morning?"

"Great. I need a shower and a change of clothes, but other than that, I'm in good shape." Forking up a mouthful of eggs, she studied him. "And you?" His aura looked clear so she figured he wasn't overly stressed.

He sat on the bed and stroked her cheek with a finger. "Well, I've already had a shower, but I'm planning on a second one with you." He chuckled at the smile she couldn't hide. "As for your clothes, I had them moved into my room."

"You did?"

"I had Sandra pack all your things this morning and bring them in here while you were asleep. Hopefully, if anyone comes back looking for you, they'll think you heeded the note and left."

He kissed her nose. "I want you sleeping in my arms, and I was hoping you wanted that, too."

"I have no problem moving in with you."

She felt a sudden rush of pleasure as she realized what she'd said. Trying not to blush, she changed the subject. "If the person looking for me is a Vampire, they'll hear my voice and smell my scent anywhere in the house. A diversion only works if people can't see through it until it's all over."

"True, again."

The smile had slipped from his face, and she suddenly wished she hadn't changed the subject to that particular issue. She avoided his eyes and started working on a piece of bacon. "This is really good breakfast food, by the way. Do the English really eat like this?"

"No, but I've been to America many times. Over the years, I've learned what Americans like to eat in the morning."

With his hand cupping her face, he stared into her eyes until she blushed then grinned at her response.

"Stop that," she ordered, furious with her body's predictable reaction to his staring. "What *do* the English eat for breakfast?"

"I can't say I've ever eaten a normal English breakfast. They do sometimes eat eggs, bacon, and toast. More often, it's things like fried tomatoes, kippers, porridge, and sausages with ketchup."

"Good, God. I hope it all tastes better than it sounds," she said, horrified.

"Millions of people can't be wrong."

"Wanna bet? How many people think Vampires are just a myth?"

Repositioning the tray, he kissed her. "Lord, you're adorable. If you've finished breakfast, let's get you that shower."

He bent over to pick her up, but she stopped him with a raised palm.

"Hold it." Suspicious, she glared at him. If he thought he was going to just bundle her up and take her to the airport now that her things were all packed, he was sadly mistaken. "What are we doing today that makes you so anxious to get me out of bed?"

She had no idea what expression was on her face, but it must have been good, because he burst out laughing.

"I'm glad you think it's so funny," she fumed. "And while you may be strong enough to pick me up and carry me into the bathroom, I can still scream loud enough to bring the entire household down here. So, fess up, buddy. I'm not taking a shower until I know what you have planned."

His laughter faded to exasperated chuckles. He moved the tray off the bed to the floor and sat beside her. "It's ten o'clock. My plan for the day is that we take a shower until the water runs cold, and then we get dressed and go see Tatyana after you have lunch."

"Oh!" She hadn't expected that. He was taking her to meet another Vampire? Why? "I have no objection to the first part of that plan. But why are we going to see Tatyana?"

Running his fingers through his hair, he sighed. "Because I don't know what else to do. If it *is* Ileana who's murdering people, Tatyana is the only one who can talk any sense into her. And if it's *Tatyana*, I want you to read her aura while she talks to us about the murder."

"Oh," she repeated. "That makes sense." She didn't know whether to feel relief or chagrin. "What time is she expecting us?"

"Just sometime early afternoon. So depending how long the hot water lasts, I figure we have more than enough time."

Buck naked, she scrambled out of the covers and crawled on his lap. She loved the surprised look on his face as she wrapped her arms around his neck and kissed him.

"Since 'early' is such a vague term and *soooo* open to interpretation," she crooned, "we could run out of hot water, go back to bed until it heats up again, run it cold once more, and still be there 'early.' Who cares about lunch?"

Roman's smile warmed her heart. "I guess we could at that."

જ્જજ

On the way to Tatyana's, Roman watched Chase's nervousness steadily increase. "Stop fidgeting. She's not going to bite you."

Her response was a half-hearted chuckle. "Literally or figuratively?"

"Either one. If she's not the killer, she'll be very nice to you. If she is the killer, I'll get you out of there immediately." He grabbed her hand, squeezed it gently. "I promise I'll protect you."

"I know. I trust you. I just can't imagine me telling you she's a killer right in front of her. What am I supposed to do, speak in code like *The Man From U.N.C.L.E.?*" She smoothed her hair back from her face, adjusted her seatbelt. "And then there's Tatyana herself. It's bad enough she's a Vampire, but she's also blond, petite, has cornflower blue eyes and a perfect face. She's beyond stunning. She's all the way to 'Oh, my God!' That's enough to make any woman nervous."

Roman shook his head. "The way you Americans express yourselves, I sometimes think we don't speak the same language."

He'd managed to coax a grin out of her. "We don't. You guys invented it. We Americans improved on it, and now that it makes sense, the rest of the world speaks it."

What a delight she was. "I think I know what you meant from its context," he said. "But who is the man from uncle?"

She laughed. "*The Man From U.N.C.L.E.* was a television show about spies who worked for an ultra-secret agency called, United Network Command for Law and Enforcement. I don't know when it was first on TV, but I think it was sometime in the 'sixties. My college roommate and I used to watch reruns on cable TV late at night when we were supposed to be studying."

"The college you went to sounds like a lot more fun than the one I went to." He squeezed her hand again. "But I don't really think you'll need to speak in code. If you see dishonesty in her aura, I'm sure the fear in yours will alert me."

"Oh, yeah, I guess so."

He lifted her hand up to his lips and kissed her fingers. "As for Tatyana being—how did you put it? Oh, yes, 'all the way to oh, my God.' I don't know how to break this to you, love, but so are you." He chuckled at her gasp. "Come now, Chase. Don't you even see the lust in the auras of the men who look at you? Can't you even *guess* how beautiful you are?"

She blushed. "Well, yes, I see the lust, but I thought that was just men in general. You know, the three-second rule—men think about sex every three seconds? But I didn't assume it had anything to do with me personally."

He burst into gales of laughter and almost missed his turn. Slamming on the brakes, he yanked the wheel and skidded into Tatyana's drive, struggling to regain his composure.

"I suppose it *is* the nature of all men to have their auras filled with lust. However, someone like you brings out that nature a little more than the average female." He took her face in his hands and stared into her eyes, deepening her blush. Kissing her tenderly, he whispered, "We're here."

The color drained from her face. She flinched then squared her shoulders and gave him a small smile. Opening the door, she eased out of the car.

He hurried to her side. "Ready?"

"Ready." She lifted her chin and smiled into his eyes.

In an unusual gesture Roman recognized as a willingness to listen, Tatyana opened the door to their bell herself, although she had several trusted servants. His spirits rose. He'd always loved Tatyana, even when he was a small child and she'd posed as a more distant relative. *Please don't let her be the killer.*

She led them to a drawing room with three plush chairs and one loveseat, told them to be seated, and offered wine. Before taking his own chair, Roman made sure to put Chase in one where he had a good vantage point to see her aura. Tatyana sat gracefully in the one remaining chair and looked at him expectantly.

How to get the answers he needed without angering her? He chose and discarded words in silence, trying to figure out how to begin. Then Tatyana took matters out of his hands.

"I assume Chase knows—I mean, can we talk freely, or do I need to guard my words?" she asked, her voice matter-of-fact.

"Yes, she knows everything about me," he admitted with a reluctant chuckle. "And if she didn't, after a comment like that, she'd keep digging until she found out."

"Good. There shouldn't be secrets between lovers."

Roman looked at Chase in shock and found her looking at him the same way.

"How did you know?" she asked in a small voice.

"Well, child, even if I couldn't see your auras, I can read it on both your faces as plain as if it were written in ink. When you've lived as long as I have, you learn to recognize these things. Besides, in all the time I've known Roman, he's never looked at a woman as possessively as he does at you." She smiled. "What was it you wanted to discuss?"

Roman took a deep breath. "You heard about the death of Melinda Carter a few weeks ago, didn't you?"

Tatyana nodded. "I did. A broken neck from a fall, wasn't it? I also heard that the police thought it was an accident, and you thought it was a murder. Is that true?"

"It is. Do you know anything about it?"

"Other than what I just told you? No, I don't." She looked from one to the other. "Should I?"

Roman glanced at Chase. She shook her head. So she'd seen nothing in Tatyana's aura he hadn't seen, meaning she was not the murderer. Both of them relaxed.

"Child, your aura just changed," Tatyana said suspiciously. "What's going on?"

Chase looked back at Roman and he nodded. She leaned forward, her hands open, palms up. "Please don't be offended. There was no dishonesty in your aura when you said you didn't know anything about the murder. Roman and I are just very pleased. We didn't want it to be you."

Tatyana hissed and leapt from her chair. "*Bloody hell*! You think a *Vampire* did this?" She looked terrifying, like an avenging angel or...well, a Vampire.

Roman saw the alarm in Chase's aura and moved to the small loveseat, patting the cushion beside him. She didn't need a second invitation and instantly snuggled against him. He put his arms around her, glad to see the fear dissipate.

It was harder to see her aura when she was right beside him like this, but it was impossible to offer her comfort when she was in a chair all by herself. Right now, she needed the comfort, and he needed to give it.

"It's okay," he whispered. "She's not mad at us. She's just mad."

Soft as his whisper was, Tatyana heard it. She took a breath. "Please forgive me, my dear. I forgot for a moment who my audience was. Roman's correct. I am not upset with you. I'm just upset at the idea." She glided back to her chair, sat, and picked up her wine. Took a sip. "I assume you have some evidence to back this up."

"Yes," he said. "First of all, her neck was broken before she landed on the ground. She didn't bleed from the injuries caused by the fall. Secondly, the night Melinda died I put sleeping powders in the tea of all my human guests before they went to bed after the party."

"Yes, we do that here as well."

"The pathologist told me the powders would have prevented her from getting out of bed on her own. There's no way she could have fallen off the balcony."

Seeing Tatyana about to speak, he added. "The toxicology report showed a sufficient quantity of the drug in her system that she couldn't have been sleepwalking three hours after drinking the tea."

"*Three hours*? No, I dare say you're right about that." Tatyana pursed her lips, one finger tapping her chin. "Still while that may prove murder, it doesn't prove one of our kind did it. What evidence do you have for that?"

"That night I didn't go out to hunt. I don't know why, but I felt uneasy. Melinda had gotten a threatening note the night before, telling her to leave or else. She was determined not to go. So I stayed in the library, and I watched and waited."

He paused and took a sip of wine to sooth his throat. "I know I would've heard and smelled a human. They couldn't have possibly gotten past me. I also would have heard Melinda get out of bed and walk outside. But I heard and smelled nothing until Melinda landed on the ground below the balcony."

"You're thinking the murderer was veiled."

"Yes."

"Did Melinda know what Chase knows? I only ask because I didn't get the feeling she was important to you. During the party I attended, she spent most of her time staring longingly at you. Yet, you barely noticed her."

"She wasn't important. Just another guest. And no, I told her nothing. If she knew, she didn't learn it from me. But she gave no sign she was aware of anything."

"So, as far as you know, she wasn't killed to silence her. A broken neck would fit that scenario, you know."

"Yes, I know, but no, I doubt it was that."

Tatyana studied them both. "Am I correct in assuming you know which one of our kind killed Melinda?"

"I think I do."

"Who?"

"Ileana."

"No!"

"Chase was looking at Ileana's aura last night. It's colored by resentment and anger. I know she still blames me for her husband's death. And Chase could have died last night." His last sentence came out choked. It hurt even to think about what might've happened. He explained about the tainted water then added, "Granted, since Chase is only half-human, the cyanide might not have hurt her."

"But she *is* half-human, so we don't know for sure what the effects might be." Tatyana shook her head. "No. It can't be Ileana. That's ridiculous. Her husband was so drunk that night, if you'd let him drive your car as he'd demanded, none of you would have lived long enough to hit the horse. Think how many innocent lives could have been lost if he'd hit another car." She paused, her exquisite face thoughtful. "You think she's trying to kill your love because you killed hers?"

They both nodded.

"But that makes no sense. Why kill Melinda? Everyone but Melinda could see you weren't interested in her."

"I don't know. Perhaps to make my life difficult. Chase got a threatening note last night. When I came to investigate, I smelled the cyanide in her water pitcher. It wasn't in the water before the party, only afterward. There were no scents, human or otherwise that shouldn't have been there. If it were one of the humans, I would have smelled them."

"Any of the servants?"

"Only the butler, Martin, and his wife, Sandra. Martin's was fresh because he brought the water before the party. Sandra's was weaker, several hours older. She cleaned the room that morning."

"Martin and Sandra have been with you for years," Tatyana said. "I think they're as trustworthy as humans can be."

"I trust them implicitly," he assured her. "When I asked them about it, their auras were clear."

"If it *is* Ileana," Tatyana told him. "The Council will have her executed."

"The Council?" Chase asked.

Roman grimaced.

"I guess Roman didn't tell you about that, did he?" When Roman shook his head, Tatyana sighed. "He's been alone a long time, dear, and must've had other things on his mind." Ignoring Chase's blush, she rose and poured herself another glass of wine. "Would either of you like another?" She held out the bottle. At their negative responses, she put it back and returned to her seat. "The Council is a group of Vampires who have been around for over five thousand years. I don't know if they are the first of our kind, or if they have just survived longer than any others still on Earth, but they *are* the oldest.

"As humans became more aware, as they began to read, write, and pass on their knowledge, the six Vampires who make up The Council were appalled to learn humans were creating legends about our kind because their loved ones were being slaughtered. These six Vampires banded together to form The Council. They set themselves over the rest of us and made two unbreakable laws. First, innocent humans—ones who do not do the unspeakable crimes such as murder, rape, child abuse, betrayal of trust, and the like—should be spared. Second, our secret must be kept at all costs.

"Because most of us are fiercely independent, this did not go over well," she said with a touch of humor. "However, after about two thousand years or so, even the most independent could see the laws made sense. Especially during the Middle Ages when so many of us were killed by angry humans grieving over their slaughtered kin. Because we gain in strength each year we're alive, the members of The Council are stronger than the rest of us. Together they are undefeatable, unstoppable.

"When a rogue Vampire breaks the law, The Council has no difficulty in carrying out the punishment. They were lenient at first, but after a while, they became much more strict. It has paid off. There hasn't been an execution in over three hundred years."

She turned back to Roman. "If it is Ileana and she claims Melinda told others about us, she'll have to prove it. The Council does not accept suspicions as proof. She'll have to provide the name of the one who told Melinda, and the names of the people she told. You will have to prove Ileana is the one who killed her. It will be a long trial." She groaned. "This is dreadful."

Roman nodded. "We won't know for sure Ileana's guilty unless we can check her aura while we question her, and I refuse to let

Chase anywhere near her. Would you talk with her, Tatyana? See what you can find out?"

"Yes, of course, I will. However, she may view me as the enemy, too. If her resentment has grown so much that it's colored her aura, there may be nothing we can do." She paused, her gaze distant as if in thought. "What colors did your young lady see in Ileana's aura that you haven't seen there yourself?"

"Tell her, love," Roman ordered.

Chase leaned forward. "A dark murky forest green, overlaid with muddy red when she looked at Roman. There was a hint of muddy pink in it, as well, and flashes of soft blue when she looked at me. It was...depressing and painful to look at it. I've never seen one like it."

"Did you know what those colors mean?"

"Yes, well, all except that shade of green. Roman had to tell me."

"I see. Tell me, child, what do you see in my aura?"

Chase started. She looked at Roman. He smiled and gave her a squeeze.

"It's beautiful. It's a lot like Roman's in that it's basically a clear red, but a little lighter than his. It's laced with yellow, orange-red, bright pink, violet, indigo, and green, as well as a hint of dark pink." She gave Tatyana a quick smile. "I know this sounds silly, but it's the most beautiful aura I've ever seen, full of contradictions—powerful, but delicate. Feminine, but terrifyingly strong."

"Thank you, my dear. She's quite charming, isn't she, Roman?"

"She is that."

Chase squirmed. "Why could I see colors he couldn't?"

"It's your cat's eyes," Tatyana told her. "They see a broader range on the spectrum than ours do, or the Lycans' apparently, so they saw what Ileana thought she'd veiled."

"I need to keep Chase safe," he interjected. "I'm open to any suggestions. She refuses to return to the U.S., and for a number of reasons, I doubt she'd be any safer there." He met Tatyana's eyes, letting all his despair show through. "I don't know what to do."

"No, sending her home won't help. If it is Ileana, she already knows how you feel about Chase. She won't hesitate to follow her wherever she goes. I know her well enough to know that." Tatyana took a long breath. "Can you veil Chase?"

"Not twenty-four hours a day. She can't go without any of her senses for that long. It isn't the same as veiling myself, where I still have limited use of my vision and hearing. Unless I'm constantly touching her, she'd be deaf, blind, and unable to feel anything around her. It would drive her insane.

"I'd have to be within a certain distance of her anyway, so I couldn't do it when I hunt, and if I'm with her, I don't need to veil her. I'm stronger than Ileana, so I can protect her."

Tatyana sipped her wine. After a moment, she set the glass on the antique cherry side table. "Let me talk with Ileana first. She may be able to veil her aura so I can't see the dishonesty, but I know her well enough to be fairly sure when she's lying. If she is behind this, we'll have to hunt in shifts. I can protect Chase while you hunt, and you can protect her the rest of the time."

"That only solves one of our problems," Chase pointed out. "There's still the other pride leader who intends to take me as a mate. I'm afraid Roman's going to be killed or seriously injured if he has to fight a challenge over me."

"What's this?" Tatyana demanded.

Roman sighed and explained about Zakhar Fedorov and the trust fund his pride wanted access to.

"Why haven't you already claimed her?"

"Chase is hesitating because we've known each other less than a week. Plus, she doesn't like being forced into taking a mate just because she's coming into heat, and I can't say I blame her." He kissed the top of her head. "Besides, if I claim her, Ileana will only be more determined to kill her."

"Ileana doesn't need to know." Tatyana turned to Chase. "If you care about Roman at all and want him for a mate, you'd better stop hesitating and let him claim you while there's still time."

Chapter 12

Chase was quiet the entire way home, lost in her thoughts. Was Tatyana right? Was it selfish of her not to jump headlong into a claiming with Roman?

She couldn't deny she cared about him and wanted him in her life.

If she really meant it when she'd told him she'd die if he sent her away, maybe it was time to put up or shut up.

Roman had been silent as well, and she didn't disturb him. She wasn't at all sure she wanted to know what he was thinking.

"A penny for your thoughts," he finally said as he drove up the lane toward Fernwood Manner.

"You can have them for free." She took a deep breath. "If you're sure you want me, I guess you'd better claim me."

"I'm more certain of this than I've ever been of anything in my life."

He parked the car, came around to her side, grabbed her, and pulled her into a rib-cracking hug.

"Can't breathe," she squeaked.

"Oh, sorry." He loosened his hold, but not by much, and seemed unwilling to let her go.

She laid her head on his shoulder. "I should probably tell David we're getting married. That will be the best lie to get him to go home and stop worrying about me."

"I'm afraid it'll take more than that to convince him to leave, but it's not a lie. We *are* getting married."

"We are?"

She could feel his breath in her hair as he chuckled. "Do you honestly think I would mate you, father children with you, and not legally marry you? After all, I'm a member of the British aristocracy. I do have my honor—and a position to uphold."

"A Vampire/Lycan with morals? How quaint." She grinned. "I just had the impression that mating involved something more than a marriage ceremony."

He guided her toward the house with his hand at the small of her back. "It does, but we'll still have a wedding to keep up appearances for David and other humans we associate with."

"Oh, well, I suppose for the sake of appearances, I guess I could agree to marry you."

"Behave." He swatted her on the rump. "You're going to be part of the British aristocracy yourself now. You have to act like a *lady*, and ladies don't pick on their husbands."

Chase stopped, stared at him, and burst out laughing. Roaring with glee, she clutched his shoulder, too paralyzed by laughter to move. Tears streamed down her face, and she had to cross her legs for fear she'd wet her pants.

After a while, the grin he seemed to be fighting won out and curved the corners of his mouth. Then, suddenly, he grabbed her and swung her around in a circle.

"I guess that *is* asking a bit much, isn't it, love?" he said, laughter leaking into his voice.

"Just a bit," she agreed between snickers. She clung to him, reluctant to be put down. "I mean, I can *try* to act like a lady, but I don't really think I have a snowball's chance in hell of pulling it off."

She cupped his face with her hands. "Do you really think the British aristocracy is ready for me?"

"Not a chance." His grin was wicked, his face filled with delight. "I can't wait to see how they react. Your language alone will flabbergast them. If I haven't told you before, love, you're absolutely perfect for me. Everything I've ever wanted—brains, beauty, and sass."

Before she had a chance to respond, the front door opened and David came out. "I heard all the noise. Are you picking on Roman or is he picking on you?"

"A bit of both, I think," she said as Roman set her on her feet, both of them still grinning. She took a deep breath and wiped the tears from her cheeks. "Roman and I are getting married."

Speechless, David stared at them, his mouth hanging open as his gaze swung back and forth between them.

Chase heard Roman chuckle beside her. "I think we surprised him."

"Yes. I think we did." She lowered her voice so only he could hear. "I've put him in a trance, and I didn't even have to use my eyes. It just took six little words."

"Good work," he whispered back. "Now can you bring him out of it?"

"I don't know." She raised her voice. "David, are you okay?"

He snapped his mouth shut and took a step toward them. "I'm not sure. I think I'm having delusions. I was sure I heard you say you were getting married."

Roman nodded. "As soon as I can get a license."

"But...but..."

"Spit it out, David." She knew this was going to be bad.

"You've known him less than a *week*," he roared, throwing his hands in the air.

She held her temper with an effort, reminding herself David was only concerned about her, and she'd probably react the same way if it were him in this situation. Still, she couldn't keep herself from making one smartass comment.

"And your point is?"

Roman swatted her ass again, but David didn't appear to notice, any more than he noticed her sarcasm.

"My point is you've known him less than a week. How can you be sure you know what you're doing?"

Roman sighed. "You know how she is, David. She's stubborn, and if this is what she wants, I have no choice. I'm powerless to resist her."

"Ouch." She elbowed him lightly in the ribs. "You make it sound like a shotgun wedding, with me holding the shotgun."

He chuckled and stroked her cheek. "I'm not sure what a shotgun wedding is, but as long as it works, I don't care what you call it. I'm much too selfish to let you go and would've mated you with or without the shotgun."

She threw her arms around his neck. It was as if he knew exactly what she needed to hear.

"Thank you," she whispered as his arms tightened around her.

David humphed. "Looks as if the only thing I can say is 'congratulations.' I guess you'll want me to go home now, but I'm not leaving until after the wedding, until I'm sure you're happy."

"No problem. I'll draw up the paperwork this weekend to turn my share of the business over to you."

"Don't do that. If this doesn't work out with Roman, you'll need something to fall back on."

"No, David, I trust him." Chase was rewarded by Roman's kisses in her hair. "I won't need anything to fall back on."

"If you're sure that's what you want." David threw Roman a dirty look. "Let's go to the study and talk it over." He turned and went back in the house, calling over his shoulder. "I just hope nothing comes along to ruin it for you."

As she followed him through the door, she shuddered, remembering how her life usually worked.

No. She shook off the depressing thoughts. This time she refused to let anything spoil her happiness.

৶৹৶

As Chase drew up papers giving David all her interest in their business and all her possessions in the States, Roman made a mental note to have Andy Wright come finalize the documents on Monday.

Watching her work and plan, and seeing how smart she was, he realized over again how lucky he was to have her. He'd claim her today, the minute they were alone, then all he had to do was make sure Fedorov and Ileana didn't get anywhere near her.

When David retired to his room to get ready for tonight's party, Roman gathered Chase in his arms. "Thank you for choosing me."

She gazed into his eyes. "I love you."

"That's a good thing, because I'm not sure I could have let you mate someone else even if you wanted to. I've discovered I'm a selfish bastard when it comes to you. I can't let you go. I love you too much."

He kissed her forehead, her eyes, her nose, and finally her lips. Her passionate response healed his weary heart. She filled him, completed him, made him whole. At last, he broke the kiss and asked the one question he feared the answer to.

"Are you sure you won't change your mind? I ask one last time because I want to claim you now."

"Why don't you want to wait until we're married?"

He searched deep within himself for the truth. "You have suitors on all fronts—Danyer and Zakhar Fedorov. Once you're mated, you're safe from them. Should either of them try to take you, retribution would be swift and sure by me, and should I fail, Drake and Gray would take over. But the most important reason is, as I said, I'm selfish and I want you. No one else, just you." He nuzzled her hair. "What I don't want is for you to regret the claiming, or to feel you didn't have a choice."

She was silent a long moment, just standing quietly in his arms with her head on his shoulder. "Do you honestly think I would agree if I felt I had no choice? Newsflash here, I don't do *anything* just because someone tells me I have to. But I realized something on the way home from Tatyana's." She raised her head, met his eyes. "Even if my *blood* was all you wanted, it wouldn't matter. I'd still choose you, Roman."

Her words stunned him. "You would choose me if I took innocent lives? You wouldn't think I was despicable?"

"That's not quite what I said, or what I meant." She gave a breathless little laugh. "If you took innocent lives, I'd be disappointed in you and do my best to convince you to stop. But nothing would keep me from wanting you or from wanting to be your mate. And aren't you lucky that's not an issue. Just imagine how good I could get at nagging you over the next several hundred years."

Overwhelmed, he hugged her tight. "If I live for a thousand years, I'll never understand you, but as long as I have you, I don't care."

"Good, because you're stuck with me."

"We've got about three hours before the party," he said, leading her into the hall and down the stairs. "How long will it take you to dress?"

"Five minutes if I hurry." She wiggled her eyebrows. "If we need more time, we'll just be late to the party."

As they walked into the bedroom together, he saw confusion flickering in her aura and on her face. "I can see you have questions about something."

"A few. Like what exactly a claiming involves." She took a deep breath and sat on the bed. "Too bad there aren't how-to books on Weres and Vampires."

"How-to books? You mean like self-help books on how to survive if you are one?"

She nodded.

He sat beside her and slipped an arm around her shoulders. "Who says there aren't?"

When she didn't respond, he glanced at her face, saw the shock. "Chase?"

"What do you mean? There are *real* books on this? Stuff that's not fiction?"

He laughed. "Of course, there are. Don't you think Vampires and Weres have libraries?"

"You have *libraries,* too. Where? Can I go? How soon? I need to get some of these books."

"Yes, you can go. Humans can't get into our libraries, but you can."

"Are these libraries here in England?"

"Two of them are. There's usually at least one in every country. America has fifteen, including two in Los Angeles and five in Salt Lake City." Her eyes widened, and he grinned. "Utah has a lot of Vampires. And I do mean a *lot*."

"Anyplace else have as many as Salt Lake City?"

"Yes. Mexico City. The number depends of the concentration of Vampires and Weres. We write the books, maintain the libraries, and make sure humans don't find out. The books can be checked out, but you can't buy your own. The longest you can keep a book at home is two weeks and only if you agree not to let a human in your house during that time. Though trusted and vetted servants and spouses are an exception. Even then, the books have to be kept in a safe when not being read. They'd be a little hard to explain if a non-aware human read one."

"I'll be damned."

He gently stroked her breast. "Anything else you want to know? Before we get distracted."

"Just one more question. The claiming?"

"It involves having skin-to-skin sex, no condom, and marking each other by sharing blood. There are also some ritual words that must be said."

"Sharing blood?"

"Yes. I bite you, and you bite me. We mark each other as additional proof we're mated, but I suggest the marks be hidden. I don't want Ileana to see them."

"Marks?"

"A ritualistic method of making it so when you come into heat, your pheromones will only work on me."

"So we do this now?"

"Yes. Then when we get the special marriage license, which should be early next week, we'll have a civil wedding ceremony."

"Okay. That works for me."

"Good."

Impatient, he tore off their clothes and pushed her down on the bed. "And now, if there are no more questions."

"None. Promise I can get some books?"

He shushed her with a kiss. "I promise. Just as soon as we can." Then he grinned. "But we don't need books for what I have planned this afternoon."

∽∾∽

Chase melted as Roman's mouth turned ravenous, his kisses demanding and possessive. His fingers trailed over her skin, playing her body like a piano, until every nerve ending was aflame.

She whimpered and tried to pull away from his clever mouth as he slowly devoured her, inch by quivering inch.

"Please stop teasing." She rubbed against him, demanding more. "God, Roman, you're killing me."

His tongue took a long, slow glide up her torso and curled around a nipple. "Oh, love, I've barely started. Why don't you lay back and just enjoy?"

Enjoy? How could she? The exquisite torture was too intense. Her core was an out-of-control inferno. She couldn't breathe. She wanted fulfillment. Now!

With his erection pressed against her thigh, he nipped, sucked, and laved her nipples. As he blew cool air on them, she wriggled and tried to impale herself on him.

He laughed, a ragged exhale, hot and moist against her over-heated skin. "Hold still, love, or this will be over much too soon."

"Too soon, my ass. Take me, damn it." She wasn't sure how much more of this she could handle without incinerating. "Stop fooling around and take me now."

He raised his head, his eyes clouded with desire. "You're a demanding wench, aren't you?"

She didn't get a chance to respond. Before she could blink, he drove himself into her. She gasped, arched, and moaned.

"Bite me." The growl seemed to come from a distance, lost in the static of Roman's deep strokes as he filled her, completed her. "Damn it, Chase, bite me."

This time his words registered. She marveled that he thought her human-like teeth could break his skin, but she turned her head and nipped the part of him closest to her mouth—the inside of his upper arm. To her shock, her teeth slid easily through the tender skin.

As blood trickled on her tongue, she felt his fangs pierce the underside of her right breast.

Ecstasy slammed into her in an orgasm so intense, she wasn't sure she'd survive it. Her consciousness exploded, shooting out beyond the universe of her mind to join with his. In a scream of gratification, her body arched and her muscles clenched around him as if trying to fuse her flesh to his.

'*Mine, all mine.*' She heard his voice in her head as her mind and body slowly drifted back to earth. '*Say it back to me, love.*'

"Yours, all yours."

He gave a strained chuckle. "No, repeat it in your head. '*Mine, all mine.*' Say it now."

Oh. '*Mine, all mine.*'

'*I love you, Chase. I'll never let you go.*'

'*I love you, too, but how are we doing this?*'

'*It's a Were thing. Weremates can speak to each other with their minds. Now that we're mated, we can communicate like this up to a range of four hundred miles. It's a secret shared only with other Weres.'* With sigh of contentment, he rolled over and pulled her close. *'You're mine now, love, and I'm yours.'*

She snuggled against him. *'Now all we have to do is keep each other safe. And alive.'*

∞∞∞

The door creaked. Drake looked up from his papers and beckoned for Gray to enter. "Thanks for coming."

"No problem. What's up?"

"When's the last time you saw Dillon?"

Gray shrugged. "The afternoon we met Chase. Why?"

"Because no one's seen him since then. His landlady called me this morning. He's missing, and she's worried about him."

"Missing?" Gray snorted. "The scumbag probably hightailed it for parts unknown. He has to know we're on to him, so I'm not surprised he didn't stick around."

"Maybe so, but why would he leave without taking his clothes or emergency cash?"

"How do you know he did?"

"I asked the landlady to search his room," Drake said. "No clothes are missing, except for the ones he was last seen in, at least as far as she can tell, and she found an envelope full of cash in his desk."

"Hmmm. So what are you thinking?"

Drake stood, fished out his keys. "I'm thinking one of my pride members has disappeared. We know he was working for Ileana, and I'd make book she was the last one to see him—alive."

"Oh, no, you don't." Holding up both hands, Gray backed toward the door. "Don't even think about giving me your keys. You know I'd do almost anything for you, Drake, but I'm not going out to see that fucking bitch again. Not even for you."

Drake chuckled. "Relax. I wasn't planning on sending you."

"You weren't?"

"No. At least not alone. You're coming with me."

"Shit. Why me?"

"Who else can I count on to watch my back?"

"That's not fair, Drake. It's a real low blow, and you know it."

"You're the best I've got, Gray. You're my second."

Gray closed his eyes, sighed. "Shit."

ℰℐℰℐ

Chase and Roman made it to the party five minutes before the first guest arrived, but only because she dressed and combed her hair in record time. She didn't bother to look in the mirror. He told her she looked stunning and that was good enough for her.

Per their agreement, as they mingled with the guests this time, Roman introduced her as his fiancée. This increased the jealousy in many of the human female guests, but nothing that seemed bad enough to incite murder.

'*Why are we here?*' she asked, after she'd listened to the last round of inane babbling from a trio of female guests.

'*We're looking at auras, love. I want to give Ileana the benefit of the doubt and check everyone who was at the parties the week-end Melinda died. Besides, not only am I not leaving you alone, you can see colors in auras I can't.*'

'*Well, I'm not seeing anything that clears her, are you?*'

'*No. I'm seeing quite a few male humans who'd probably like to kill me over you, but none of the women seem to have that level of violence in them.*' He hesitated then sighed. '*Of course if it were a spur of the moment crime, a crime of passion so to speak, it might not show up in her aura.*'

'*Roman, it has to be a Vampire. If it had been a human or a Were, you'd have heard her and smelled her with those marvelous senses of yours. I know you don't want to believe it, but there really is no other logical explanation.*'

'*Unfortunately, it won't be enough to tell The Council we saw her aura and know she's guilty.*'

Realizing it probably looked like they were giving each other the silent treatment, she reverted to speaking in a whisper. "What do we do?"

There were no Weres or Vampires attending this evening so she figured she wouldn't be overheard.

His smile told her he understood and approved. "I'm not sure. We may have to set a trap. That spy show you told me about this afternoon, did your man from uncle ever set any traps?"

She gave a short bark of laughter. "Not that I can remember, but even if they had, I don't think Napoleon Solo or Illya Kuryakin ever dealt with Vampires."

"No, but the basic principles would be the same. We'd have to adapt it, of course, but it would help if we had an idea to start with."

"We really need to ask David about that. He's the one with the creative imagination."

"Ask me what?" David said from behind her and made her jump. "I'm not giving you two advice on sex. So let's just leave my creative imagination out of this, shall we?"

Roman chuckled, but Chase dissolved into helpless laughter, thinking of their afternoon love-making session and the warm, pulsing mark on the underside of her breast. Advice on sex, indeed.

"We need to set a trap to force a confession from our suspect, as we don't have any proof," Roman said. "I don't think auras will be considered as proper evidence for the...authorities."

Her laughter only increased over his hesitation. She knew he'd been about to mention The Council.

He arched a warning eyebrow at her. "Chase just thought you might have some creative ideas on how to set up a sting—I think that's the right word—to expose the killer."

"Oh. Sure, we can use my creative imagination for that." David thought for a few moments then shook his head. "I can't come up with one off the top of my head, but let me think about for a while, and we'll meet in the study after the party."

"Thank you."

He nodded and headed off to do more mingling. As Chase watched him walk through the crowd, she noticed something.

"You know, I never realized it before, but David's quite good looking. See how many female auras fill with lust when he passes?"

"You became mated and engaged to *me* this afternoon," Roman growled. His tone was stern, but she could hear the suppressed amusement in his voice. "And *now* you start noticing other men? This is not what I'd consider a good sign."

"You'll just have to keep me occupied, so I won't have time to notice them, won't you?"

He grinned. "Believe me, I intend to."

Before she could answer, another passel of guests stopped to pay their compliments. She had to smile and be polite, all the while thinking about Roman and wishing they were both downstairs in bed.

She struggled to keep her scowl off her face as the last of the group moved on. "Will we have to do this often after we're married? Parties, I mean."

"Lord, I hope not. The two this weekend are the only ones I've given in years. The rest were my father's idea." He tightened his arm around her and kissed her hair. "Thankfully, his matchmaking isn't necessary anymore."

"I knew there was a reason I chose you," she said wrapping one arm around his waist and hugging him back. "Apart from all the other reasons, I mean."

"Just as long as you did, I don't care what the reasons are." He gestured with his chin. "I hear some late guests arriving. Let's wander over that way and mingle."

ᴄ⌇ᴇ⌇ᴐ

June 8th:

The party ended at midnight. By the time everyone not staying at the manor had left, and Martin had taken the houseguests in for tea, Chase was dead on her feet. She took off her shoes for the walk to the study, dropped them on the floor by the couch, and collapsed into its deep cushions. "Thank God, that's over."

"Amen," agreed Roman.

David snorted. "Wimps. I thought the English liked parties and dress-up things."

Roman poured them each a glass of wine and went to sit on the couch with Chase. "'The English' is a very board term. Some of my countrymen do like that stuff. I've just never been one of them. Most of the parties I have gone to in the past have been force fed to me."

"Right. To find you a wife. I remember the first day we were here, you thought that's why your grandfather hired Chase and me." David's voice was calm, but there was a grim set to his mouth and tension in his aura. "It looks like this time he hit pay dirt."

Roman glanced at Chase, a question in his eyes. She grinned. "Pay dirt just means he succeeded. He got what he was digging for."

David chuckled. "This is going to be a great marriage. You guys will have to hire an interpreter." When she stuck out her tongue at him, the chuckles erupted into laughter. "And Chase is such a *lady*. Just what English high society needs."

She snuggled against Roman, remembering his similar words earlier that afternoon. "So, did you come up with any creative ideas, David?"

"Not really. But in most of the cop shows I've seen, the suspect usually confesses to whomever he's going to kill as he's telling him why he's going to kill him. You know, the guy says, 'I killed Sam and since you found out, now I have to kill you.' That's usually when the cops show up. I doubt that'll work in this case, because the suspect probably already knows it's been considered an accident by Scotland Yard, and the case is closed."

He focused his attention on the wine in his glass before zeroing back in on Roman. "I don't know how well you know this person, but would she believe you if you told her you wanted to kill someone, too, and needed to know how it's done? Could you get her to confess that way?"

"I doubt it. Still, it's not a bad idea. Perhaps I can get her to confess if I confront her." He rose and went to his desk. Pulling a tiny digital tape recorder out of a drawer, he tossed it to Chase. "Have you ever used one of these?"

She nodded and began playing with the buttons. It was similar to ones she used in her work all the time.

Roman picked up the phone. "I wonder if Tatyana was able to talk to her. Maybe she'll have some ideas."

He dialed, waited. "Tatyana? Roman. Did you have a chance to talk with Ileana?" He frowned. "No word all afternoon? And no one at her house knows where she is?"

As his jaw tightened and a tic formed over his right eye, Chase studied his aura. The apprehension in it didn't reassure her.

"Yes, we're sticking to the plan. Call me when you finish and we'll coordinate. Thanks." He placed the phone in its cradle, returned to the couch, and put his arms around her. "Ileana disappeared this afternoon."

"She's casing the joint," David said. "Watching the house and waiting for Chase to be alone."

"Yes," Roman agreed. "I think you're right."

"What do we do now?" she whispered, slipping the tape recorder into the side pocket of her gown. She shifted her wine glass to her other hand so she could snuggle closer to him. "We need a plan of attack."

"The plan is, we don't leave you alone. We see you have protection at all times. As soon as I can, I'll take you far away from here. We have real estate in several different countries." Roman rested his cheek on her head. "I'll protect you, Chase. I promise."

"I know you will. I trust you." She leaned into his shoulder, taking strength from his scent, as well as his words. "I mean, how do we get her talking about the—"

At a loud boom from the front of the house, Roman bolted to his feet. "David, stay with Chase," he ordered as he charged out of the study.

She stared after him. What could David do against Ileana? But then, Ileana wouldn't make that kind of noise. She'd be silent and stealthy. It was probably just a dog knocking over the trashcans. She glanced up and met David's eyes.

He rose, came over to her, and pulled her up into a hug.

"Are you really sure about this? I mean really, really sure?"

She returned his hug with one arm, her wine glass still in her other hand. "Yes. Roman's what I want."

He suddenly collapsed into her. Dropping the wine, she grabbed him under the arms.

"David," she cried, easing him down to the floor. "David, are you okay?"

She reached out to check his pulse. Then something grabbed her and she screamed.

℘℘℘

The crash had come from the front yard. Charging from the study, Roman veiled himself, the second he was out of sight of Chase and David, and raced through the house to the spot where he figured the noise had originated.

Ileana wouldn't make such a racket. She was too silent and skilled to be that clumsy. Unless she'd hired an assassin so she could honestly tell The Council she hadn't killed Chase.

A bench, one that had been beside a fountain on the front lawn, was now *in* the fountain—both the fountain and bench nothing more than a pile of large, jagged, concrete pieces, gleaming in the last rays of predawn moonlight. No single human could have lifted that bench and thrown it into the fountain. The thing was solid concrete and must've weighed four or five hundred pounds. It would've taken at least four men. Possibly, a half a dozen.

Something Chase said at breakfast flashed across his mind: '*A diversion only works if people can't see through it until it's all over.*'

He heard her cry, "David! David, are you okay?" Then she screamed.

Bloody hell! Terror clutching his heart, he tore back to the study and found David unconscious on the floor next to a spilled glass of wine.

Chase was gone.

Chapter 13

Chase slowly opened her eyes. At least she thought she did. It was one thing to be unable to move, but to not feel, see, hear, taste, or smell anything—other than the saliva in her mouth, the furious beating of her own heart, and the air going in and out of her lungs—terrified her.

A shudder ripped through her. This must be what Roman referred to when he talked about her being veiled.

Ileana!

She fought to tamp down her panic. By sheer force of will, she locked her fear in a small box deep inside her. If she wanted to survive, she had to remain calm and use her head. To outwit Ileana, she had to learn her game plan and thwart it.

Logic said they were moving. Ileana would hardly have left her in Roman's study. But since she couldn't feel or see anything, it was just a guess. Trying not to think about what Ileana had planned for her, she concentrated on her afternoon with Roman.

Their lovemaking. Their mating. Their love.

She'd find a way to stay alive for him. She had to. He wouldn't make it if she died, especially by Ileana's hand. The guilt and self-recrimination would kill him.

The moment she landed on a rough, stone floor, she discovered her senses were functioning again. The boat-necked, cinnamon-colored silk gown, she'd worn to the party, provided little in the way of protection or warmth. Wrapping her arms around herself, she shivered and surveyed her surroundings.

Across the room, a kerosene lantern gave off a pale yellow light, enough for her to see Ileana standing nearby. Her waist-length, auburn hair was windblown, her golden brown eyes cold and hostile, and her voluptuous body rigid.

She was probably the most physically beautiful woman Chase had ever seen—if one didn't notice her aura. It looked darker than on Friday. In an effort to keep panic from showing in her heartbeat or aura, Chase sat up, rubbed her hands up and down her arms, and focused her thoughts on the self-help books Roman had told her about.

Determined to face whatever was coming on her feet, she rose. Something bumped her hip. *The tape recorder! I've got it in my pocket. If I can get Ileana talking—*

She concentrated on the Vampire and Were books to keep any deception out of her aura and, easing her hand into the small side pocket of her gown, ran her thumb over the buttons on the machine. She pushed the one she hoped was "record."

Ileana turned away and walked through a barred door that looked like it belonged on a jail cell. She pulled it shut, locked it, and tossed the key to the other side of the large space outside the cell—where Chase couldn't possibly reach it.

"I'm not going to kill you tonight. Now that you and Roman are mated, I'm going to wait for a time, while you starve, and he suffers. Then after I kill you, I'll dump your emaciated body on his porch, so he'll see what he's done—That is, if he survives the en-forced separation," she said in an eerily calm voice. The peaceful tone made her words more threatening, not less.

"If by any chance you happen to be pregnant, he'll suffer that much more when he reads the autopsy report."

As she imagined the grief this would cause Roman, Chase's temper flared, bolstering her courage. Tossing her hair back, she tut-tutted. "You grabbed me too soon, Ileana. Roman and I haven't mated yet. We decided to wait and get married first, once the spe-cial license came through."

"You lie!"

Her eyes narrowed and slipped out of focus. Chase knew Ileana was checking her aura and concentrated on the fact she and Roman weren't married yet.

"Humph." Ileana lips curled in a sneer. "Are you really dumb enough to believe he actually wants to marry you?" She shook her head. "He wants sex from a willing partner so bad, he'd do anything to get it. Even mate someone he doesn't love."

"Then why kidnap me before the ceremony?"

She smirked. "If you die, he'll just find someone else. And I'll kill the next one, too. And the next one. Until he's afraid to even look at a women."

"Ileana, please, you don't have to do this. Roman didn't mean to kill your husband. It was an accident. Swerving to avoid a horse is instinctive. If you'd been driving, you'd have done the same thing."

Ileana's screech of agony made Chase wince. It sounded like a huge metal slab being ripped in two. She wouldn't have thought the sound possible from a living creature.

"You don't know anything about it!" She stomped to the cell door and shook the bars. Apparently satisfied they were solid, she stepped back. "He's arrogant. He thinks he's such a good driver. But he always drove too fast. My husband offered to drive when we left Tatyana's, but no, Roman wouldn't have it. Didn't trust anyone else with his precious car."

"According to Tatyana, your husband was too drunk to drive. None of you would've survived if he'd been behind the wheel."

Her eyes widened then narrowed. "My husband was my *life*! Sooner or later, Roman will find a mate, and I'll get my revenge." She turned away.

"Wait, Ileana," Chase called.

She had to get the confession on tape. When Ileana ignored her and kept going, Chase changed tactics.

"Isn't all this angst over a human a little melodramatic?" she asked. "After all, he would have grown old and died in a few years anyway."

With a screech of fury, Ileana spun and flew at the bars. Chase stumbled backward, wondering if they'd hold. They did.

"You really are stupid, aren't you?" Ileana hissed. "No wonder Roman hasn't claimed you. Well, for your information, you dumb cunt, humans who mate Weres or Vampires are immune from aging."

"Immune? How?"

"A hormone in the saliva of the 'others' transfers to the human mates, so they gain our ability to heal the flesh—unless they're decapitated in a car accident, like my husband." She pivoted and headed for the stairs. "Now, if you'll excuse me."

Not yet. I need a little more. "Why did you kill Melinda Carter? Roman never loved her."

Ileana glanced over her shoulder. "What do you care?"

"I just wondered. I mean, it didn't really cause him much pain." She tried to make her shrug look casual. "And since I'm going to die anyway, you've nothing to lose by telling me."

"She defied me. Usually when I steal their things, put dead animals in the garden, and leave notes on their beds, they run away and never come back. But not her.

"She followed him around like a puppy, her aura glowing with lust. And those sighs, if he so much as spoke to her. All the while, she made these stupid, little remarks about how good she'd be for him. It was disgusting."

She waved a hand. "She should have left when I told her to. I figured Roman was probably entrancing her for sex. Reason enough to kill her."

"So what's the plan now?" Chase asked. "Are you just going to leave me here and let me die of hunger and thirst?"

"Hardly. I have a much more unpleasant death planned for you." Ileana's evil smile chilled Chase to the marrow. "I spent all afternoon preparing this place for you. I've left you a sleeping cot and a barrel of drinking water. The water's stale, but clean. There's a chamber pot in the cell next door. I've made you an access through the connecting bars. You'll see it once it gets light. The bed's under the window."

"All the comforts of home," Chase muttered. "But no food?"

"Oh, no, dear," Ileana said sweetly. "I want you to be as emaciated as possible when Roman sees your body. I want him to know how much you suffered. Besides, don't you know food attracts rats?"

She lifted her hand and wiggled her fingers in a goodbye gesture. "Now that I've satisfied your curiosity, I'll say goodnight. Enjoy your stay." Blowing out the lamp, she disappeared.

Rats? Ugh. Alone in the dark, Chase shuddered, reached into her pocket, and shut off the recorder. She longed to hit the playback button and confirm she'd gotten the confession. But if Ileana was within a half a mile, she might hear her own voice and come back.

Good thing she stuck this in her gown, rather than giving it back to Roman. At least when he found it on her body, he'd have the evidence he needed for The Council.

She needed a better hiding place for it, she decided, taking the little machine out of her pocket. Her bra? Perfect. That way they'd find it at autopsy. Though if the pathologist or police listened to it, God knew what they'd think. She could only hope Roman would check her body before turning her over to the authorities.

Don't think like that. He'll come for you. They were mated. She couldn't, *wouldn't*, give up on him.

Exhausted, she wanted to lie down. On the cot if she could find it. The idea of spending the night on the floor wasn't appealing.

With a sigh, she turned to her left and walked forward, her hands stretched out in front of her, her bare feet edging across the cold, rough stones. She prayed there weren't any large holes in the floor big enough for her to fall through.

"I hope David's all right," she muttered then winced as her voice echoed in the empty space surrounding her.

Her hands hit solid stone. She turned left again and went on, using the wall as a guide. The stone changed to metal bars. Probably the other cell, the one containing the chamber pot—which, according to her secret stash of historical romance novels, was a toilet. Of sorts. Oh, joy, another fun day in the dungeon.

Moving her hands from bar to bar, she continued on until she again found stone. She followed that to the corner and once more turned left. This wall bulged outward in a convex shape. Maybe the outside wall of a tower?

Following it, she felt her shins connect with an edge. She bent down and discovered a small cot. It even had a blanket. Sinking gratefully onto the bed, she wrapped herself in the warm material.

"I guess she doesn't want me freeze to death, either," she said under her breath, but even the soft whisper sounded too loud in the empty silence.

Roman would come for her. He'd find her. He would. Trying to believe it, she closed her eyes and let sleep overtake her.

കാരു

Frantic, Roman searched the house and grounds, though he knew it was no use. Ileana would have taken Chase somewhere to taunt her before killing her.

Terror assaulted him at the thought of what Chase would suffer at Ileana's hands, but he refused to allow himself to panic. She needed him now. If he lost control, he'd destroy any chance to find her.

There was no scent to follow. That alone told him she'd been veiled. It also meant a Vampire had taken her. Ileana was the only one with a motive, and she had disappeared.

Waking Martin, he told him what happened and asked him to go to the study and look after David. "Call Dr. Zindart if you can't bring him around. I have to find Chase."

He didn't wait for Martin's response but hurried into the library to call Tatyana. Hopefully, she hadn't started on her hunt. She answered on the first ring.

"Tatyana," he breathed, swamped with relief. "I was afraid you'd left."

"I did. I'm halfway to London. I forwarded the house phone to my cell phone before I left in case you needed me. What's happened?"

He fought to keep his voice from shaking. "Chase has been kidnapped."

"*What*? When?"

"About fifteen minutes ago. It's my fault," he groaned. "I was stupid. We were in the study and heard a noise at the front of the house. I left her with her human friend and went to investigate. By the time I got back to the study, David was unconscious, and Chase was gone. There's no scent to follow, neither Chase's nor anyone else's, so I know she was veiled."

"Did you search the house and grounds?" she asked then answered her own question. "Yes, of course, you did."

"We're mated. What am I going to do?"

"Don't panic," she said. "I know Ileana better than anyone does. Meet me in the woods south of my house as soon as you can get there. Run. Don't drive. We've no time to waste."

"On my way." He hung up the phone and raced out of the house, still in his tux.

Speeding through the dark, he realized since they'd bonded, he should be able to locate her. Why hadn't he thought of it before?

Chase? Chase, can you hear me? Where are you?

Nothing. Christ, why didn't she answer? Perhaps she was sleeping, or veiled, or...No, he wouldn't think that. He couldn't bear the thought of losing her.

It struck him that Ileana wouldn't know about their ability to communicate. Not only was it a closely guarded Were secret, she was a Vampire and thought all others were beneath her. What else wouldn't she know, and how could he use it?

By the time he reached the woods, Tatyana was already there. Her smile told him she'd come up with something, and there was hope.

He snatched at it. "What is it?"

"We're in luck. If Ileana did what I think she did, we may have time to save Chase."

"Tell me."

"I stopped by Ileana's and bribed the maid. She was a wealth of information."

"She knows where they are?"

"Not exactly. But she told me that yesterday afternoon, Ileana got a visit from Drake Gatos and one of his men. Apparently, the maid was working in the hallway and overheard everything."

Roman closed his eyes and fisted his hands. "Get to the point, Tatyana."

"Okay, okay. Drake questioned Ileana about someone named Dillon. He's missing, and Drake seems to think she had something to do with his disappearance. He also told her Chase had chosen you as her mate, so if Ileana saw this Dillon guy again, she should just tell him not to waste his time spying on Fernword Manor. As soon Drake left, Ileana changed her clothes and ran out. She hasn't been back since."

"All that means is Ileana was probably watching my house waiting for Chase to be alone. I don't see what—"

She put a hand on his arm. "Think. Did you see any sign of her or smell her scent, anything, to make you think she was nearby?"

"No, but I wouldn't if she were veiled."

"She couldn't have gained much information if she were veiled."

"True." He ground his teeth to keep from shouting. "But it's not information she was after."

"She wasn't there, Roman. She was off preparing Chase's prison."

"Her prison?" He groaned as the words slashed through what composure he had left. "But Ileana wants revenge, and the best way to get that is to kill Chase. To destroy my love as I destroyed hers."

"Yes, but if she thinks you've mated with Chase, she's more likely to want to weaken you first through an enforced separation."

"If Chase sticks to the plan, she won't admit to being mated."

"What about the mark?"

He shoved his hands in his pockets so he wouldn't slam his fist into a tree trunk. "Short of stripping Chase and checking her inch by inch, she'll never find it."

"Good, but it doesn't change anything."

"What do you mean?"

"Think about it, Roman. Ileana wants to torture you. She wants you riddled with guilt and self-doubt. In her mind, she'll have a better chance of accomplishing that if she holds Chase without food and waits until she's emaciated before killing her. So when she dumps the body on your porch, she can watch you suffer."

"Oh, Christ." He buried his face in his hands, struggling to control his emotions. The thought of Chase alone and frightened was bad enough, but the image of her alone, frightened, and *starving* in some dark prison filled him with a bottomless well of dread.

"Don't." She put her arms around him. "Try to think of it as a gift. It gives us time to save her. At least a week. Two, if we're lucky. But only if you control yourself and hide the effects of the enforced separation."

"Where, Tatyana?" He grabbed her hand as if it were a lifeline. "Where would she take her?"

"I don't know, but it will be somewhere no one can hear any cries for help. Somewhere she can leave and let Chase fend for herself. She won't stand guard. That's work for servants. But she's not going to involve anyone else. Ileana trusts no one, her servants included."

"Considering how you bribed them, she has good reason."

"True." She tapped her chin with her finger. "She's always been fascinated with ancient ruins, and as I recall, a lot of these old castles have dungeons and tower prisons that are still fairly sturdy, even after centuries of abandonment and neglect. It wouldn't take much work for her to correct enough defects so Chase couldn't escape."

Roman pictured it in his mind. "It won't be a place we're familiar with, but it will be one that she is. She didn't have time to find a place from scratch and get it set up, so it has to be a place she already knows about. The problem is finding the right one." His jaw tightened. "Let's run over to Ileana's and see if we can find anything that will give us some idea of where she might have hidden Chase."

"What if she's home? Or if her servants are awake?"

He took her hand. "I know how to veil, don't you? Maintain your scent veil the entire time we're there. If she thinks we're on to her, she may panic and act sooner than she intends to."

Holding hands so they could sense each other through their veils, they took off into the night, running at their fastest speed. Normally, running exhilarated Roman, but tonight it only fueled his fear-driven fury. Ileana could have taken Chase anywhere on the isle of Great Britain in the hour since she disappeared from his study.

Would she really wait to let Chase become emaciated before killing her? He could only hope Tatyana was right.

Ileana's house was dark and quiet. They jumped to the balcony outside a second floor bedroom and slipped inside. Ileana's scent was several hours old, the same strength as Drake's and Gray's. Proof she'd left the house immediately after their visit and hadn't returned.

Tatyana led the way to the library. She was a frequent visitor to Ileana's, while Roman never called on her if he could avoid it.

Once inside the room, he dropped Tatyana's hand and all but his scent veil, signaling for her to do the same.

They rummaged through the books looking for anything that might give a clue as to what Ileana was thinking. Though they had only the starlight filtering through the curtains, it didn't hamper their ability to read.

He picked up a battered copy of *Wuthering Heights* and handed it to Tatyana. She thumbed through it, raising her eyebrows in question.

"It's the only book not on a shelf," Roman whispered in a voice too low for human ears to hear. "Is it a message or a clue?"

"Bring it. It was her husband's favorite book," Tatyana answered in the same decibel. "So it's either a clue, or she thinks it will mislead me. If she knows you suspect her, she'll assume I'm helping you."

"Keep looking," he said. "See if you can find a book on castles or ruins anywhere in England, Scotland or Wales. I don't think she'll try to take her over water. It's too hard to keep her veiled. So let's stick to Great Britain. For now."

She scanned the room. "She must know we will come here to look for clues, so any we find we have to look at both ways."

"Do you really think she's that smart?"

"Her anger and thirst for vengeance have made her unstable, not stupid." Tatyana went back to searching the books. "Here's something. A book on ancient ruins in Scotland."

"And here's one on England. So all we need now is Wales."

"If we don't find one, that's where we start searching." She climbed a ladder and started on the very top shelf. "No. This one includes England, Scotland, and Wales. I wonder why it was up here." She retrieved the book and climbed back down. "Have you found anything else?"

Roman shook his head and took her hand as a signal to re-veil. Once veiled, they climbed the winding staircase to Ileana's lavishly appointed master bedroom on the third floor. They searched the room from top to bottom but found only one more book on ruins in Great Britain.

"I think that's all we're going to find," he breathed. "Hand me those and let's go."

When they were far enough away that Ileana wouldn't be able to detect their voices from her property should she return, they stopped.

"We must assume Ileana's been spying on me since Chase got here. I suspect she killed Melinda, so Chase is her second victim. The second one is supposed to be easier."

He squeezed his eyes shut and forced back the fear. "Ileana's probably aware of everything I've done and said to this point, including my visit to you. From this point on, you don't know anything but that I'm falling apart."

"Good idea," she said. "I'll spread the word to my servants, and they'll spread it to hers. But if I'm correct about what she's doing, we have a little time."

He cupped her face. "I don't want to lose that by scaring her into acting too soon. Understand?"

She nodded and took the books out of his arms. "I'll take these with me and go through them, gather what information I can before dawn, then put the books back where we found them. You didn't hunt last night, so you need to do that now."

When he opened his mouth to protest, she shushed him. "Don't argue. Ileana may decide to come for you, too. We don't know how far her need for revenge will go. You won't help Chase if Ileana catches you unawares and kills you before you get to her. So go hunt. You need your strength."

"Yes, mother," he said with a twisted grin. "I can't tell you how much I appreciate this, Tatyana—you being here for me." He raked his fingers through his hair. "I don't know what I'd have done if you hadn't been."

"For being in shock, you've handled it well. I can already see the wheels starting to turn in that brain of yours." She poked a finger into his chest. "So do as I say. Hunt. Then go home and rest. Meet me in the morning at ten in the barn on the Keller estate. They've gone to Russia and don't have a live-in caretaker. Their man just comes in during the week, not on weekends. So we can talk there without fear of being overheard. Be sure to veil yourself before you leave the house. I wouldn't put it past Ileana to follow you if she sees you leave."

As he stepped away, she grabbed his arm. "You need to call that inspector—Clayton, isn't it?—and tell him Chase is missing. She's clever. If Ileana leaves her alone long enough and there's any way she can get free, she will. If she does, she may need help, so you want the human authorities to be looking for her, too. I'll call The Council and let them know what's happened." She turned then stopped. "Oh, and we'll need to be armed from now on. So pull out your sword when you get home."

He nodded and took off toward London to hunt as Tatyana instructed. She'd lived for centuries, and she was the only one of his relatives who hadn't abandoned his mother when she mated a Lycan.

She was right. He was in shock and maddened by fear for his mate. Chase needed him strong. If that meant hunting, he'd hunt. If he was a little more violent than necessary in the kill, he justified it. The man's aura had been coal black—a sign he'd preyed on innocents far too long.

When he returned to the house, Roman went to the safe in his study and removed a compact, thin-bladed, short sword from its hard leather case. No matter what happened, he vowed, he'd make Ileana pay for this.

∽∾∽

Chase woke to find a gray light filtering through an opening in the stone wall, high above her cot. The window held no glass, only metal bars. Outside, rain pounded the tower. Huge drops blew through the bars and ran down the wall.

Cold and uncomfortable, she lay under her blanket and stared at nothing while she mulled over her predicament. She remembered the tape recorder, pulled it out of her bra, and checked the tiny screen. Something had indeed been recorded on it since Roman had given it to her.

She wondered if Ileana had waited in the area to make sure she didn't escape. No, she wasn't the type. Much too arrogant. Since she'd prepared this place, Ileana would assume it was escape proof. Whether it was or not remained to be seen.

Satisfied with her logic, she turned the volume on the recorder down as low as it would go, selected the only recording on the machine, and pushed "play."

Ileana's voice, ice cold, beautiful, and deadly calm, whispered from the tiny speaker, "I'm not going to kill you tonight." Chase quickly shut it off, stuffed it in her bra, and feigned sleep in case Ileana came back.

She snuck a peek at her watch but wasn't sure how long to wait. Roman told her vampires could run four hundred miles an hour and hear accurately up to half a mile. She waited another five minutes. When there was no sign of Ileana, Chase decided she must've gone home.

She sat up and surveyed her prison. In the morning light it looked like a jail in an old tower. The floor, walls, and ceiling were made of light-colored stone, while the inside walls were stone interspersed with metal bars. Her cot was situated under the only window in her cell. From what she could see through the bars on the other side, there was also a window in the next cell. The cell with the chamber pot.

Chase remembered what Mr. Wright, Roman's attorney, had told her about the English upper class not thinking women were smart enough for undercover work. Ileana was a member of that class. If she was as arrogant as she appeared, she might not have taken enough precautions. Especially if she held a low opinion of Weres and not just women. If there was a way out of here and back to Roman, Chase was determined to find it.

Standing, she decided she'd better find the chamber pot first. Her bare feet made soft padding noises on the cold stone floor. Damn it, she wanted breakfast, a hot bath, a change of clothes, and shoes. And Roman. God, she missed him.

Forget what you want. This is what you've got, so deal. The pep talk didn't reduce the longing, but it did straighten her spine. Deal, she would. One minute at a time.

Okay, first mission, find chamber pot. She walked toward the bars of the other cell and spotted the access Ileana had mentioned— a small thigh high door cut in the bars. Crawling on her hands and knees on the filthy stone floor, she skittered through the opening. The chamber pot sat in the corner: a brightly patterned enameled bucket with a lid and two rolls of toilet paper beside it.

Looked like Ileana had thought of everything.

A strained chuckle escaped as she considered the irony. Ileana thought starving her was okay, but leaving her without toilet paper would have been uncivilized.

'*Chase, can you hear me? If you can, think your answers, don't speak them.*'

She squeaked at Roman's voice and almost fell off the pot. '*Roman, is that really you? Ileana took me!*'

'*Yes, love, I know. Are you okay? Did she hurt you?*'

'*No. She's pissed me off, but she didn't hurt me.*'

His relief was almost tangible. '*Thank God. I'm coming to get you, love. Where are you?*'

'*How the hell should I know?*'

'*Well, look around and tell me everything you see.*'

'I think I'm in some kind of tower. It's like a jail cell. But not at ground level. There's no traffic near me that I can hear. No animals.'

'Is there a window? Can you see outside?'

'Ah, not at the moment.' Despite the situation, she had to swallow a laugh. He'd picked a hell of a time to "call." *'I mean, there's a window, but it's up high.'*

'Can you find something to stand on to reach the window? If I knew what the terrain around you looked like, it would help me find you.'

'Sure. Give me a minute.' She finished her business, hurried into the other cell, stood the cot on its end, and climbed to the window. *'I was right, I'm high up. At least a couple of stories. It's cold and rainy.'*

'What's the ground around the tower look like?'

'Mostly rolling hills covered in low-growing grasses and something that looks like some kind of heather or sage plant.'

'Sounds like you're on a moor. Somewhere. Right, I'll be in touch soon. Don't give up hope, love. Tatyana and I are looking for you.'

'Might want to get Drake's pride involved, too.'

Silence answered her. Stubborn man. Tigers could scent her before his wolf could.

A moor somewhere? What the hell did that mean? How many moors did England have? "Shit, with my luck, moors will be the most extensive habitat on the Isle of Great Britain."

She repositioned the cot and went back to finish checking out the other cell. In spite of the fresh air, it smelled musty. She stared up at the window. The bars were securely fastened in cement. New, sturdy cement. Rats. It would take a sledgehammer to loosen it.

Next, she examined the locked cell door. Ileana had ensured the key was out of reach, and Chase couldn't find anything to pick the lock with.

Convinced that if Ileana had made a mistake it would be in this cell and not the one where she was sleeping, she spent hours examining the small enclosure for weaknesses and became increasingly frustrated when she drew a blank. Ileana had to have made a mistake. Arrogant people always did. It was an unwritten rule of life.

Thirst finally drove her to the water barrel in the other cell. Ileana had positioned it on the opposite wall from her bed. It was wooden and knee-high, the type farmers used to catch rain in places like Oklahoma and the Midwest. When she'd studied the Great Depression in school, she'd seen pictures of farmhouses with these standing out by the corner of the porch.

Made of upright wooden slats fastened together with metal bands, she was surprised it held water without leaking. She was also glad she hadn't tripped over it on her journey to the cot last night.

Looking around for a cup and not finding one, she sighed. The water smelled clean enough to drink—not that there was any other option. She wiped her hands on her dress, with little effect. The rain? Climbing on the cot again, she stuck both hands out through the bars and let it wash off what it could of the filth. She pulled her arms back in and grimaced. Her hands looked cleaner, but not by much. Still, it was better than nothing.

She dried them on her gown then bent over and used her hands to scoop up water, drinking as much as she could hold. The water was cool and tasted old, but not unpleasant. As Ileana had said, stale but clean.

The barrel lid leaned off to one side against the wall. Thinking the lid was meant to keep the water clean, she put it back in its rightful place. Like the barrel, it was made of wooden slats held together with metal bands. A long band went around the circumference. Three thick, heavy metal strips were laid across the top and secured with weird-looking square nails.

One of the strips was loose, most of the nails missing. If she could get the rest of them out, she could use strip as a crow bar. Assuming she could find something to pry.

She grinned, reminded of a joke David had once told her. '*If we had some strawberries, we could have strawberries and ice cream. If we had ice cream.*' She missed David and hoped Ileana hadn't hurt him, though he was bound to be frantic with worry over her disappearance. Unless Roman had wiped his memory. No, he wouldn't do that.

She tried to contact Roman, but there was no response.

With a sigh, she examined the rest of the cell. Much like the other one, she could find no weaknesses. The metal strip on the lid was too wide to pick the lock on the door, the nails too short. She glared at the key under the lamp. Damn. It was too far away to use the strip to snag it and pull it within reach.

Stymied and discouraged, she turned her attention to the bars on the window. The concrete on these bars looked older than in the other cell. A dirty gray in color, it looked solid enough, but in the early morning light she could see tiny fractures. She climbed onto the cot, stuck her fingernail in one of the cracks, and pried. Her nail broke, but the crack widened as small fragments flaked off.

Ileana had made her mistake!

The concrete looked solid, but it wasn't. If she could get the strip off the barrel lid, she could use it to knock the concrete off the bars. She'd only have to free two or three bars to be able to squeeze through. It would take her forever, but it wasn't as if she had a pressing engagement.

Why couldn't this be on the window in the other cell? That way, if Ileana did come back before she was finished, it wouldn't be immediately obvious. As it was, there was no way to hide the excavation. Shit. Then again, if she didn't escape, she'd die anyway.

The drop would be about the same as falling from a second story balcony. People survived falls like that all the time. Besides, it wasn't as if she had to jump. She could cut the blanket into strips and make a rope.

It was a good plan. Now to put it into action. She repositioned the cot, grabbed the lid, and began working the nails loose from the strip.

Chapter 14

After Roman finished speaking with Chase, he lay in bed for several minutes, mulling over their conversation. It had given him hope, not that he could tell David. He knew he should send the man home but doubted he'd leave.

Then there was Chief Inspector Clayton. Roman decided to ask David to brief him. That would keep them both out of his way, and David knew nothing incriminating. Only that someone had knocked him out, and Chase was gone when he came to.

After he talked to David, Roman was going to see if he could find any trace of Ileana's scent leading away from her estate. She might not have veiled herself all the way to and from Chase's tower. As arrogant as she was, there was a chance she'd made a mistake, and he refused to be idle for the three hours before he and Tatyana were scheduled to meet.

He jerked on a pair of jeans and pulled a heavy sweater over his head then attached the sword to his belt. Finished, he called Clayton at home. After explaining his fiancée had been kidnapped last night, he told him about David.

As expected, Clayton promised immediate and total action, including sending tech crews out to tap the phone lines for when the ransom calls came in.

Roman knew there'd be no ransom calls, but he held his tongue. He wanted the human authorities involved in case Chase wandered up to a constable somewhere wearing an evening gown and no shoes. They needed to be on the alert for her, and this was the best way to accomplish it.

After he hung up, he went in search of Martin. He found him in the dining room, setting out dishes, while David stared at a cup of coffee.

When Roman walked, in David jumped up. "Where's Chase? What's happened to her?"

"She's been kidnapped," he said without preamble. "I've been out searching for a trace of her, but I haven't found one. So far." He did his best to keep the bleakness from leaking into his voice. From David's expression, he hadn't succeeded.

"She's dead, isn't she?" he moaned into his hands. "I should have taken her home when we first realized there was a threat."

He didn't want David to bear the burden of his guilt, so Roman put a hand on his shoulder. David looked up, surprised at the contact. Capturing David's eyes, Roman radiated comfort. He needed the man functioning. As some of the despair eased from his aura, Roman removed his hand and sat, still maintaining eye contact. "David, this isn't your fault. You did everything possible. Chase is still alive. She's being held somewhere for ransom. If they'd killed her, I'd have found a body."

He hated to lie, but no way could he admit the truth—they'd talked to each other via telepathy. He needed David to brief Clayton, but he had to be careful what he said in case Ileana was listening.

"I've called Scotland Yard, and they're on their way here to talk to you and put taps on the phones. I need you to brief them for me. Tell them everything you can remember, but don't mention any suspects, because we have no proof."

David nodded, much calmer than before.

Roman released his eyes. "I'll find her in time, David. I promise." He wasn't sure if the promise was to David or to himself.

Following Chase's lead from Friday night, Roman went to the study and thought long and hard. Then he wrote a lengthy note to David and Martin explaining the kidnapper could be listening to all conversations in the house, and they needed to be extremely careful about everything they said to each other as well as to the inspector.

He told them if they needed to speak to each other or to him about sensitive information to please do so in writing. He asked them not to mention Ileana to each other or to the inspector, as he didn't want to give her a reason to kill Chase. Finished, he went back to the dining room and gave David and Martin the note. Martin read it with a look of comprehension, David with raised eyebrows. When they'd each nodded their acquiescence, Roman turned to leave.

"What are you going to be doing?" David asked.

"Well, I've been up all night trying to find her, and I'm dead on my feet. So right now, I'm going to take a short nap," he lied. "After that, I'll head back out and start looking for her again."

"You'll find her—you *have* to."

"I know." Roman patted him on the shoulder and left. Once out of the dining room, he veiled himself and slipped through an open window in the drawing room. Satisfied he'd covered his tracks, he headed across the fields searching for any trace of Ileana's scent.

Wherever she'd hidden Chase, she had to have gone there at least once before she grabbed her. Roman thought it unlikely that Ileana had driven there. No, she ran. He was sure of it. According to Chase, there were no traffic or animal sounds nearby. That meant the place was remote. It also meant there probably weren't any roads leading to it.

The thought of his mate sitting in some rat-infested dungeon infuriated him.

'*Hang on, love,*' he called. '*I'll find you.*'

⁂

Drake groaned at the knock on his door. If he kept getting interrupted, he'd never get his damn paperwork done. When the thump was repeated, this time with more urgency, he cursed and tossed his pencil on the desk.

"You might as well come in," he growled. "You've already destroyed my concentration."

"Sorry, boss," Gray said, poking just his head in. "But Roman's here to see you. He says there's a problem. Chase is gone."

"She's gone? You mean she left him?"

The door flew open as Roman pushed his way past Gray without waiting for an invitation. "Hell, no, she didn't leave me. We've mated. She's been kidnapped."

"Kidnapped?" Drake repeated.

"By Dillon?" asked Gray.

Roman blinked. "What? No, by Ileana. Who's Dillon?"

"Never mind," Drake ordered. "Just tell us what happened."

As Roman brought them up to date, Drake picked up his pencil and rubbed his fingers over it like a worry stone. How in the hell had he missed it? He'd investigated Dillon's relationship with Ileana and should've put two-and-two together. He hadn't, so he now had to bear some of the responsibility for what had happened to Chase.

He didn't realize how hard he was squeezing the pencil until it snapped in two. Disgusted, he threw the pieces in the trash. "How can we help?"

"I need trackers," Roman said. "I talked to Chase this morning by Werespeak, and Ileana's got her locked up in some old tower on a moor somewhere. But I've no idea where to search."

He glanced at his watch. "I'm meeting Tatyana at the Keller estate in thirty minutes to see if she's come up with anything. If not, we may have to search every ruin on the island."

"Gray, get a hold of Danyer." Drake fished his car keys out of his pocket. "And alert the pride. I want every available man here waiting when I get back." He beckoned to Roman. "Let's go."

☙❧

Inside the Kellers' neat, well-kept barn, Roman found Tatyana sitting on a bale of hay. Dressed in a beige silk pantsuit and Italian shoes, with a sword identical to his on her belt, she looked utterly out of place.

She glanced up as he and Drake came through the door. "Ah, good. You brought us some help." Smiling, she rose to shake hands. "Hello, Drake."

"Tatyana." He brought her hand to his lips. "As beautiful as ever, I see."

"And you're as much of a charmer. Have you been brought up-to-date?" When he nodded, she moved on to Roman. "It looks like you took my advice about food and rest," she said. "I'm proud of you."

"Well, as you pointed out, I'm no good to Chase if I can't function." He gave her a quick peck on the cheek and settled himself on a bale of hay beside Drake. "What have you found out?"

"I spoke to Ambersey at The Council this morning." She retook her own seat and crossed her legs. "He's furious that Ileana would risk our exposure like this. I told him we have no proof that the culprit really is Ileana, but everything points to one of our kind, and she's the only one with motive. He understands, but he's sending out a 'locate and hold order' on her regardless, which means if we find her and she resists, we're authorized to destroy her. If they do pick her up and she can convince them she's innocent, they'll probably let her go and rescind the order."

"I may be able to add some weight to your argument," Drake offered. "I caught one of my pride spying on Roman's place just after Chase arrived. An investigation into his whereabouts over the last month leads me to believe he and Ileana have been planning this for a while."

Roman stared at him. "How so?"

"On Ileana's orders, Dillon made a trip across the pond shortly after Roman's father did, first to New York, then to California. Los Angeles."

"He followed my father to New York.?"

"Not to attack him," Drake assured him. "He just told him about Chase being part Were and suggested he go to California. Apparently, Dillon kept them both under surveillance while in Los Angeles. Then he flew back to England the day before Chase and her human partner arrived at Heathrow."

"So Ileana set it all up," Tatyana mused. "Why would Old Man Fernwood go along with it? He loves Roman. He'd never do anything to hurt him."

At Roman's muttered curse, Drake grinned and winked at her. "Yes, but his attempts to find him a wife are the stuff of legend. Some of my pride started a betting pool on whether or not he'd mate a human, just to get the old man off his back." He looked from one to the other. "Will your Council accept evidence from someone other than a Vampire?"

"Not as a rule, but the members of The Council aren't fools. They've been around a *very* long time, and Ileana's young by the standards of our kind. If they can question her, they can break her. But first we have to find her."

"And do it soon enough to save Chase," Roman said.

She nodded. "Yes. Ambersey agrees finding your mate is our first priority. He suggested sending out a call for volunteers to help find her, but I said no. If we put out the word to our kind, someone might tip Ileana off. We can't take that chance."

"I'm assembling a group of trackers who know how to keep their mouths shut."

Drake's tone left no doubt in Roman's mind what would happen to anyone who spoke out of turn. Hope resurfaced. Chase had been right about involving him. With enough tigers to help in the search, they might find her before nightfall.

"Have you had any luck narrowing down our search areas?" he asked Tatyana.

"Yes and no." She grimaced. "I think that we should start on the moors. *Wuthering Heights* takes place on the moors. Not that I'm suggesting that we start looking in Yorkshire. But I think the idea of a ruin on the moors, with the turbulent weather and violent storms that are common there, would appeal to Ileana's sense of dramatics."

"I agree," Roman said.

Damn, he wished he could tell her he'd spoken with Chase this morning and knew she was on a remote moor, but he couldn't. He caught Drake's eye and guessed he was thinking the same thing. It was forbidden to reveal Werespeak to anyone who wasn't a Were.

"Also, I've been thinking," she said. "Ileana wouldn't use anything she found in these books. Because if she had, and she knew you suspected her, which she must have if she was watching your house, she'd have hidden or destroyed the books. Since she didn't, we have to assume they're false clues."

Roman stood and raked his fingers through his hair. Christ, he hated all this lying, subterfuge, and role playing. "So we're back to square one?"

"Such a pessimist," Tatyana scolded. "Sit down and have a little faith. As I was saying, she won't use a ruin in the book. She'll use something still undiscovered by humans. However, as the humans have learned, where there is one ruin, there are usually more.

Not to mention there are also hundreds of follies on private property."

A slow grin curved Roman's lips. "These books will tell us where the discovered ruins are, which is what Ileana used them for, isn't it?"

"Exactly. I think the book to concentrate on is the one I found out of place on the top shelf in the library. I looked through that book thoroughly last night, and I think that some of the remote areas in that book would be best."

She pulled out a large map of Great Britain with red circles drawn on it. "Some of these areas to the north are quite remote at least for Great Britain, and they were in that book but not the others. I think we should start there."

"That's quite an area to search," Roman complained. "I also had an idea earlier. I think that Ileana probably scoped out the place where she took Chase to make sure it was escape proof so—"

Tatyana cut him off. "Scoped out? You need to hire an interrupter. I think you've spent too much time around Chase."

Reminded of the laughter in the study last night, Roman chuckled. "Not enough time, Tatyana, love. Not nearly enough time."

"I know, dear." She patted his arm. "Go on with what you were saying."

"I want to start at Ileana's and back track all her recent scent trails. If you're right, and I think you are, Ileana moved up her schedule because of pressure from Drake on Saturday afternoon. So she must have settled on this place between Drake's visit and when she grabbed Chase. I figure she made at least one trip, probably unveiled, to prepare the place prior to kidnapping Chase."

"That's a good point. She wouldn't have seen the need to veil for trips she made from her place." Tatyana tapped her fingers on her chin. "If we're to follow Ileana's old trails as well as seek out these ruins, we'll need a lot of help. How many tigers can you spare?"

"Ten," Drake said. "Eleven if Danyer is still—" His cell phone jingled. "Yeah, Gray, what is it?" He listened, his eyes narrowing. "He did what?" His breath huffed out in a long exhale. "Call Danyer back, tell him the situation, and suggest he get his ass over to my place pronto. I'm on my way."

Snapping his phone shut, he turned to Roman. "Zakhar Fedorov arrived this morning. He's demanding custody of Chase, or else he'll challenge me for leadership of my pride."

"Jesus," Roman muttered. "Can't you just tell him she's mated and left to be with her mate?"

"I can try." He took Tatyana's map, studied it, and handed it back. "I'll get my pride to follow Ileana's scent. You guys start on the ruins," he said as he headed for the door.

Roman watched him leave, concern furrowing his brow. He couldn't leave Drake to fight off Fedorov and his minions alone.

"He'll be okay, Roman. The other pride leader won't challenge him if there's no chance of claiming Chase."

"We can only hope." He sighed. "Okay, where were we?"

"We need more help. Can you think of anyone we know we can trust not to report to Ileana?"

"What about that French couple who came to Ileana's wedding? You told me they were very good friends of yours, but they don't like her."

"Claude and Marie! Yes, that's a good choice. And you're right, they don't care for Ileana. I'll call them right now."

She flipped open her cell phone, dialed, and spoke rapidly in French for several minutes. When she shut off the phone, she was smiling.

"We're in luck. Claude has four houseguests and when they heard the situation, they decided to come and help. He has a lot of influence, and he's more than willing to do anything he can to thwart Ileana. Especially when he heard The Council is after her. They're leaving France within the hour and will call me as soon as they get here."

"Tatyana, flights between Paris and London are usually sold out way in advance."

"Claude's a pilot and has his own jet."

"So by late this afternoon, we'll have eight of us, plus the tigers, searching. That improves our chance of finding her."

"Yes. Until they get here, we should start with these ruins in this smaller area here." She circled a spot on the map with her finger. "It's much closer than those other places I wanted to search."

"That's fine. I'll search with you until your friends come, and then I'll take one person with me and head over to Ileana's and start backtracking trails. We need to work in groups of two or more. I don't want anyone searching alone, in case they happen upon Ileana."

"That a good point. We'll need Chase's scent for our searchers. When we hear from Claude, can you go home and get some of her clothes and catch up with us later?"

"That won't be a problem." Roman stood and pulled Tatyana to her feet. "If you're ready, I suggest we get started. Every minute she's missing, she's that much closer to death."

⌖⌖⌖

By the time Chase got the strip off the lid of the barrel, it was nearly sundown. All but one of her nails were broken, her hands were filthy, and the front of her gown was torn and dirty. But she held up the metal strip in triumph.

Now if it would just work. She climbed on the cot and began to pick at the concrete with the end of the strip. At first, it was slow going. Her hands were tired and sore and her bare feet were freezing from being on the stone floor all day. Not to mention, she was hungry. God, was she *hungry*!

She wasn't sure if she was as hungry as she thought, or if it was that she knew she had nothing to eat that made her stomach complain so loudly. When the light faded to the point she could no longer see the cracks in the concrete, she laid the metal strip on the floor under the cot.

As she hobbled over to the barrel for a drink, she realized the rain had stopped, and she had no way to wash her hands. Disgruntled, she removed the lid and bent over the barrel. Sticking her face down to the water, she drank her fill. She'd get out of this place, and when she did, Ileana would pay.

A little queasy after her drink, she went back to the cot and curled up under her blanket, thinking about Roman. She'd tried to contact him several times and gotten no response. Once she'd thought she heard his voice in her mind, but when she called to him, he didn't answer. Now that it was night, maybe she should try again.

'Roman? Are you there? Can you hear me?'

'Chase! Thank, God. I've been trying to reach you all day.'

'What do you mean? I've been right here. Where the hell have you *been?'*

'Searching for you, love. But I don't know which sections of the island to search.'

'How much of Great Britain is moorland?'

'Quite a bit, I'm afraid. But don't worry. We'll find you.'

'Hurry. Please. If Ileana comes back and sees what I'm doing, she won't wait to let me starve.'

'What are you talking about? What are you doing?'

'I'm digging my way out. What the hell do you think I'm doing?'

'You're digging your way out of a stone tower?'

He sounded so exasperated she nearly smiled. *'Did you expect me to just sit and wait for her to kill me?'*

'No, but I suppose it would be too much to hope for that you'd wait for me to rescue you.'

'If I could be sure you'd find me.' Tears stung her eyes. *'I miss you, Roman. I'm cold, hungry, and I'm...I'm scared.'*

'I know, love. Christ, Chase, I'm so sorry I got you into this. If I had known—'

'Don't!' She could hear the anguish in his voice, and it broke her heart. *'Don't blame yourself. That's just what Ileana wants you to do. None of this is your fault. I'll get out of here. I found something I can use as a pry bar, so I'm knocking the concrete off the bars in the window of my cell.'*

'Jesus, love. You said you're two stories up. The fall could kill you.'

'I've got a blanket. I'll make a rope.'

'Oh, of course. Why didn't I think of that?' The sound of his sigh in her mind was oddly comforting. *'Just be careful, okay. And don't give up. I will find you. I promise.'*

'I know. I trust you.'

'Sleep well, love.'

Sleep well? Yeah, right. She hadn't had the heart to tell him about the suspicion growing in her mind. If she was right, he'd find out soon enough, anyway.

∽∾∽

Roman searched for ruins with Tatyana. While their superior vision allowed them to find several old towers—though none the humans hadn't already discovered—none of them had a dungeon or tower prison holding Chase. And there were thousands of these things in Great Britain.

When Claude called from Heathrow, Tatyana ran to meet them while Roman headed home. Thankfully, the drawing room window was still open, though someone had pulled it partway closed. It was a close fit, but he made it.

Still veiled, he sped through the house to his room. Then he dropped the veil and started going through Chase's clothes, pulling out those with the strongest scent. He'd just decided he probably had enough, stuffed everything into a bag, and was preparing to veil again, when there came a quiet knock on the door.

"Come in."

Martin stepped into the room. "Ah, sir. Do you have a moment? I need to see you in the study."

"I'm rather in a hurry, Martin. Is it important?"

"Indeed," Martin said, with a nod and a finger to his ear.

Roman understood. This was something Martin couldn't say aloud. "Certainly." He followed Martin up the stairs to the study. "How did you know I was in my room?"

"I didn't, sir. I've been knocking every ten minutes for the last two hours."

"I see." Roman shook his head, amazed at the old man's devotion.

Martin walked over to the desk, picked up a note he'd obviously written in between his constant trips to Roman's bedroom, and handed it to him.

> *Your father called this afternoon. He'll be finished with his business early, by the end of the week, in fact, and wants Wilson to pick him up at the airport. I told him some things had come up and I would need to speak with you and call him back. He wanted to know what the problems were, but I told him I couldn't say. I'm afraid, sir, he's not very happy with me at the moment. But I did get the number of the hotel and his room number.*

His father! With everything going on with Chase, Roman had completely forgotten about his father. He patted Martin on the shoulder and sat down at the desk. Hell, his father was supposed to be in New York for a month. Why did he want to come home early? No matter. He couldn't. Ileana might take him hostage, too, and kill him, along with Chase, to inflict maximum pain.

"Martin, can you find David and ask him to come to the study?"

"Certainly, sir."

After he'd gone, Roman picked up the phone and called Andy Wright at home. "Andy, it's Roman."

"Roman. What can I do for you?"

"I'm sorry to bother you on a Sunday, but I'm badly in need of your help."

"Anything, old chap, anytime."

"What's your schedule like for this week?"

"Clear. What's up.

"Can you get away to make trip for me?"

"Of course. Anything I'm working on that can't wait until I get back, my partner can handle for me. Your family is always my first priority, Roman. You should know that by now."

"Thank you."

"What's the problem?"

"Chase Alcott has been kidnapped."

Silence. Roman could feel the tension on the line. "Andy?"

"Er—she was—kidnapped? She didn't just get pissed and go home?" He cleared his throat. "Naturally, I'll help, Roman. Anything I can do. Anything at all."

"I need you to pack for a weeklong trip to America, leaving today. But before you go to the airport, I need you to come out here and bring any stamps or seals you need to legalize some transfer documents. Can you do that?"

"Yes. I can be there in half an hour."

Roman glanced up as David entered the room "Thank you, Andy. I'll be waiting."

Motioning David to a chair, he handed him a bank draft.

"What's this?"

"Payment for the work you and Chase performed. The job's finished, and you were successful at finding the murderer."

"But it's more than twice what your grandfather promised us."

"I understand that, but I have another commission for you. One that will help Chase if you're willing to take it on."

David looked up, hope glowing on his face. "Absolutely."

"Great. Then go pack your things and meet me back here in half an hour."

David looked confused but didn't argue. Once he'd gone, Roman wrote a note to Martin asking him to open the drawing room window a little farther and not to allow it to be closed. When he'd given Martin the note, Roman veiled himself and slipped through the window. Running as fast as he could, he headed away from the estate. He covered over thirty miles in five minutes. Deciding that was far enough away Ileana couldn't hear him from any point on or near his estate, he called Tatyana on his cell phone.

"Roman. Where are you, dear? We're waiting at the airport for you."

"Sorry, but Father called. He plans to come home next weekend. I'm sending Andy Wright over there to stop him and need another hour. Why don't you take them back to the Kellers' barn, and I'll meet you there?"

"You think your father coming home is a problem?"

"Don't you? What's to prevent her from killing him, too?" He swallowed hard. "I have to concentrate on Chase. I can't afford any more distractions."

"Yes, of course. I understand. We'll meet you there in an hour."

Roman hung up and called the airport, booking two tickets to New York on a flight that evening for Andy and David. Then he called his father at his hotel in New York and explained what was going on. His father was relieved he'd finally found someone to marry but horrified he'd lost her again in such a manner. He agreed to wait for Andy and David in New York and go with them to Los Angeles until Roman gave the all clear for him to come home.

Since he'd done all he could to resolve this latest crisis, Roman veiled himself and took off for home. When he got back to study, David was waiting for him.

Roman went to his desk and wrote a note detailing the problem with Lord Fernwood and the need for David to fly to New York with Andy, pick up the old man, and take him to Los Angeles.

Finally, he added a line asking David and Andy not to discuss this until they were aboard the plane. He handed the note to David.

As he read it with slowly widening eyes, David's already strained face paled, but he gave a "thumbs-up" and mouthed, "Okay."

"Thank you, David. I promise I'll call you the minute I have any news one way or the other. Try not to worry too much. I will find her."

"Yeah."

Roman rose as Martin showed Andy into the study. "Thanks for coming."

"What documents did you need legalized?"

Roman handed him the documents Chase wrote out on Saturday afternoon. "Chase is transferring all her property in America to David. She prepared these and signed them with me as a witness. Do we need to do anything before David can take legal possession of the property?"

Andy cleared his throat. "America's a stickler for what they call 'notarized signatures.' We don't have anything quite like that, but as your attorney, Roman, and based upon your word, I will attest she signed the documents."

Roman and David both swore it. Andy took Roman's seat at the desk, opened his briefcase, and went to work.

"There, that should do it," he stated half an hour later. "I added a couple of seals to make it look official. As Americans are quite impressed with seals, this should be good enough."

He passed the papers to David as Roman handed him the note. Andy read it with his eyebrows sliding up his forehead.

"Your tickets are waiting for you at the British Airways ticket counter at the airport," Roman said. "Please don't delay."

Once they'd left, both looking a little dazed, Roman ran to his room and grabbed the bag of Chase's clothes. Veiling himself and the bag, he slipped out the drawing room window and headed for the Kellers' at maximum speed.

As he walked in, Tatyana and her six Vampire friends were looking at her map and jabbering away in rapid French. Five of the six had short swords like his, attached to their belts. The sixth, whom Roman recognized as Claude, had a long Scottish broadsword in a scabbard strapped to his back.

"Finally!" Tatyana said when she saw him. "I've already been to Ileana's for a bag of her clothing, but we need Chase's."

Roman distributed Chase's clothing to everyone present. As the Vampires memorized her scent, Roman paced, his hands balled at his sides, trying not to lose his temper.

Words such as, "Heavenly," "Delicious," "Delectable," "Enchanting," and phrases like, "If the young lady looks as good as she smells, I may kidnap her myself when we find her," all uttered seductively in heavily-accented English, had him clenching his teeth so hard if he'd been human, he might have broken his jaw.

Only Tatyana seemed aware of his discomfort. "Relax, dear," she said, laying a hand on his arm. "They're French. What do you expect?"

Roman nodded but couldn't relax. When the guests were sure they could recognize Chase's scent, Roman yanked her clothes away from them and stuffed them back into the bag.

"Roman and I will search the scent trails leading away from Ileana's house," Tatyana said. "The rest of you search for ruins."

Roman snorted. Smart move. She was probably worried he'd throttle Claude or one of his friends. She was right.

After agreeing they'd search until midnight and then meet back at Tatyana's, they all exchanged cell phones numbers and promises to call with any news, no matter how trivial. Then they veiled themselves and took off into the setting sun.

Holding hands so they could sense each other through the veils, he and Tatyana headed for Ileana's. Once there, he led her toward some of the trails he'd discovered that morning. When he halted their momentum, they dropped everything but the scent veils so they could confer.

"How far are we from Ileana's northern boundary?" Tatyana breathed in a voice so quiet Roman almost couldn't hear her.

"About a mile," he answered just as quietly. "But we don't know where she'll be hiding."

"No, we don't. But even Ileana can't be in two places at once. So she can't be here and watching your house at the same time. I think we're safe."

"Are you sure that she's still watching my house?"

"I am. You've been veiled every time you left or returned, but she's still able to hear what's going on inside. She's probably camped somewhere on your property listening to your conversations and rejoicing at the pain in your voice while you rush around trying to find Chase."

A low, deep growl rose in his throat. "When I get my hands on her—"

"Should we go over there and try to find her?"

He shook his head. "No. Even if we found her, we couldn't make her talk. Let the Council deal with her." He glanced at his watch. "They should be here soon. You told them to start looking at my place?"

"Yes. So what do you want to do here? Do you want to split up?"

"Let me think." He ran through the options in his mind. "I need someone to watch my back. I'm stronger than Ileana, but her thirst for revenge has made her dangerous. If someone wants to kill you so badly that they don't care whether they survive the fight, they're more fierce and unpredictable." He shrugged at her raised eyebrows. "The Japanese used that tactic in the human's Second World War."

"Then we'll search together."

"We'll have to go unveiled or we won't be able to smell her trails."

"So where should we start?"

"We'll pick one and start tracking it to see if it heads in a likely direction after a while." He pointed out one that looked promising. "Let's follow this until we know where it's going. If it doesn't lead anywhere useful, we'll double back and start over."

Roman left the bag containing Chase's clothes in the high branches of a tree at the edge of the woods so it wouldn't conflict with Ileana's scent but missed the comfort the smell of her clothes gave him. Tatyana took his hand, as he stood beneath the tree looking up at the bag, and led him to the trail they'd selected.

He tried several times to contact Chase and, when he got no response, prayed she was only sleeping.

Ileana's trails ran through the neighborhoods and countryside, but none of them led off in a direction that would take them out of the inhabited parts of Great Britain to the moors.

Finally, Roman called a halt, telling Tatyana to go home to her guests. They agreed to meet back at the point where they'd stopped as soon after first light as possible, but for now, they both needed to hunt and get some rest.

As he was collecting the bag of Chase's clothes, he heard her voice in his head.

'*Roman? Are you there? Can you hear me?*'

'*Chase! Thank, God. I've been trying to reach you all day.*'

As Chase updated him on her situation, his heart swelled with pride—and drummed with terror for her safety. She was digging her way out, but Christ, if Ileana discovered it—

He could only hope The Council caught the murdering bitch soon.

He sensed Chase getting weaker and noted her hesitation when she admitted she was scared. Part of this, he knew, could be the enforced-separation-psychosis. Yet, he also knew her human side and his Vampire side should minimize that problem. Still, he feared she was withholding important information about her condition.

When their conversation ended, Roman wrapped himself in the scent from her clothes and headed off to hunt.

Why couldn't he find the tower? What was he missing? Had Ileana prepared Chase's prison long ago in hopes it would someday prove useful? Had she intended to use it for Melinda then changed her mind? If so, he might never find it.

A Vampire's scent lasted for weeks, despite rains that could wash away a Were's scent in a matter of hours. But it didn't last forever, and if it had been more than two months since Ileana made the trail to Chase's tower, he wouldn't be able to track her.

Discouraged to the point of losing his appetite, he forced himself to hunt and, in the back streets of London, saved a man from being murdered by having the murderer for dinner.

Chapter 15

June 9th:

Chase woke to a gray morning. Rain splashed on her face. A raging wind blew sheets of water through the window and onto the bed.

Her dreams had been filled with Roman. Images of their passionate lovemaking lingered in her mind.

'*Roman? Can you hear me?*'

Silence.

She groaned as the lust pooled in her groin—and it wasn't just because of her dreams. Her heat was growing stronger.

When she tried to sit up, she groaned for another reason. Her arms and upper body ached, her muscles complaining about the abuse she'd heaped on them. Hunger raked its claws through her belly, yet thinking about food made her nauseous. She told herself to stop whining and get on with it. Throwing the blanket off, she struggled to her feet.

The room spun and tilted.

"Whoa, head rush," she moaned as she flopped back on the bed. "Better try this a bit more slowly."

Easing her legs over the edge of the cot, she rose to a sitting position then cautiously stood.

"That's better. It's going so long without food that's making me woozy. I hope. Wonderful crash diet, though. I'm bound to lose that stubborn ten pounds and more. It'd be perfect, except for the side effects, dizziness, nausea, and oh, let's not forget death."

Sighing at her own black humor, she headed off to the chamber pot and then to the water barrel. As she looked at her filthy hands, she cursed Ileana again for not providing a cup. How could it have hurt to leave her a drinking utensil? What was Ileana afraid she'd do—saw her way through iron bars with a tea cup?

Stupid, frigging Vampire.

Thank God, it was raining again. She stalked over to the bed, sat it on end, climbed on it, and stuck her hands out the window. The rain was so heavy, her hands and arms were soaked in minutes, along with her hair, face, and the top of her gown.

Rubbing her hands together vigorously, she cleaned off as much of the dirt as possible and climbed down.

She started to rub her hands dry on her dress then had a better idea. With the metal strip from the lid, she cut a large piece of fabric from the gown and dipped it in the barrel until it was soaked. Then she washed her face and cleaned the rest of the dirt from her hands. Much better. Though she was in desperate need of a shower, she felt almost human again—well, as human as a half-weretiger got.

After getting her drink, she tried to contact Roman again. When he still didn't answer, she grabbed the metal strip, crawled on the cot, and continued her excavation of the window bars.

She worked slowly but steadily and refused to stop even when she was so dizzy and nauseous she was sure she was going to puke. By the time it was too dark to continue, she managed to dig out almost three bars. *One more day*! *If Ileana stay's away tomorrow, I'll be out of here by noon.*

Where the hell was Roman? She hadn't heard from him all day. If he didn't come soon, he might as well not bother. She'd just get out by herself.

Exhausted, she crawled under her blanket, but the lust that had plagued her while she worked kept her tossing and turning on the cot, unable to sleep.

"Stop it," she growled at her body. "I'm too worn-out to be horny."

Damn it all to hell! Someday, by God, she'd make Ileana sorry for this. She really wanted that bitch to pay.

e/ɔe/ɔ

When Roman met Tatyana at first light, Claude and his friends, along with Danyer, and Drake and his men were waiting with her. Roman organized them into pairs and set them to retracing the scent trails they hadn't gotten to the day before.

Before Drake could take off, Roman snagged him by the arm. "What happened with Fedorov?"

"The man's an ass," Drake growled. "No wonder he doesn't have a mate. I told him Chase was mated. I also told him she'd disappeared, and no one knew where she was. Though I'm not sure he believed me on either count."

"Is he sticking around?"

"He didn't say, and I didn't ask, but I wouldn't put it past him. I'm glad you've already claimed her, but..."

"But, what?"

"I seriously doubt the fact she's mated will stop him. It looks like you were right. It's going to get ugly."

Roman looked around and spotted Tatyana embroiled in an argument with Claude and Marie. He turned back to Drake and lowered his voice. "I've been in contact with Chase twice. Then suddenly yesterday I couldn't reach her."

"You may have been out of range. Werespeak is only effective up to about four-hundred miles, give or take fifty or so. Where were you when you spoke to her?"

"Once at my place. The other time at Ileana's."

"She neighbors your place. Where we are here is quite a ways south of there. Can you contact her now?"

Roman tried, shook his head.

"That means wherever Chase is, she's between three hundred-fifty to four hundred-fifty miles north of your place."

"Scotland?"

"It could well be. Look, I'll take Gray and see if we can find any connection between Ileana and any place in Southern Scotland."

"Thanks. I'll have the searchers head north." As Drake headed off with Gray, Roman turned to the group. "I'd like to concentrate our efforts in a ninety-degree fan due north of Ileana's house."

He and Tatyana started down a promising scent trail, only to dead end in a meadow.

Trail after trail proved no better, but Roman was sure they were on the right track. "We just have to keep trying," he told Tatyana. "We'll have better luck tomorrow. We've narrowed down the remaining options and there aren't that many left."

"Most of these trails lead to places Ileana likes to go on her daily runs. If I were trying to hide a trail to some place secret, this is how I'd do it."

He kissed her cheek. "Go home and hunt with your guests. Meet me back here at first light. We'll finish the rest of the trails tomorrow, and if we don't find anything by midnight, we'll give up and start searching ruins. How long can they stay and help?"

"Claude says they'll stay as long as it takes," she said with grin. "Apparently, he's having a marvelous time, and he's determined not to give up a chance to make things difficult for Ileana."

She gave him a quick hug and took off. Roman headed for London to hunt, feeling in his soul that he was close. He'd find her prison tomorrow. He had to!

c⁄ɔc⁄ɔ

June 10th:

Chase woke feeling weaker, dizzier, and more nauseous. Raging lust had kept her from sleep most of the night. She was beginning to understand what Roman meant when he said she'd take any male that offered. Thank God, they'd mated, and she'd been saved from being a slut. Though it wasn't much help to her now, damn it.

She clenched her thighs together. Christ, where was a dildo when you needed one?

Lying under her blanket, trying not to scream with anger and frustration, she forced herself to concentrate on escaping.

She rolled slowly out of bed and stumbled through her morning routine—chamber pot, water barrel, metal strip. She figured she had several hours of work left, but if she could keep going, she'd have an opening big enough to squeeze through. Determined to escape, but certain Ileana would return before she finished, she worked as diligently and feverishly as her weakened condition allowed.

Her frayed nerves twitched with every thrust of the strip into the concrete. Hating the noise, convinced Ileana would hear it, she compelled her muscles to continue the action repeatedly—strike, thrust, and pry. Strike, thrust, and pry.

When she finally levered the third bar out of the window, she nearly burst into tears. She'd done it!

It was still raining, so she couldn't see the sun, but as close as she could tell it was early afternoon on Tuesday. She'd been missing for three days! Why hadn't Roman found her? How hard could it be to find a stupid tower on a moor? If he could Werespeak to her, surely, he could locate her prison. Of course, she hadn't heard from him since the day before yesterday. He sure as hell had some explaining to do when she got home.

But first, she had to get out of this damn tower.

She grabbed the metal bar and used the end of it to start tears in the blanket, ripping the material into wide strips. These she knotted end to end to make a rope. Praying it would hold her weight, she tied one end to the bars still secured in the window, propped the cot up on its end, climbed up, and struggled through the hole with the rope clutched securely in her hands.

Frigid rain slapped her in the face, while the wind tore at her, threatening to rip her away from the tower. Gritting her teeth, she planted her feet on the outside wall and, using the rope as a counterweight, leaned backward and repelled her way down to the ground.

She was free! Tears ran down her checks and mixed with the rain, as she realized the magnitude of what she'd accomplished. Now all she had to do was to get as far away from here as possible before Ileana returned.

'*Chase?*'

'*Goddammit, Roman, where are you? I've managed to get out of the frigging tower, but I don't have a clue where in the hell I am.*'

'*Calm down, love, just—*'

'*Don't you tell me to calm down! You have no idea what I've had to do to escape. You said you'd come for me, but you didn't even answer when I—*'

She broke off, horrified. Why was she acting like this? She wasn't usually such a bitch.

'*I'm so sorry, love. I tried to contact you, but you must have been out of range or—*'

'*No, don't, Roman. None of this is your fault. I'm the one who should apologize. I don't know what came over me. It's not like I don't know how hard you're trying.*' She took a deep breath, wiped her eyes. '*I'm not really blaming you, even though it sounds like I am.*'

'*It's all right, love. I understand. Now, look around you. Tell me what you see.*'

'*Pretty much just what I saw out the window. Rolling hills, covered with this coarse-looking grass.*' She bent down and plucked a blade of it, rolled it between her fingers. '*The grass is thick, rough, and sort of sharp, not at all like what's in a lawn. There're lots of these purplish, flowering plants. I can't smell them with the rain and the wind, but if I had to guess, I'd say they were heather.*'

'*Have you ever seen heather?*"

'*I've seen pictures.*'

'*Okay. Anything else?*'

She looked around. '*There're some mountains in the distance almost the width of the horizon, but they're a long ways off.*'

'*Can you still see the tower?*'

'*Yes.*'

'*Describe it to me.*'

She glanced over her shoulder, turned. '*It's made of beige stone. Short, only a couple of stories, and squat, um, fat, I guess you could say. No, wait, I think it had another story, but that one's crumbled. There're building stones all over on the ground. What else? Oh, yeah, it's sitting on a little rise. Steep, but not really high.*'

'*Okay. Are there any other buildings around? Is the tower part of a larger structure?*'

'*There's nothing around but the tower. It doesn't look like it was part of anything. Just a tower in the middle of nowhere.*' The bareness of the landscape made the hair on the back of her neck prickle. '*Roman, I can't stay here. There's no cover. If Ileana comes back, I'm screwed.*'

'*Then get as far away as you can. Try and find some place to hide.*'

'And if I can't?'
'Just keep moving. I'll find you.'
'Hurry. Please.'
'I will. I love you, Chase.'
'I love you, too.'

Picking a direction at random, she started running. She had no idea where she was going, but wherever it was, it had to be better than where she'd been.

When the tower was no longer visible behind her, she dropped to the ground, panting—and sobbing—from pain, exhaustion, and frustration. She'd practically dug her way out of that frigging cell with her bare hands, and by God, she deserved a warm bath, a hot meal, and some scorching sex!

Since she wouldn't get any of them lying on her ass in the rain, she forced herself to her feet.

The land around her became harsher and harder to traverse as the day wore on. Or maybe she was just weaker and more exhausted. How much of this was from lack of food, and how much was from the enforced separation from Roman—or for other reasons—she didn't know, but she knew she had to keep going.

She tripped and fell countless times, scratching her face and hands on the rough vegetation, ripping her dress, and once even tearing a hunk of her hair out by the roots.

Her smell was spread all over the ground behind her, making it easy for Ileana to track her. Would the rain wash away all traces of her scent? She couldn't count on it, so she looked for a river or stream. She'd heard stories of people who, when being chased by bloodhounds, trekked down the middle of a stream to hide their scent from the dogs. With her luck, a Vampire's noise was sure to be more sensitive than a bloodhound's.

Stumbling over some kind of plant root, she fell to the ground again, so tired and weak she could hardly breathe. The rain pounded down on her. The wind whipped her hair about her face and pressed her sopping wet dress against her body, chilling her through and through.

She didn't want to get up and move but she knew if she didn't, Ileana would find her and drag her back. Or she'd freeze to death where she lay. Summoning her remaining willpower, she forced herself onto her hands and knees, then to her feet, and staggered forward.

ϵ∕つϵ∕つ

As Roman talked with Chase, terror for her filled him. She was out of the tower, but nowhere close to being out of danger. God help him, but he wished she'd stayed put. If she chose the wrong direction, she'd put more distance between them.

Adding to his worries was the fact the building she'd described resembled no ruin he'd ever heard of, nor did the land sound familiar. Damn it, she had to be within four hundred-fifty miles of him, so why the hell couldn't he find her?

As he followed yet another trail with Tatyana, his cell phone rang. He yanked it out of his pocket, flipped it open. "Yeah?"

"Roman, it's Drake. I think we've found it."

"Thank God! Where?"

"Southern Scotland, near the upland moors. Ileana had a lover a few years ago, a Scottish Vampire named O'Malley."

"I've never heard of him."

"He's a bit of a recluse. His name came up in my investigation of Ileana, so Gray and I tracked him down at his house in London. Turns out he owns a huge chunk of real estate in Southern Scotland. There's an old folly on the property, a tower, out in a remote section of heath."

Roman closed his eyes, prayed. "Do you know what it looks like? Is there a description of it?"

"According to O'Malley, it's fat and round. Used to be three stories, now it's only two."

"That's got to be it."

"Yeah, that's what I thought. We're heading to the airport. Claude and the others are with us. We're taking his plane. But at the speed Vampires can run, you two can probably get there faster that way."

"Just tell me where to go."

"Head for Dumfries. There's a small landing strip not too far from there, where the glider club meets. O'Malley's people will meet us there and take us as far as the quarry. I've got a map to the folly. We'll find it."

"Can O'Malley be trusted?"

"I'm not sure any Vampire can be trusted, but considering O'Malley's reaction when we mentioned The Council, I think it's safe to say he won't tip off Ileana, if that's what you mean. He's not too pleased with her for involving him in the first place."

"Okay. I'm on my way." Roman snapped his phone shut and beckoned to Tatyana. "Drake found it. Let's go."

By the time they got to the airstrip, Drake and the others were piling into four Range Rovers.

"Hop in." Danyer called, waving them over to one of the cars. "We're heading for something Drake here calls a folly, whatever the hell that is."

"A folly's a structure built mainly for decoration," Roman said as he and Tatyana climbed into the Rover. "Usually one that doesn't serve much purpose."

Danyer shook his head. "You English are something else."

Their driver rolled his eyes, started the car, and pulled onto the main highway, at the head of the convoy. Once on the O'Malley property, he turned down a narrow dirt road and headed east, toward a sky growing darker and more ominous with every passing minute.

By the time they reached the spot where the road dead-ended in a quarry, a raging storm buffeted the car.

Reluctantly crawling from the warmth and protection of the Range Rovers, they set off on foot, following Drake's map. They trudged over the moorland in silence, battered by fierce, gusting winds that hurled sheets of icy rain at them, biting their exposed skin and leeching the heat from their bodies. Roman shuddered to think how Chase was faring, barefoot and dressed only in a thin, silk gown.

Two hours into their ordeal, they crested a hill and came upon the tower, standing like a beacon on the next rise.

Roman stopped dead, staring at it. It was exactly as Chase had described it. Forlorn and solitary, it rose up toward the sky like a giant admonishing finger. Building stones from the crumbling third floor littered the ground. A doorway at ground level held the broken remnants of a wooden door.

Drake and Danyer came up beside him.

"That has to be it, don't you think?" Danyer said.

"Yes, but she's not there."

'Chase, I found the tower. Where are you, love?'

'I'm lost, damn it. I don't have a frigging clue where I am.'

'Which direction did you go?'

'How the hell should I know? There's no sun in this goddamn country so—wait, toward the mountains. I headed toward those mountains on the edge of the horizon.'

'Okay. Find a place to hide and wait for me.'

'I can't. Someone's following me. I don't know if it's Ileana, or someone else. But I can't let them catch me.'

Fear slammed into him, twisting his insides. *'How do you know someone's there, love? Have you seen them?'*

'No. Not exactly.' She hesitated. *'I've...sensed them.'*

'Chase, you—'

'Look, damn it! Don't ask me to explain it. I just know they're back there.'

'Keep moving then, heading toward the mountains. I'll catch up with you as soon as I can.'

"What is it?" Drake asked as Roman broke contact with Chase.

"She says someone's following her. She sensed them."

Drake cocked an eyebrow. "You say that like you don't believe her."

"Of course, I believe her, but she's—"

"She's tuning into her tiger," Danyer interrupted. "It's a survival thing. In the wild, tigers are solitary animals. They don't have the advantage of a pack or a pride. They have to depend on themselves. As Weres, we sense danger before it hits us. Chase is half tiger, son," he said, his voice hard. "She's not a Vampire or a wolf, so you'd better be prepared to accept her for what she is. 'Cause you ain't gonna change her."

Roman's jaw clenched. "I don't want to change her. I just want her back."

"Good." Danyer clapped him on the shoulder. "Let's go find her."

cscs

Battling the gale that fought her for every inch she gained, Chase stumbled through the afternoon, putting as much distance as possible between herself and the tower.

She hadn't meant to be so bitchy when she spoke with Roman, but she couldn't seem to help it. Sighing, she pressed a hand to her churning stomach. Between the pain of her tiger trying to shift and this unrelenting nausea, it was hardly surprising she was in a foul mood. Not to mention, the whole situation just plain sucked!

As the light faded, she came upon a large lake. It wasn't a stream, but it *was* water.

The only drawback, other than getting hypothermia, was that if Ileana noticed her footprints going into the lake, all she had to do was run around the perimeter until she saw the footprints coming out. Still, it would slow her down and give Chase more time to get away.

She had no idea how far civilization was, or in which direction. She'd just have to keep moving until she found help. Debating her options, she realized she was stalling. The water looked freezing, and she was already so cold her skin was turning blue.

Gritting her teeth and grasping the tattered remains of her will-power, she took a deep breath and stepped into the lake. Not knowing what water would do to a digital tape recorder if she had to swim, she kept close to the edge.

The rain beat down on her head and shoulders. Mud oozed between her bare toes. As she slogged around the lake, she was more miserable than she could remember being since the night of her parents' death. It took her over an hour to make her way far enough around to suit her.

Her feet numb, her teeth chattering so hard she was sure they'd be knocked loose, she staggered out of the water and dropped to the ground just beyond the mud line. She shook violently, her whole body jerking. If she stayed here, she'd die of hypothermia. She had to get up. She *had* to. Still, it took her almost fifteen minutes to force herself to her hands and knees so she could crawl onto the rocky ground surrounding the lake. Struggling to her feet, she stumbled on.

Though the terrain here wouldn't retain her footprints, they'd still be visible in the mud along the shore, and it wouldn't be hard to discover where she'd come out of the water. There had to some way to throw Ileana off her trial.

For another hour, she followed the shoreline around the lake, going in the same direction she'd been traveling when she walked through the water. If the rain failed to wash away her scent, the precaution was pointless, but it was the only plan she could come up with. When she reached the point where the shore curved back toward the tower, she turned and continued heading for the mountains as Roman had asked.

If this doesn't work, I've wasted a lot of precious time. No, it would work. It had to.

She rubbed her arms vigorously, trying to warm herself. It didn't help. Tired as she was, she couldn't stop to rest. Even if Ileana didn't find her, she'd freeze to death before morning. Her only defense was to keep moving.

By the time the rain stopped, the moon was setting, and she was several miles away from the lake. She found a small depression that was fairly dry and filled it with grass. Covering herself with vegetation to keep warm, she slipped into an exhausted slumber, praying she'd wake tomorrow.

೮∕೨೮∕౩

Roman led Drake and Danyer over to join the rest of the search party gathered around the tower.

Claude was staring up at the window Chase had obviously escaped through. The blanket rope she'd tied to the remaining bars was still there.

"This woman, she is very clever, no?" Claude said. "I see why someone took her. I would have taken her myself."

Roman growled, but before he could do anything more, Marie walked up and slapped Claude across the face hard enough to knock him to the ground. Laughing, he jumped to his feet, grabbed her, and kissed her passionately.

Drake raised his eyebrows.

Roman shrugged. "They're French. What do you expect?"

He scanned the group. "Chase has been on the moor for about three hours now. It's raining, so we won't find her scent. We need to cover as much ground as possible, keep going in a northward fan toward the mountains. We'll work in groups, with each group taking a different direction. Criss cross back and forth so you don't miss any clues."

He turned to Tatyana. "Would you mind going with some of Drake's tigers? I'd like to put a Vampire with each group of tigers so we make the best use of our diverse abilities."

Her eyes narrowed, but she nodded, turned, and joined three tigers heading northeast.

"Somehow, I don't think she bought that," Danyer whispered under his breath.

"No, I don't think she did. But I needed you, Drake, and Gray with me. I told Chase to head for the mountains, but that covers a pretty broad area."

Roman could hear the others in the distance calling, "Chase!" and wondered if she'd answer a stranger's voice. Maybe. As long as it wasn't Ileana's.

By midnight there was still no trace of her and everyone dispersed to hunt. Roman was tempted to stay out and keep searching.

Drake clapped a hand on his shoulder. "We all need food and rest. Even after we find Chase, we still have to deal with Ileana and Fedorov—and however many bad asses they bring to the party."

"He's right, son," Danyer said. "And you can bet your ass the bad guys will be in top form. They always are."

☙❦❧

June 11th:

They regrouped at first light and started searching again. Roman headed off in the same direction as he had the day before, with Drake, Gray, and Danyer close on his heels. They grid-searched, looking for any sign of her. Now that it finally quit raining, they had a chance to pick up her scent.

Suddenly Drake yelled, "Roman, over here."

On the stub of a broken branch of a heather plant was a small piece of cinnamon colored silk. On a plant right next to it were a few strands of cinnamon colored hair.

"At least we know which direction she took," Gray said. "Shall we call the others and all of us search this direction?"

"Yes." Roman phoned Tatyana and asked her to bring the others over.

They didn't have to wait long. Soon seven Vampires and eight tigers could be seen streaking across the heather. Once reunited, they all began following the path of broken heather and pieces of silk.

Claude laughed and held up a much larger piece of Chase's gown. "At this rate, by the time we find her, she'll be nude." The glee in his voice had Marie hissing at him.

"Either Marie's going to kill him," Drake growled softly to Roman. "Or I will."

"Marie really should be used to him by now," Tatyana whispered. "They've been together four hundred years, so none of this should come as a surprise to her."

Marie looked over and winked at them. Obviously, she'd heard them, but Claude was too busy expounding the virtues of finding Chase nude to eavesdrop. Roman reined in the urge to teach the Vampire some manners and focused on the search.

The sun was high in the sky when they came to the lake. Roman found Chase's bare footprints on the shore.

"Was she getting a drink or wading through the water, do you think?" Gray asked.

"Well, her footprints go in, but I don't see them come out," Roman replied. "She's still trying to disguise her scent." He sighed. "I'm glad she's smart, but if she keeps this up, I'll be chasing her forever."

Looking for more footprints, they walked along the lakeshore. It was Claude who found the next set, showing where she'd come out. It erased some of Roman's anger toward the Frenchman, until he mentioned what sexy feet she must have to make such delicate footprints.

Figuring her new direction from the angle of her footprints, they returned to searching for her scent, hoping at last their ordeal might come to an end.

'*Chase, we're at the lake. Where the hell are you?*'

Deafening silence was the only response.

გარ

Chase slept until midday when the discomfort of having to pee finally woke her. In a daze, she relieved her bladder, struggled to her feet, and plodded on again. Weak, nauseous, tired, and aching, with her feet torn and bleeding, she concentrated on the simple task of taking one step after another. *I will not give up. I will not give up.* She repeated the words over and over in her mind like a mantra.

I will NOT give up!

After walking for what seemed like days rather than hours, she came to a small stream. Too parched to care if the water was safe or not, she scooped it up in both hands and drank. Deeply. When her thirst was finally satiated, she paused to take a closer look at the barren landscape.

Her gaze suddenly sharpened as she focused on a field of coarse grass just beyond the stream. Birds' nests. Dozens of them. It surprised her at first, but as she glanced around, it made sense. Where else would they nest? There weren't any trees.

She waded across the stream. At her approach, the birds fluttered away from their nests, leaving left their eggs, small but plentiful, lying within easy reach.

Finally, some luck!

Without knowing or caring what kind of birds they were, she picked up an egg and shook it, trying to see if she could hear it slosh. She didn't want baby birds, only raw eggs. That thought made her already-queasy stomach churn even harder.

No, she told herself, she couldn't afford to be finicky. When she was in college, her roommate had a brother on the football team who'd eaten raw eggs for breakfast every morning. If he could do and even enjoy it, Chase figured she could handle swallowing a few in an emergency.

Cringing, she cracked one open then sighed with relief when it was just an egg. So hungry it actually looked appetizing, she scarfed it down without even tasting it then did the same with a half a dozen more. She went back to the stream for some water to wash them down, grabbed a few eggs for the road, and took off again, thinking she might actually make it back to Roman.

The land started changing, the coarse grass and heather-like plants slowly giving way to other types of vegetation. A few trees appeared. Here and there she passed a cottage, but when she went to ask for help, she found them abandoned. She was utterly alone out here. She hadn't washed for days, hadn't had a regular meal.

Still, she'd had raw eggs and water, and she was alive. What more could she ask?

She was from Los Angeles, after all, and those people were tough. She'd show that stupid English bitch she couldn't kidnap an American, lock her in a tower, and expect her to just stay put and take it!

She looked behind her, wondering how far she'd come—and how far she still had to go.

'*Damn it, Roman, where are you?*'

Chapter 16

June 12th:

Swamped by despair as June eleventh became June twelfth, Roman refused to stop to hunt or rest. Instead, in the wee hours of the morning, he returned to the lake with Drake, Gray, and Danyer in tow.

"Chase can't tell me the exact direction she headed, because she doesn't know, and there aren't any landmarks in the area to give us a clue. She said she tried to outsmart Ileana, but I think somehow she's outsmarted us all."

He was losing her. Every time they talked, he could feel her growing weaker and more despondent, suffering from exhaustion, hunger, her heat, and the enforced separation. Although the effects of the separation were reduced thanks to their Werespeak and the fact they were both half-breeds, he still felt her personality being altered. She was angry and resentful one minute, weeping and needy the next. If he didn't find her soon, there'd be nothing left of the woman he loved.

Their only chance to find her was to catch a scent trail she'd left after the downpour ceased. He thought back to when the storm ended and tried to calculate how far Chase might have gotten before then.

"Try to think like a cagey private detective," he told his three cohorts, pointing to the remnants of her bare footprints. "One trying to throw off any pursuit."

Drake nodded. "Which is undoubtedly why she walked through a lake of ice-cold water during a raging storm. It's not like she wouldn't have been wet enough already."

"What are the chances that fucking Vampire's really behind her?" Gray asked.

"Chase senses someone following her, but doesn't know who it is," Roman said. "I'm as worried about Fedorov following her as I am about Ileana."

Drake picked up a small stone and skimmed it across the surface of the lake. "Or they could both be following us, waiting for us to lead them to Chase."

At his words, they all scanned the landscape. While there was no sign of Fedorov, that brought Roman little comfort. Ileana could be standing right beside them, and if she was sufficiently veiled, they'd never know.

A chill skittered down his spine. He shook it off. First, he'd find Chase then he'd deal with the consequences.

Damn it, he wanted her back! His fear for her life was punishing—a constant terror and an aching loneliness in his heart, more painful than anything he'd ever known. He'd been too young to really comprehend the night his parents died, so the anguish he'd suffered then had been mild compared to this.

"Spread out and head in some unexpected directions," he ordered. "And let's see if we can outsmart Chase for a change."

*e*ɔ*e*ɔ

Chase moaned as another wave of pain tore through her gut. If Roman was right, it meant her tiger wanted to shift. She wished to hell the cat would get it over with. But no. The ache was continually increasing then ebbing. Increasing then ebbing.

"Shift, goddammit." She groaned and pressed both hands on her stomach. "Put me out of this misery."

Her body was already in agony from her deteriorated physical condition—weak and nauseous from hunger and thirst, her feet bleeding, her skin dry and irritated. Why did her tiger side insist on torturing her, too? Shouldn't there be some advantage to having these special genetics?

Other than her enhanced abilities of sight, hearing, and smell—

all of which had grown exponentially in the last few hours—her tiger half had brought her nothing but a clawing pain in her belly and a lust so fierce she'd screw a frigging tree, if she could find one with smooth enough bark. And she feared before the day was over, she'd be so horny she'd even risk the splinters.

God, she missed Roman, and not just for the sex. She missed his scent, his warmth, his understated British humor, the way he looked at her.

His voice and emotions radiated increased concern, every time they talked. Who could blame him? She'd been acting like an idiot. A bitch one minute, a sniveling baby the next. Their conversations had grown uncomfortably tense over the past day, and she knew it was her fault. She just didn't know what to do about it.

Oh God, not again. She lurched forward and doubled over as her stomach purged its meager contents. "How can I keep puking when I've hardly had anything to eat?"

As she wiped her mouth off on the skirt of her gown, her arm brushed her chest. She winced. Her breasts, tender and sensitive, throbbed where her arm had touched. She could think of only two reasons for her breasts to be that tender. Either her heat was affecting them, or she was pregnant. She'd suspected it for some time and could no longer convince herself she was imagining things. Pregnancy would also explain her violent mood swings and constant nausea. Her hormones were going crazy.

She had to keep it from Roman. At least until she could tell him face to face. If she didn't make it, it would kill him to know his child had died with her.

But damn it, how the hell could she still be so horny if she was pregnant? It hardly seemed fair. Shouldn't her heat have ended at conception? Or was this something else she didn't know about cats.

The moon was setting. Unable to sleep due to the lust, and now with perfect night vision, she'd just kept walking. According to her watch, it was now two in the morning.

Her ears twitched as she caught the sound of something familiar. Was that a cow mooing? Instinctively, she opened her mouth and tasted the air. Yes. Cows. Their scent was faint, probably because they were a long way away. The problem with having superhuman senses was they gave you information about things too far away to do you much good. Still, the scent of prey gave her a direction.

She headed for them then paused. If she did shift, the clothes she was wearing would be shredded unless she had time to remove them first. Unlikely, considering it was her first time, and it would probably be instinctive. She looked down at her gown. It was torn and ragged, but she had enough material for what she needed.

Tearing pieces out of the skirt, she removed the tape recorder from her bra, fashioned it into a long necklace, and hung it around her neck. If she ended up naked, at least she wouldn't lose her evidence.

Satisfied, she headed in the direction of the cows. Cows meant people, and people meant help. They could tell her where she was, and Roman could finally come for her.

൦ൟ൦

Roman inhaled deeply, searching the air. "Chase says she scents cows, and she's heading in that direction, but I can't smell a thing."

"Sounds like her sense of smell has finally caught up with her tiger side," Danyer said. "If so, those cows could be miles away."

Drake studied his map in the fading moonlight. "There's only one village in this area, and if that's where the cows are, we're going in the wrong direction."

"Shit," Gray growled. "It'd be nice if we could get a break. One fucking break is all I ask."

Roman looked over Drake's shoulder at the map. "We may have just gotten one. Since we know where she's headed, we can meet her there."

"Unless the cows aren't at the village," Drake pointed out. "Though, I can't imagine they'd be roaming free out here. O'Malley said he doesn't allow free-range domestic animals."

Roman calculated direction and distance to the tiny dot on the map, his heart easing for the first time in days. "It's the best lead we've got. Unless, you guys have a better idea, I say we head for the village."

CRACR

Roman filled his nostrils with Chase's scent, which was slowly but steadily getting stronger. Finally, they were on the right track.

It would be light in a few hours. His energy was flagging. He needed to hunt soon, or he'd collapse. But he couldn't take the time to do it now.

They were closing in on Chase, and his need for her was critical. He could always hunt later. Lord above, but he hoped she'd listened when he told her to wait in the square by the fountain.

He didn't want her interacting with humans in her weakened condition—unless absolutely necessary—since he couldn't guarantee she wouldn't shift at an inappropriate time.

He couldn't wait to hold her and comfort her and see for himself if she was okay. When Drake first told him about the village, Roman had wanted to head north at Vampire speed. However Drake, Danyer, and Gray had convinced him that leaving the three of them behind was folly. He might need their help to defend Chase.

Still, running flat out at the other three's fastest speed, they'd made good time, covering over a hundred miles in just under two hours. As exhausted as the four of them were, Roman could feel the adrenalin start to thicken the air as they neared the village. The long ordeal would soon be over. Once he got Chase back, he was never letting her go again.

As he crested a hill and saw the village below, he heard her voice in his mind. His blood turned to ice.

'Roman, help!'

CRACR

Drake saw the look on Roman's face and grabbed his arm. "What is it?"

"Chase's in trouble," he growled, jerking free.

Danyer sniffed the breeze. "Fedorov and his men. I can smell them."

As Roman took off so fast he was nothing but a blur, Drake stripped off his clothes, signaling for Gray and Danyer to do the same. "How the hell did they find her?"

"Could be they're the ones who were following her," Gray pointed out.

"Most likely," said Danyer. "Or else they split their forces, since there are four of them. Had a couple following her, and the others glued to our asses. Probably communicating by cell phone."

"Bastards." Naked, Drake set his tiger free. Chase was a member of *his* pride, damn it. No one was taking her against her will. If Roman couldn't take out that arrogant Lithuanian asshole, Drake bloody well would.

Racing toward danger with Gray and Danyer at his flank, his blood fired at the thought of a showdown.

Fedorov would soon learn not to mess with *his* family.

☙❧☙

Chase found the cows in a field adjacent to a small, picturesque village. She stumbled into town so weak and tired she could barely put one foot in front of the other. She'd made it. She was safe! Roman knew where she was, and he was coming for her.

The village was bigger than she'd expected. There was a pub, a gas station, a church, several dozen quaint little cottages, and a lighted, red payphone booth. To her right was the village square with a fountain and several benches.

Roman had told her to wait for him by the fountain. Dragging with exhaustion, she tottered over to one of the benches and collapsed onto its wide wooden seat. She closed her eyes and tried to tune out the numerous aches and pains in her battered body. It didn't work. Then a scent drifting on the breeze registered in her tired brain. Her eyes shot open, and she tensed.

Two men watched her from across the street. Something about them raised her hackles. Her nostrils twitched again.

Tigers? What the hell were they doing here? Were they part of Drake's pride, looking for her? Or from some other pride? If so, how had they found her when even she didn't know where she was? As she studied them in the starlight, she saw their auras were almost black.

Oh, God, these were the ones who had been following her. She recognized the air of menace radiating from them as the same one she'd sensed on the trail.

She couldn't stay here. She had to find help. Struggling to her feet, she hurried away as fast as her aching body would allow. They followed, keeping their distance. One of them pulled out a cell phone.

Shit.

As adrenalin surged through her, easing her aches and pains and chasing away exhaustion, she picked up her pace, slipping down a side street. Not a single house showed lights inside. Where were the people? Oh, right, they were asleep. It was still the dark side of dawn.

The side street was shadowy and unwelcoming. She decided to turn at the next corner and head back to the main part of town. She needed to find a place to make a stand.

If she had to fight them, she wanted to do it soon, before reinforcements arrived. With a little luck, she could do enough damage to make them decide there was easier prey somewhere else. She'd just about reached the corner, when two more men came around it, cutting her off.

'*Roman, help!*'

Out of options, she backed up to the wall of a building that edged the street and braced herself. One of the men beckoned to her, a sneer on his face. His scent was feral, his eyes filled with a dark hunger. When she shook her head at him, his smirk widened. Her tiger responded, clawing at her stomach, drunk on anger, fear, and adrenalin.

'*Chase?*'

'*Roman! Where the hell are you? I've got tigers up the ass here and could really use some help right about now.*'

'*I'm coming, love. Try to hold them off a few minutes until I can get there.*'

'*Don't think they're going to give me a choice. Oh, shit!*'

The men closed in.

'*Chase? What is it? What's happening?*'

'*Busy, here. Can't talk now.*'

'*No! Chase!*'

Ignoring Roman's terrified scream in her head, she focused on the one who'd gestured to her. He was bigger than the others and seemed to be the leader of the pack. With his dark hair, intense eyes, and arrogant demeanor, he radiated male power as he sauntered toward her. He came to a stop in front of her, his eyes silently commanding her to submit.

Like hell, she would.

Her chin shot up. His eyes narrowed, hardened. Then he slapped her.

She gasped and cupped her stinging cheek. "You bastard!"

Running her tongue over her lip, she tasted blood. Pain seared her stomach. She wanted to scream, from the agony and the fear of what was happening to her, but she knew better than to show such a weakness.

Between one heartbeat and the next, her whole reality changed. Her bones and muscles stretched, liquefied, expanded, and re-formed—heavier, stronger. Massive. Powerful. Ready to defend. She heard her gown rip, felt her clothes fall away.

Her head and chest surged forward, her front paws hitting the ground. '*Yes!*' her tiger roared with joy. '*Free. Free, at last.*'

Energy surged through her veins, setting her blood aflame. Like a series of electric shocks, it pulsed from her nose to the tip of her tail. Power. Pure, unadulterated power. *Oooh. Mine.* It felt sooo good. So right. She tingled with glee. *Oh yeah, I could really get used to this*!

She shook her head, rolled her shoulders. Her eyes focused on the big male. Now also in tiger form, he loomed over her, growling. As if he could intimidate her. The son of a bitch had struck her. Payback time.

Her battle cry a scream of rage, she charged him, claws extended, canines bared.

ფოც

As Roman raced for the village, he heard Chase roar and knew she'd shifted. Although, he wished he'd been there to help her through the transformation, he was grateful she'd managed it on her own. As a tiger, she'd have a much better chance of defending herself.

Charging into the village, he followed the sounds around the church and down a side street—a dark, narrow lane, filled with tigers.

Three unfamiliar males stood in a semicircle, watching another male, who had to be Fedorov, fend off an enraged, white-coated Siberian female. Chase!

Snarling and spitting, she charged Fedorov, but she was no match for him. Despite the adrenalin that had to be swarming through her system, she was too weak from the hunger and exhaustion he saw in her aura to be much of a threat to the huge male. Silent as a thought, Roman rushed toward the fight.

Fedorov lunged at Chase, knocking her off her feet. His teeth clamped on the back of her neck as he tried to straddle her.

Roman plowed into him without bothering to shift. He'd discovered in his last battle with a tiger that a wolf was no real threat to a big male. He'd have to fight as a Vampire. They rolled into the street, the cat's mammoth claws ripping huge gashes in Roman's flesh.

Instead of backing away to catch her breath as Roman expected, Chase plunged into the battle. Before he could shout at her to break off, she leaned back on her haunches with Fedorov's tail clamped in her jaws. Fedorov snarled, spun, and slashed her with his claws.

Roman saw the blood, spreading like red dye over a white sheet. His mate's blood!

Blinded by rage and fueled by a hatred so dark it nearly erased his conscience, he gave the soul-deep hunger inherent in his Vampire nature control of his mind and body.

Nothing mattered but draining his target. No life remained in his universe but himself and the man who'd dared to harm his mate. Pain, love, fear, and exhaustion vanished from his existence.

Freed from all distractions, Roman's vision narrowed to the male's throat, while his fangs strained toward the jugular. He lunged and hit the tiger mid-back. The momentum sent them rolling into a stone fence. As they slammed to stop, Roman flipped the beast on his side and sank his teeth into the vein in Fedorov's neck.

Hot blood flooded his mouth and raced down his throat—life-giving blood, chock-full of the adrenalin of anger, lust, and "flight or fight." Strength flowed through his veins, healing his injuries, washing away the weakness and growing psychosis of the enforced separation, returning power to his weary body.

He drained Fedorov completely and felt a surge of satisfaction when he felt the man's heart sputter to a stop. Finished, he stood and tossed the body aside.

Chase sat on her haunches a few feet away, watching him quietly. He started for her then hesitated as he realized what she'd witnessed. Would she still believe he wasn't a monster after seeing that?

She cocked her head and studied him. Then she reared up on her hind legs, propped her front paws on his shoulders, and licked his face, her sandpaper-like tongue catching on the rough stubble on his cheeks.

Choking on laughter and relief, he hugged her furry body. She shifted, and suddenly his arms were full of naked woman. They tightened around her, pulled her close. '*Mine.*'

'*Mine,*' she echoed.

A snarl at his back had him spinning around and shoving her behind him.

Two tigers Roman recognized as Drake and Gray—and a massive beast that could only be Danyer—stalked toward the three remaining tigers who tucked their tails and ran. Judging by the way Drake and the others gave chase, Fedorov's men wouldn't get very far.

Roman returned his attention to Chase.

"Are you okay," he asked, taking off his jacket and slipping it on her.

"Yeah, but I'm—" She put her arms around his neck and wriggled her groin against his. "Horny, hungry, dirty. And I think I'm pregnant."

"Well, let's get you home, so you can get clean and—what?" He stared at her, certain he hadn't heard right. "Did you say you thought you were pregnant?"

She nodded. "Pretty sure, considering how nauseated and bitchy I've been."

On the heels of the joy that had him crushing her against him came the fear of what her ordeal might have done to the child. "Are you sure you're all right? Don't you need to lie down? You shouldn't be standing up in your condition." He couldn't think.

Didn't know what he needed to do for her. "No, wait. I should take you to the doctor right away. I—"

"Stop." She laughed and halted his babbling by putting her fingers on his lips. "I'm fine. We're fine. Shifting healed all my injuries. We just need food, a bath, and you. God, I need you."

"Then we're even because I—"

"Well, isn't this a lovely family reunion?"

Rage and fear boiled up in Roman's mind. He pushed Chase back and turned around to face his enemy.

"Ileana."

She stood several feet away, with her sword in her hand. Tension rolled off her. Roman could almost see it in the air as she stared at Chase. He knew what she was thinking. The vengeance she longed for was so close. If she could distract him, she could have her revenge with one quick stroke of her blade. He drew his sword and stepped toward her.

"How did you find us?" he asked, his voice light and conversational.

She sneered. "I've been following you for several days. I came back to the tower to check on her and discovered she was gone. Then I heard your voices in the distance. So I veiled and followed." She gave him a mocking smile. "I knew you'd find her eventually. You led me right to her."

"You'll never touch her. I'll never let you near her."

"Oh, really? How are you going to stop me?"

He could hear the madness in her voice and see it in her eyes. He wouldn't have thought vampires got mental illnesses. Apparently insanity was one disease they were susceptible to.

Ileana watched him warily. "I won't do it tonight. I'll do it sometime when you least expect it. Sometime before the baby's born. Let you get used to the idea. It'll hurt more that way."

"The Council's looking for you. Once they find you I don't think you'll be hurting anyone."

Hysterical laughter bubbled from her throat. "I'll just tell them it's all a misunderstanding. I'll say I went to my house in Romania after your party on that Friday night and have been there ever since. All my servants will swear to it. You have absolutely no proof." She jerked her chin at Chase. "And your sweet little detective's testimony won't hold any evidence value." She twirled her sword around in a circle. "So for the next several months, no matter what you do or where you go, you'll constantly have to worry about when I'll show up to take your family away from you."

Chase moved out from behind him to stand at his side. She looked exhausted and more than a little ragged around the edges, holding his jacket closed with an arm across her chest. Her head high, she stared Ileana straight in the eyes. Roman put his arm around her shoulders.

"I'm afraid, Ileana, that his 'sweet little detective' *does* have proof."

Ileana just sneered at her. "What, you think they'll listen to you because you're half-Were? You're also half-human, and you don't count. No matter who you are."

Chase pulled a long piece of cloth from around her neck and unwrapped his digital tape recorder. "They may not believe me, but I'm sure they'll believe you. Everything you said on the night you kidnapped me is recorded. I imagine The Council will recognize your voice."

"You're lying," Ileana snapped. "I don't know where you got that, but you didn't have it around your neck the night I carried you to the tower. And even if you did, you've been out in the weather so long, it won't even work."

Chase rolled her eyes and played with the buttons on the machine. She held it up. Ileana's voice came out of the recorder clear as a bell, musical, cold, calm. It sounded very deadly.

"I'm not going to kill you tonight."

Ileana hissed.

Chase smiled sweetly and shut the recorder off, before sticking it in the pocket of his jacket. "See, I told you. It's all on there. Melinda's murder. The dead animals in the garden. The missing items from the house. Oh, I want my pearls back, by the way."

Her voice was calm and matter-of-fact. "I have your whole confession. All of it. I wonder how The Council will feel about you risking the exposure of Vampires by killing innocent humans."

Ileana stared at her. The horrified disbelief on her face might've been amusing, if she weren't insane and lethal.

Pride filled him. Chase had kept her head and given him what he needed to stop the bitch. He tightened his arm around her, all the while keeping his eyes on Ileana.

A snarl ripped from Ileana's throat. She raised her head. Something about her body language told him she was getting ready to attack, not him but Chase. He started to push her behind him, but she was already moving, probably tipped off by the same thing.

Ileana charged at her, the sword raised high above her head. Roman stepped forward and parried her thrust. Their swords sang from the blows. He was stronger than Ileana, but her desperate need for vengeance made her fearless. She screamed at him and tried to lunge around him. She didn't want to fight him at all. She only wanted to get at Chase.

He and Ileana swung, thrust, and parried, almost as if dancing on the cobblestone street. Though their movements were soundless, the clang of their swords rang out, harsh and loud, in the still night. He hoped no humans came to watch.

Out of the corner of his eye he saw three naked men standing next to Chase. Drake, Danyer and Gray. Obviously, they wouldn't interfere. Confident if he lost the fight, they could protect Chase and his child, Roman relaxed just a little.

Sashaying from side to side, he and Ileana continued their deadly dance. He was hampered by his need to stay in front of Chase, to protect her. Ileana was hampered by her need to find an opening to kill her. Their distractions made them evenly matched.

This could go on all night! He had to find a way to end it. He was sure Ileana could see the men standing by Chase, but she didn't seem to consider them a threat.

Perhaps he could use that. He began moving to the side, slowly easing away from Chase, trusting Drake and the others to protect her. Initially, Ileana mirrored his moves. He shifted another few inches sideways, all the while parrying her vicious thrusts. Ileana eyed the opening he'd created. She hesitated for a fraction of a second. Roman moved again.

It was too much of a temptation for her. She lunged around him, heading for Chase. Drake stepped in front of Chase just as Roman stepped behind Ileana. She didn't seem to register the danger. She was too focused on Chase. Roman lunged forward and, with one sure blow, sliced off her head. It rolled away into the street.

It was over!

Before Roman could secure his blade, Chase was at his side, hugging him fiercely, kissing every part of him she could reach.

He picked her up and swung her around in a circle.

"Don't do that," she pleaded. "You'll make me throw up."

"Sorry," he murmured, stopping his swing and setting her on her feet. "Lord, I've missed you so much! Are you sure you're all right?"

"I will be. As soon as the world stops spinning." She raised a hand to her head.

"Chase?"

"I'm fine, don't worry."

He caught her as she fainted.

ᴇⱭᴇⱭ

Chase came to on Roman's lap, his arms wrapped around her, his lips kissing her filthy hair. They were sitting in the middle of the dark side street. She opened her eyes and looked up at him.

"What happened?"

"You fainted."

"We need to move, Roman," Drake whispered urgently. "Now that the noise has stopped, the humans may come to see what caused it."

"I know." He got to his feet, still holding Chase cradled in his arms. "You go ahead. Don't wait for us." As Drake and the others turned to go, Roman called out to them, his voice barely more than a whisper, but fervent with gratitude. "Thank you—for everything."

"Most fun we've had in years," Gray gave Roman a mischievous grin. "I imagine Claude will be rather disappointed that he wasn't here when we found her, especially considering her state of undress."

Roman tensed. "Indeed."

Chase didn't understand his reaction. She was about to ask who Claude was when Roman crushed her against his chest and charged from the village.

Her vision dimmed. She blinked. Instead of the pre-dawn morning, they were surrounded by a thin, black fog the thickness of a gauze veil. "Are we veiled?"

"Yes."

"Oh, well, this isn't so bad. Nothing like what Ileana did to me."

"The bitch could have done it this way, but she probably wanted to terrify you."

"It worked. But..."

"But what?"

"If we're veiled, why are you running so slow. You said you could run four hundred miles an hour."

"I can." He hesitated. "You're pregnant. I have to take it easy with you."

"I see. And how far are we from home?"

"About three hundred and fifty miles, more or less."

Exasperated, she rolled her eyes and glared at him, though the anxiety in his expression made it hard to maintain. "At this rate we won't get there till August."

"You're in a delicate condition."

"Because I'm pregnant?"

When he nodded, she sighed. "What is it about men that they think pregnant women are invalids? We've been known to work until going into labor and even deliver our own babies. I don't think you need to coddle me." When he didn't pick up the pace, she snarled, "If you don't mind, I would like a meal, a bath, some hot sex, and a long sleep in a bed. Now. So *move* it, buster!"

He broke into a grin, tightened his hold on her, and took off. She loved it. Laughing breathlessly, she leaned back and let the world fly by.

"Almost there," he said after a while. He slowed his run and pointed to the house rushing to meet them. Slipping noiselessly in through the side door, he carried her to his room.

Dropping his veil and releasing her, he let her slide down his body, pleasuring them both. "Go take a shower. I'm going to go get you some broth. You need something easy on your stomach after fasting for so long."

She dropped his jacket on the floor and grabbed her toiletry bag. In the bathroom, she indulged in the almost sensual pleasures of brushing her teeth, washing her face and hands, and trimming off her broken fingernails.

She was combing the debris from her hair when Roman came back with a large cup full of the most marvelous smelling liquid.

Dropping the comb, she reached for the cup with a small moan of longing.

He laughed at her reaction, picked up the comb, and continued working on her hair, but not before she'd seen the naked hunger in his aura as he looked at her.

The rich broth hit her system with the force of an adrenalin rush, warming her insides and giving her a sense of well-being. She finished it quickly, placed the cup on the counter, turned into his chest, and wrapped her arms around him, breathing deeply with contentment. He dropped the comb and returned her hug. His arms felt wonderful. He was the only man she'd ever want.

And boy, did she *want* him! She was about to tell him when he beat her to it.

"I love you so much, Chase. You can't begin to know how much I missed you and wanted you back in my bed."

She swiveled her hips against his erection. "I think I have a tiny clue."

"I want you so much right now, it's all I can do to keep from losing control. I know you're in no condition at the moment, but that doesn't change how I feel."

She could hear the yearning in his voice, and it thrilled her. "So are you planning to take a shower with me?"

"Do you want me to?" he whispered, his voice low and husky with desire. "Are you sure you're up for this?"

Soft laughter bubbled up inside her. "Oh, yeah. I'll even let you help me wash. Cats like to be clean, you know. So you better hit *all* the spots."

She squealed as he chased her into the shower.

THE END

If you enjoyed Blood Fest: Chasing Destiny, turn the page to read an excerpt from the next book in the series:

Blood Fest

Cursing Fate

by

PEPPER O'NEAL

Chapter 1

A weretiger compound outside a remote Lithuanian village, eighty miles from the Polish border, June 16th:

It had to be tonight. Now, while the house was quiet. While the pride leader and his henchmen were out of town, and the human guards they'd left behind were sleeping.

Right *now*. Before someone came in and discovered what she'd done.

Tabbi closed her eyes and swallowed hard, guilt and fear clogging her throat. Her gaze skittered to the floor then away. Dear God, she could scarcely believe she'd really done it—but the guard had left her no other choice.

She eased off the bed, trying to ignore the complaints of her broken skin and bruised muscles. Weretigers healed rapidly, especially if they shifted into their tiger forms. But there was no time for that now. If she could just stay alive long enough, she'd be okay.

Wincing, she pulled on jeans and a T-shirt and secured her flyaway, waist-length hair in a ponytail. After she'd gathered the few personal items she owned, she removed a loose floorboard and retrieved the neck bags she'd hidden underneath. It had taken her six months of planning and scheming to make the bags and gather the needed supplies—and some critical information—but she and the children couldn't travel without these minimal necessities.

The guard's body lay cooling beside the bed. Tabbi had originally planned to overpower him when he locked her away at night, but his ever-rampant lust and cruelty had forced her to kill him. She cringed at the claw marks on his face, and the gaping wound in his neck, but his fate had been decided the moment the pain from his fists caused her to shift. At least this time, she'd escaped being raped.

She knelt and emptied his pockets but pulled out only crumpled money, coins, and rolls of hard candy.

Damn it all, where were the keys? He had them when he came in because he'd locked the door behind him. Struggling to control her mounting panic, she rolled him over and almost passed out from relief when she heard the metal-on-metal jingle. She unhooked the key chain from his belt loop, grabbed the bags, and crept to the door.

In her rush to get out of the room, she fumbled the keys and dropped them. The harsh clatter as they hit the floor echoed through the silent house, nearly stopping her heart.

Shit!

She held her breath and listened. Nothing. Either she'd gotten lucky and hadn't woken the guards—or they were lying in wait for her. *Get a move on*, ordered a little voice in her mind. *It's too late to back out now*.

After a few minutes of trial and error, she found the right key, unlocked the door, and peered out into the deserted hallway. She prayed the dead man in her room had been the only one on duty tonight. If so, by the time the other guards discovered their absence, she and the children would be far away from here. If not...she shoved the thought away, locked the door behind her, and slipped into the shadows of the dimly lit corridor.

Tiptoeing down the hall to the third door on the right, she unlocked it and snuck inside. "Wake up, Cat," she whispered at the first bed. "It's time to leave."

The four-year-old Lycan blinked and yawned. "I's awake, Tabbi. Is we 'scaping now?"

"Yes, but you have to be quiet. We can't make a sound, or the bad men will catch us."

"I know. I be good. I no want more hittings."

"Oh, sweetheart." Tabbi forced back the bitter tears stinging her eyes and gave Cat a hug. No child should have to live like this.

"You're the best good girl I know. Get your clothes on now, while I wake the others."

She set the bags on the floor, went to the next bed, and shook the sleeping wereleopard's shoulder. Echo woke quickly, without complaint or noise. They all knew the score. If the guards caught them, they'd lock them up so tight, there wouldn't be the slightest chance of escape.

Once the girls were awake and dressing, Tabbi dashed across the hall to get Zane. The fourteen-year-old half-human/half-weretiger opened his eyes with a jolt of fear Tabbi understood all too well. She put a finger to her lips. He nodded, threw back the covers, and climbed out of bed, fully dressed. He even had his sneakers on.

She blinked. "How did you know it would be tonight?" she whispered at a decibel too low for his human roommate to hear.

"Didn't," he said, equally quiet. "Been going to bed in my clothes every night. Just in case."

Tabbi shook her head. Zane never failed to surprise her. He picked up his pillow, revealing a small cache of clothes, one thin spiral notebook, a squashed candy bar, and a battered paperback book—all he had to show for the eleven years he'd spent in this hellhole. Tabbi's heart ached for him. Someday, she swore silently, she'd make sure he had car magazines, a baseball and glove, and all the other things teenage boys dreamed about. Maybe then, his nightmares would fade.

Her own collection of personal gear was little better than Zane's, even though she'd been here almost twice as long. But then, she hadn't cared about possessions since she'd arrived at the compound at the age of twelve and Zakhar had sold her to a pervert for an hour—the first time. From that moment, all she'd dreamed about was revenge.

Stripping the case off his pillow, Zane scooped up his treasures and stuffed them inside it. Then together, they snuck into the hall. Tabbi felt like a traitor for leaving the others—whether they were Weres or humans—but she couldn't take them all with her. So she was taking the most vulnerable three, the ones who needed escape as badly as she did. Someday soon she'd come back for the others and shut this place down for good.

After she'd relocked the door, she and Zane crossed to the girls' room. Once inside, she gave a neck bag to each of them and slipped the fourth over her own head. She heard a soft giggle and glanced down. Echo was helping Cat fasten her sneakers and had managed to coax a laugh out of the young werewolf, despite the fear and adrenalin clogging the air.

At twenty-eight, Echo would be coming into her first heat in less than two years. Yet in spite of the abuse heaped on her since childhood, she'd remained remarkably sweet and shy. Tabbi refused to let the girl go through what she had when she'd turned thirty.

No. She couldn't afford to let those memories in. Not now. She had to be strong. The others were counting on her to get them out of this living hell. Locking her pain, fear, and anger back in its cage in a far, dark corner of her mind, she concentrated on what came next.

"Now, we go downstairs to Zakhar's office. I think the guards are asleep, but just in case they aren't, try not to make any noise."

Zane put a hand on her arm. "There's always at least one on duty, sometimes two."

"I think tonight there was only the one, and he's no longer a problem."

He studied her battered face a moment then nodded, a grim smile flickering at the corners of his mouth. "Good."

"I don't know if I'd call it good, but it *was* necessary."

She picked up Cat and led the way out the door. Relocking it, she headed downstairs to the main floor. At the door of Zakhar's office, she tried the guard's keys. None of them fit.

God, no! They had to get in. Everything depended on it. Fighting renewed panic, she tried each key again, slowly, though every second felt like an hour. They were completely exposed out here with no way to prevent their recapture. Her heart racing, she wiped the sweat out of her eyes and struggled to force a key into the keyhole with fingers that refused to stop shaking.

"Let me." Zane pulled a straightened paperclip from his pocket and went to work on the lock. Forty-five seconds later, the door clicked open.

"Where did you learn to do that?" she whispered as she shut and locked it behind them.

"I've been practicing on our door upstairs. In case you didn't come through, I was going to see what I could do." When she stared at him, he shrugged. "What?"

She put Cat down and pulled Zane into a hug. "You're a genius. I'm so very proud of you."

He blushed and ducked his head, but not before she'd caught a glimpse of his ear-to-ear grin.

Looking around at her three charges, she wondered how the hell she'd get them from Lithuania to France and over the channel into England. She had to admit she had only a vague plan. There were just too many unknowns. Still, whatever happened to them out on the road could hardly be worse than what was happening to them in here.

Thank God, they all spoke fluent English and would likely be taken as tourists, at least in Western Europe. Except for Cat, of course, who had trouble pronouncing some of the words. Hopefully, the little girl's butchered language would be misinterpreted as a toddler's natural progression.

Zane touched Tabbi's shoulder. "Now what?"

"Now, we rob the safe."

"How?"

"There's a key in the desk."

"How do you know that?"

She shook her head. "You don't want to know."

No way would she admit how Zakhar had used her.

The drawers of his solid mahogany desk were locked tight. The guard's keys were no use to her here, nor had she expected them to be. Crawling under the desk, she retrieved a key from its hook on the underside. A key she'd seen there on the night—no! She refused to darken her mind by thinking about what a sick bastard Zakhar was.

She got to her feet, unlocked the middle drawer, and felt around inside for the special key she'd seen the pride leader toss in it that night before he'd started on her. Her fingers brushed it, curled around the ornate handle, and pulled it free. The shaft was thin, nearly four inches long, and had small slots along its length that held microchips embedded with special codes. It looked much like the key to Zakhar's Maserati, though it was longer and thinner.

Swinging a painting away from the wall to reveal the safe, she inserted the key into a barely visible slot near the bottom edge. Zakhar thought he was so clever, sticking a fake dial on the safe. After one spin, any safecracker worthy of the title would know the dial was bogus and start checking around for a digital key. It might've worked on her, though, if Zakhar hadn't gotten careless—which shouldn't really have surprised her, given he thought all women were brain-dead.

Ignoring any miscellaneous documents, she took all the cash and gemstones from the safe—money she and the others had generated by suffering at the hands of countless men—and stuffed it into her bag. Just as she tossed the key back in the drawer, someone rattled the doorknob. They all froze. Hardly daring to breathe, Tabbi signaled for quiet, but it wasn't necessary. No one made a sound.

"Oleg?" barked a harsh voice. The doorknob rattled a second time. "Is that you in there? You damn fool, if you're messing with the females again, there'll be hell to pay."

A scratching sound was followed by a muttered curse. Tabbi's heart pounded in her ears so loudly she was surprised the man didn't hear it.

"Hell, there isn't a key on this damn ring that'll fit this." He pounded on the door. "If I have to, I'll get the master pass key after I finish my rounds, so you'd better be out of there and doing your job when I get back."

His footsteps tramped away down the hall and upstairs. If he went into her room—Oh, God, they were running out of time.

"We have to go," she whispered. "Look around for a hidden button somewhere on the wall by the bookcase. I know Zakhar has an escape route of some kind. I once saw him enter through a hidden panel in that wall. There has to be a latch on this side, too."

While they searched, Tabbi booted up Zakhar's computer and tapped in a series of keystrokes that would trigger a virus she'd planted weeks ago—one she created with what she'd learned when Zakhar hired a geek to teach her to hack into banks and steal money for him electronically.

"What are you doing?" Zane whispered.

She glanced over her shoulder and checked that Cat and Echo were absorbed in hunting for the button. Zane needed to know this, though, in case anything happened to her.

"I'm activating a virus that will destroy the system and hopefully buy us some time—among other things. If something goes wrong and I don't make it, there's information you'll need in my bag. Promise me you'll take care of the others."

He hugged her and nodded.

She patted his shoulder. "Don't watch me. Look for the button that will get us out of here."

It was Echo who found it, hidden behind a book in the bookcase. She touched Tabbi's arm to get her attention, pushed the button, and grinned as the door slid open.

"Good job."

With a tight smile, Tabbi shut down the computer. Within ninety seconds after the next person booted it up, the pride would get a *very* unpleasant surprise. Satisfied, she headed for the secret door. Beyond the threshold, a flight of stairs descended into black nothingness.

"I think this comes out at the silo, although I'm not sure. But wherever it goes, it's our only way out."

The pitch-black tunnel made even Were eyes useless, and she hadn't thought to steal a flashlight. Too late now.

She took one of Cat's hands, told Echo to take Cat's other one, and Zane to grab a hold of Echo's. With her free hand on the wall as a guide, she led them through the tunnel. The corridor seemed to go on forever. Cat grew tired and began to whimper. Tabbi hauled the child into her arms and guided Echo's hand to the waistband of her jeans.

"Hold onto it," she said and kept walking.

Finally, they came to another staircase. At the top, they hit a blank wall. Tabbi gave Cat to Echo and ran both hands over the wall until she touched a button. When she pushed it, a door slid open. They piled out into a room filled with thirty-kilo bags of grain. Zane cursed as he tripped over one and landed in a heap on the floor.

"English," Tabbi ordered. "It's vital you speak only in English from here on out, *especially* when you swear."

"Where is we?" Cat asked.

"We're in the silo, kitten." Zane scooted over to the window and peered out. "Something's happening over at the house. People are running around outside. I can see the light from their flash-lights."

Tabbi joined him at the window. "I'd say they've discovered the guard's dead and the four of us are missing. If they're searching the yard, either they don't know about the tunnel, or don't realize we used it."

She glanced at Echo, who leaned against the wall, holding Cat. "You did put the book back after you pushed the button, didn't you?"

"Of course. What do we do now?"

Zane snorted. "We get out of here, that's what. I know Zakhar keeps some cars and stuff in the garage here. I was looking out my window once and saw him drive in. I just didn't know where he went from here."

Tabbi nodded. "I saw him, too. More than once."

"I bet the scumbag kept the cars out here in case of a raid, so he could get away and leave everyone else to get caught." He started for the door then hesitated. "They'll hear us drive off. You think we can outrun them?"

She ruffled the boy's hair. "They're not going to hear us. We'll push the car to the road before we start it. It's only a half a mile from here, but it's nearly three quarters of a mile from the house."

"Won't we need the keys?" Echo asked.

"If Zakhar kept cars here so he could make a fast getaway, the keys are probably in them. Or at least somewhere nearby." Tabbi took Cat and headed for the garage. "And if they aren't," she added, winking at Zane, "I bet I know someone who can hotwire one."

⌘⌘⌘

The estate of Drake Gatos, Radlett, England, June 17th:

Drake glared at his computer monitor. *Quicken is not respond-ing.* "What the bloody hell does that mean? It's a goddamn software program, for Christ's sake. I don't need it to talk to me. I just need it to work."

Gray sauntered into the study. "What are you bitching about now?"

Drake beckoned him over and waved a hand at the screen. "Look at this shit."

"You and that computer. I swear, you two are worse than an old married couple. Maybe I should recycle both of you and get new models."

"That's a hell of a way for a second-in-command to speak to his pride leader."

"I didn't realize I was talking to my pride leader. I thought I was talking to my friend. What the hell's eating you lately? You've been a pain in the ass ever since we got back from rescuing Chase in Scotland." Gray cocked his head and studied him. "You're not upset she chose Roman instead of you, are you?"

"No." He shoved away from his desk and paced. "Chase wasn't for me, Gray. As much as I would've liked a chance with her, fate picked her for Roman."

"Then what is it?"

"I'm...not worried, exactly. More unsettled."

"About?"

Drake sighed. "About the man we let escape in Scotland."

"Jesus, boss. You still got your panties in a twist over that? What is it with you? It's like you've gone hyper territorial all of a sudden." Gray threw up his hands. "What's the big effing deal? Of the four guys from that pride who came after Chase, Roman took out Zakhar, and we got two of his men. So what if one lone weretiger got away? The guy's hotfooting it back to Lithuania with his tail between his legs." He snorted. "Literally. He's not coming back to hassle us."

Drake shot him a glare, his canines lengthening momentarily. "And you know this, how?"

"Logical thinking." Gray held up one hand and ticked off points on his fingers. "Chase has been claimed by Roman. Hell, she even married him in a human-type ceremony. On top of that, she wrote an ironclad will leaving her money to Roman, or to her old partner if something happens to both of them. There's no way anyone from her father's old pride can get to the thirteen mil in her trust fund. Therefore, with both Chase and her money out of reach, we don't have anything her old pride wants."

"What's to stop one of them from trying to kill Roman so he can mate Chase when she's widowed?"

"You're joking, right? Didn't you see the way he took out Zakhar? I knew Roman was half Vampire, but—Jesus." Gray shuddered. "He drained every drop of blood from that cat's body. Shit, I nearly pissed myself, and I *like* Roman."

"Can you blame him?"

"Hell, no! The son of a bitch had his woman. I'd have killed the bastard, too, though I might've used a less dramatic method. But I can only imagine how shitting terrified the guy who escaped is. When he gets back and tells the rest of the pride, they'll think twice before coming to England, looking for trouble. Believe me."

Drake rubbed his hands over his face and sighed. His weretiger pride now included not only Chase, an American human/weretiger half-breed, but also her new mate, Roman, a half-Lycan/Vampire. *And damn it, I haven't had a moment's peace since she stepped off the frigging plane in England.* Life as a weretiger pride leader was hard enough without all these added complications.

Still, Gray did have a valid point. With Chase officially mated, there was no reason for Zakhar's pride to come looking for trouble. And as quickly as his men had abandoned him during the fight, it was unlikely they'd try to avenge him.

"I certainly hope you're right." He glanced over to see Gray grinning at the computer screen. "What now?"

Gray patted the monitor. "As much as I've enjoyed this little chat, I think your break time's over. Quicken's responding again, so I'll leave you to your paperwork."

"Thanks a lot, shithead." Drake managed to stifle his grin, though his lips still twitched. "You'd better be right about Zakhar's pride."

"Trust me. Since we put the fear of God in them, they'll behave themselves."

"You hope," Drake muttered as he went back to his bookkeeping. Now if he could only put the fear of God in this stupid computer.

എന്റെ

Poland, approaching the Polish/German Border, June 21st:

The last rays of the sun were fading as Tabbi slowed Zakhar's black, S-Class Mercedes and pulled off the paved road onto a small dirt lane. She had no idea where the new road led, but it looked promising. As she drove, she searched both sides of the narrow dirt strip, looking for—there. That little copse of trees and underbrush should do just fine.

She came almost to a stop, turned the wheel, and eased the car into the underbrush, edging it forward until the brake lights reflected on the leaves of the vine-like foliage closing in behind her. Exhausted, she cut the engine, dropped the keys on the floor, and rested her head on the seat back, giving into a yawn that caught her unawares.

It had been a long four days.

They'd crossed into Poland at Trakiszki. At first, Tabbi was hesitant to drive the car across the border, afraid that without passports or identification they'd be arrested. Then Zane had come up with a brilliant idea. He and Echo stripped, shifted, and raced by the border guards as a tiger and leopard. The guards deserted their posts and ran after them, trying to round up what they apparently thought were escaping zoo animals.

Once the crossing was clear of guards, Tabbi drove the car through.

After leading the locals on a merry chase, Zane and Echo pranced up to where she waited on the shoulder of the road, twenty miles from the border. They'd been more than a little pleased with themselves—and rightly so.

That had been the easy part. The hard part had been avoiding the main highways and finding her way across Poland on the small back roads, such as there were. The maneuvering had added an extra two days to their trip.

She rubbed her churning stomach, trying to shake off the stress of the journey. Terrified they'd be stopped, arrested, and taken back to Lithuania and Zakhar, she hadn't relaxed since the night she'd killed the guard. By now, the other guards must have notified the authorities. In the age of modern computers, the alert would've gone out to every nation in Europe. So she was bound to be stopped at the German border.

Lithuania wasn't part of the EU, so with Lithuanian plates on the car, she wouldn't just be waved through.

They'd been lucky so far, but it couldn't last. If only she could get to a computer, she could hack into Interpol and cancel any alerts or warrants. But she had no idea where to find an accessible terminal without heading for a major city and exposing the four of them to more danger. She'd have to find another way.

She doubted Zane's ploy would work to get them across into Germany. The Germans were far too organized and well trained. She raked her fingers through her hair in frustration and conceded to defeat. As much as she hated the idea, it was time to abandon the car.

Zane was asleep in the passenger seat beside her. Echo and Cat were conked out in the back. She wished she could join them in slumber, but night was fast approaching and they needed to hurry.

She shook Zane's shoulder then did the same to the girls. "Wake up, guys. It's time to go."

"Where are we?" he asked.

"About thirty kilometers from the German border."

"We can't take the car across, can we?"

"No, I'm afraid not."

"Oh, man," he grumbled. "I'm really going to miss these wheels."

"Me, too."

"I's hungry, Tabbi," Cat said with a yawn. "I want Frosted Flakes."

"Sorry, sweetheart, you'll have to make do with sandwiches and fruit," she said, handing out the food she'd purchased in the last village they'd passed through.

"Can I have Frosted Flakes next day?"

"I don't know, baby. I don't know where we'll be tomorrow. But you can have them once we get where we're going. I promise."

She popped the trunk and climbed out of the car. Once she'd removed the neck bags and closed the trunk lid, she walked to the little dirt road to make sure the car couldn't be seen. Satisfied, she went back for the others.

"We need to get across the border, but because I'm pretty sure the car's been reported stolen, we can't drive. Before we leave, let's use the rags I bought and wipe down the car—inside and out. No fingerprints, no DNA."

Zane stared at her. "So we're just going to walk across the border?"

"Yes, but I don't think we should do it as humans."

"You want us to shift?" Echo asked in wonder. "What if we're seen in animal form?"

"We'll try to avoid that. But if it happens, it's better for the humans to see four animals crossing the border than four people. They won't try to arrest the animals."

Zane snorted. "No, they'll just think we're after their livestock and shoot us."

"I doubt that. Most likely, they'll figure we've escaped from some zoo, so they'll try to catch us. Once we're over the border, we can shift back and continue our journey as humans."

"But we be necked," Cat pointed out.

Tabbi smiled. "No, sweetie. We won't be naked. We'll put our clothes in these bags and put the bags around our necks so we can carry them as animals. Here, take off your clothes and shift, and I'll show you."

"'Kay."

When Cat had shifted to her wolf form, Tabbi put her clothes in the bag and draped it around the child's neck, adjusting it for a comfortable fit. Then she scratched her behind her ears and kissed her muzzle.

"Just like that. See?"

Cat nodded her furry, gray head.

Zane watched as Echo shifted into a sleek leopard beside him. "We'd move a lot faster if we stayed in our animal forms," he said. "It'll be a long walk to France as humans."

"I know. I've considered that, along with the fact the authorities probably have our human descriptions." She rubbed at the tension in the back of her neck and sighed. "I was thinking we might steal another car, but that could be dangerous in Germany. The German police are very sophisticated, and I doubt we'd get very far."

Zane shifted into a tiger. Tabbi draped his bag over his neck then did the same for Echo. "We'll go as far as we can as animals, but we'll have to travel at night and sleep during the day. Keep close together, and whatever you do, don't lose your bags."

She'd just taken off her clothes when Zane suddenly turned back into a human.

"What is it?" she asked.

"What happens if one of us gets caught?"

"If one of you gets caught, whether as a human or an animal, stay calm and wait for me to rescue you." Tabbi looked each one in the eye. "I *will* come for you. Understand?"

They all nodded.

"You're not going back," she told them. "I don't care what I have to do or who I have to kill, I promise you, none of you are going back to that hell."

As she stuffed her clothes in her bag and hung it around her neck, she said a silent prayer of thanks that none of them had noticed she hadn't included herself in that statement. Because she *was* going back, and when she did, she'd avenge them all.

About the Author

Award-winning author, Pepper O'Neal is a researcher, a writer, and an adrenalin junkie. She has a doctorate in education and spent several years in Mexico and the Caribbean working as researcher for an educational resource firm based out of Mexico City. During that time, she met and befriended many adventurers like herself, including former CIA officers and members of organized crime. Her fiction is heavily influenced by the stories they shared with her, as well her own experiences abroad.

O'Neal attributes both her love of adventure and her compulsion to write fiction to her Irish and Cherokee ancestors. When she's not at her computer, O'Neal spends her time talking long walks in the forests near her home or playing with her three cats. And of course, planning the next adventure.

CPSIA information can be obtained
at www.ICGtesting.com
Printed in the USA
BVHW031704170419
545820BV00003B/7/P